Business as Usual
by
Adam Parish

*Book 4 of the
Jack Edwards and Amanda Barratt
Mystery Series*

Also by Adam Parish
*The Quartermaster (1)
Parthian Shot (2)
Loose Ends (3)*

To sign up for offers, updates
and find out more about Adam Parish
visit our website www.adam-parish.com

This is a work of fiction. Names, characters, organisations, places, events and incidents are either products of the author's imagination or are used factually. Any resemblance to actual persons, living or dead is purely co-incidental.

Text copyright @2021 by Adam Parish

No part of this book may be reproduced or stored in a retrieval system or transmitted in any form or by any means (electronic, mechanical, photocopying, recording or otherwise) without express permission.

Thanks to Helen for her
help, humour, and patience,
Fran, Sandy and Hamish
for their ideas and time
and Mandy for everything

Chapter 1

The cleaning staff had gone home. The lift doors opened. On the upper floor was a narrow corridor, through which white beams from street lamps laid down a path of light. What was that number? A quick look at the phone. Punch in code. The door slid open noiselessly.

Six curved, high-resolution screens flashed into life, and it was time to sit. The pedals were out of reach; a lever remedied that. That was the easy bit. Now some expert keystrokes – complicated code, but not for this operator.

Gotcha, full wireless control.

A countdown timer burst onto the screen. Two minutes and thirty-four seconds to target. Loss of connection now would be catastrophic.

With steady hands and ice-cold professionalism, the operator got to work. It wasn't an easy drive at this speed. From somewhere, a powerful pleasing roar of a beautiful engine.

100mph now. Not bad.

Damn, little bit of oversteer but back in control. Twenty seconds to target. Now the straight. Nothing ahead.

170mph now. A 30mph hairpin.

The screens fade to black.

Sweep digital footprint.

Job done.

Chapter 2

Jack Edwards sat on a cliff-edge bench in his extended, irregular garden and reviewed an epic scene. Mascar was a hamlet of about one hundred people, and Jack's expansive baronial sandstone mansion stood atop a cliff above the bay in isolated splendour. A classically semi-circular bay and precipitous, crumbling sandstone cliffs provided a stunning enclosure. The beach was mostly sandy but mottled with numerous seaweed-covered black rocks. This spoilt the picture-perfect scene for some, but not for Jack. He loved everything about it, and he got to call it home.

The breeze danced through his hair. It did that every day, but in May, with a cloudless sky, it was soothing and warm. He looked out over the endless sea – calm near the shore, but a few miles out simmering with elemental rage – and then back, always back, to the cliffs and their resident seabirds. Gannets were diving expertly in the bay. He watched them for a while and sighed with pleasure.

Had it really been six years since his late aunt's bequest? Enough money to take only ten minutes to decide to chuck his job as a university lecturer. Since then, he had lived a solitary life, but it had been the right decision. Sometimes he acknowledged that he needed a fuller life, but how could he force things? Interesting possibilities floated in and out of his head from time to time, but he couldn't hold on to them.

Business as Usual

It would probably have been different if Marion had lived, but she had died. He thought about her a lot, nearly every day, but the memories were starting to feel a little more distant. He could still see her face, but with every passing day he had to work a little bit harder to do it, and he hated that. For more than a year he had visited her grave every day, but it didn't really work. She knew he had loved her. She would have called him an idiot.

Death preoccupied him today, but not just Marion's. When you were forty you weren't meant to lose your partner, and you weren't supposed to lose your best friend either. Now Jack had achieved both of those unwanted milestones.

Paul Riordan had been a friend, his best friend, since university. Many hours had been spent together: on the golf course, the football pitch and the Scottish hills. Once, Paul had saved his life. Long before mobile phones, it wasn't easy to get rescued when stranded miles from a main road, especially to be taken off a snow-capped mountain with a badly broken ankle. Paul had carried him out on his back in atrocious weather and over rough ground. Jack wondered whether he would have been able to do this had the roles been reversed.

After university, both had drifted into academic life: Jack as an undistinguished political economy lecturer and Paul as an alpha physicist, tipped for the top. After exceeding expectations for a year or so, he committed the ultimate academic betrayal. He resigned and moved to the City of London.

Physicists were the rocket scientists of the City. The only ones who had the brains to understand and model the new financial theories. As an employee, Paul-earned a huge salary and bonus, but after a few years learning his trade, he made millions as a founder and managing partner of one of the earliest hedge funds. That sort of money nearly always changed people, but it hadn't changed Paul, and they had stayed friends.

Jack was godfather to Paul's daughter. He was ashamed to admit that he couldn't remember her name. Well, it had been about twenty years ago. In a depressing further coincidence, Paul had lost his wife as well. Jack had been abroad and missed the funeral. And now Paul was dead.

He would miss him; Paul was perhaps Jack's only real friend. A depressing thought.

The funeral was on Monday. It was Saturday now, and he wished it was over. He lit a cigarette in a rage against mortality and looked out to sea. It made him feel small, which helped to soften the thought of death, but it didn't last long, so he went back into the house.

Externally, the house was in good shape. Jack had commissioned pointing and roofing work when he had arrived. Internally, he had done nothing. It might have been laziness, but he didn't think so. Every day he walked through the rooms which Marion had walked through, and it comforted him. But recently there were signs that, maybe, he was ready to move on.

He had made a minor start by kicking off an ill-planned project aimed at converting one of the many unused rooms into a purpose-built library. This wasn't just a vanity project; Jack had a lot of books, and his late aunt had accrued even more. Her enthusiasm for collecting, always keen, had grown to something of a mania in her final years. Six years on, Jack was still finding books in the unlikeliest of places. A recent audit on the collection had generated an estimate in excess of twenty thousand, making the library project something of a necessity.

He liked books and had been surprised to find that he enjoyed designing the room. Being able to afford whatever he liked helped. He hadn't stinted. The house had lots of rooms, most of them spacious and high ceilinged, and most unused. The height of the ceilings allowed for a mezzanine level, circular stairs and the best of mock cherrywood shelving.

With construction complete, the empty shelves stared at him, demanding to be filled. Simple: arrange the books in order, any order. So many classifications were theoretically available, and making a final decision had caused months of delay. That's what Jack told himself, although the delay was equally attributable to him falling down on the job by reading books as he went along.

Given these challenges, it was impossible to produce a realistic completion date, but he wasn't interested in project management issues, certainly not this weekend. Sitting on the floor drinking coffee and reading books was a far better way to spend time when counting down to the funeral of a friend.

At just past nine o'clock, Jack threw down a book about silent films and, on a whim, decided to go. The funeral was in Buckinghamshire, in one of the Chalfonts, so he would go to London tonight, spend Sunday there, then drive to the country village early on Monday morning. It was a long drive to London, and Jack preferred the peace of the night. It didn't take long for him to get started. He had all the clothes and stuff he needed in the London flat, and after locating a bottle of water and a packet of cigarettes, he was ready.

The Maserati was joyous to drive, but Jack wasn't feeling joyous, so he clambered into his SUV and got started. The sun was close to setting, but as always in the Highlands in good weather, the night wouldn't be dark. The road was empty and pothole-free. Despite that, he wasn't driving fast. He was thinking. Thinking about Paul and how he had died.

Late at night, a balmy early summer evening and a deserted road in the south of England. Feeling the supercar holding the road perfectly balanced, right up to the limit. And then, beyond the limit.

The car and Paul's body were well designed, but a quarter-of-a-mile roll down a steep slope – and an explosion and fireball – had proved too much for both. He wondered what Paul was thinking about just before he died, but that was tough to think about and impossible to answer, so his mind wandered onto another impossible question.

Whilst Jack could, at a stretch, be described as religious, Paul had been a confirmed atheist. To him, religion was man-made, unfounded in reason and all smoke and mirrors. Jack had fought back, partly for the sake of argument and partly because, for reasons he couldn't explain, he just believed in a God of some sort. Paul would know the answers to these eternal questions now.

Chapter 3

Jack had arrived in London very early on Sunday morning and spent a restless and idle day at the Bloomsbury flat. Smaller than his baronial mansion at Mascar, it was convenient and comfortable. In cash terms the flat was worth far more, but it wasn't worth more to Jack.

Jack had liked London once - he'd completed a set of summer lectures in the capital – but he didn't much like it these days. Too busy, too dirty and too difficult to get around. You could do anything you wanted in London, but Jack didn't want to do much these days. He was tired of London. He thought about Dr Johnson's aphorism. Was he tired of life?

Concentration on anything other than tomorrow's funeral proved impossible, so he went to bed early, intending to get a fast start out of the capital and to the Buckinghamshire village.

This plan worked, and at about five-thirty the next morning he was up and dressed and out of the flat. Leaving London on a Monday morning proved easier than commuting the other way, and in less than an hour, Jack arrived in the south Buckinghamshire village of St Simon. He drove slowly past a row of shops, a pub and a church with a Norman tower and that was the end of the village. Half a mile further, spotting a bold sign which indicated a hotel, he pulled into its tree-lined driveway.

Adam Parish

Inside, the hotel was moderately busy, and Jack ordered breakfast and hung around until a slow-moving clock struggled to half past nine. He secured permission from a polite receptionist to leave his car in the car park and started walking back towards the village. This was a wealthy place, and the houses on the village outskirts, each one larger than the last, were set far back from the main road in leafy grounds.

The road split after a few more minutes' walk and Jack headed into the village. A welcoming sign dated the village's founding to the year 1100, which seemed about right. There was a small Co-op store in the village centre, the only vulgar intrusion from the twenty-first century. The remainder of the buildings were an eclectic, irregular mix of styles and ages. He passed a war memorial and headed towards the church.

The planning authorities of the dark ages had made a mistake. Car parking provision at the church was inadequate, and the narrow approach lane was packed with badly parked, luxury vehicles. The well-dressed owners of these cars stood chattering in groups outside the church. It was a quarter to ten, fifteen minutes before the start, so Jack withdrew to a sheltered path partly hidden by a line of yew trees and lit a cigarette. No one else was smoking, but he didn't care. He was the best friend of the deceased. The discreet path ended and he drifted to the periphery of the crowd of mourners. He stood alone and looked at them. No one looked back. Most – too many – of them were smiling and a few were buzzing from group to group, taking full advantage of this networking opportunity. Maybe that was fair enough? There was more money at this funeral than in most British cities. The fact that he himself contributed a decent amount to this imbalance didn't help. Was he like these people? He hoped not, but he couldn't be sure. It was a worrying thought.

There was nowhere to throw his cigarette in the perfectly tended churchyard, so he had to roughly extinguish it with his fingers and thrust it into his coat pocket as a woman with a big hat looked on disapprovingly. The crowd thinned as ten o'clock approached, and Jack made his way into the packed church and secured a seat at the back.

Business as Usual

The service was typical High Church of England, which was all a bit complicated for Jack. On the upside, the service was short, and the mourners were soon back outside in the churchyard and uncomfortably surrounding a newly dug grave. Jack didn't push to the front and instead waited until the crowd had cleared. He moved to the open grave and looked down at the coffin, plain and pine. What use was money? Silently, he uttered a goodbye to his friend and turned to leave.

Lost in his thoughts, he hadn't heard her approaching. A tall, blonde girl of maybe twenty stood beside him. She was dressed in a heavy coat with a wide black hat which drooped over her face. She pushed the hat brim back and looked at him with intense blue eyes. "Are you Jack Edwards?"

He wondered who she was.

As he hadn't answered her question, she repeated it and helped him out with some information about herself. "I'm Pam, Pam Riordan. I'm your god-daughter."

He couldn't disguise the fact that he had never met her since her christening, and he didn't try. He took her hand and shook it. "Well, yes, nice to, er, meet you at last."

She flashed him a thin smile. "Yes, first time in nineteen years. Not much of a godparent."

He accepted this criticism with a sheepish acknowledgement and wondered what to say next, but, again, she got in first.

"Come on, where's your car?"

"At a hotel, about half a mile down the road."

"That'll be the Manor Hotel. Let's go."

"Is the reception there?"

"There is no reception, but I do want to speak to you."

Once in nineteen years didn't seem too much to ask, so Jack said nothing, and she linked her arm with his and walked him along the road. They didn't talk as they walked. They didn't know each other, but they had a powerful mutual love for a dead man, and the walk wasn't uncomfortable.

Just before they reached the hotel, she turned off the road and followed a tree-lined path. It led down a steepish hill which opened onto an unexpectedly wide road running parallel and behind the hotel. This road continued for another quarter of a mile, wooded on the right-hand side and, on the left, walls and gates, beyond which sat houses that could be better described as mansions. After passing a couple of these massive gated houses she stopped.

"Here we are." She fiddled with her phone and a moment later, with a deafening groan, the thick, solid-iron gates separated.

This revealed a large mock Tudor mansion, two or three storeys high, which sat in extensive grounds, the front entrance set back from a grass and gravelled approach.

Jack said, "I didn't see you in the church."

"No, I couldn't face it. I walked around the village until it was over."

"And no reception?"

"Well, I thought about it, but Dad was a bit of a loner. Really, he didn't like most of the people you saw today. Mostly they're just work colleagues or business associates. I don't know any of these folks either, and I didn't feel up to it."

Jack nodded. Good for Pam.

She opened a sturdy oak front door and led him through a bright reception area and into a front-facing bay-windowed sitting room. "Do you want a tea or coffee? Or maybe a drink? We've got everything."

He wanted a bourbon but asked for a black coffee.

She made two coffees and took his coat, and they then settled in opposite armchairs. He regarded her while she sipped at her drink.

Jack was already impressed. She was pale, and her hands were clasped tightly on the arms of her chair, but she was in control, confident beyond her years. He wondered what, if anything, she did. Whatever it was, she would be good at it.

She looked at him closely. "So, Jack, we meet at last. Dad used to talk about you quite often."

"That's nice to hear. We had a lot of good times and a lot of laughs."

"Yes, he talked about climbing and drinking. I think he missed those days."

"So do I," Jack lamented. "We kept in touch a bit, but mostly the odd phone call in the last few years. He was so successful, very talented. I knew he would succeed. He was a clever guy."

"Yes, it was all work with Dad … an obsession really." Her voice temporarily cracked. "Especially after Mum died." She looked at him carefully. "You didn't make it down for her funeral."

"Sorry." What else could he say?

She didn't probe further, but her lips tightened for a moment. Perhaps it was only just dawning on Pam that she was now alone. Millions of people had it worse, but Jack was thinking only about the teenage girl opposite. She had privilege and money, but these things weren't always enough. He wondered if he could help. "What do you do?" he asked.

"Nothing."

"Well, I don't expect you need to work."

She laughed and said, "That's true, but I'm not idle. I've just finished university. I got a first. My graduation ceremony is due next week." She wiped her eyes. "Dad was happy about that. He was looking forward to going up."

"He would have been proud, I'm sure." Pam had been the most important thing in Paul's life, and Jack cursed him a bit for leaving her. It was pretty careless of him. Godparent was an honorific title, and having met Pam for the first time in nearly twenty years he could have left it that way. But Jack was a man that needed something worthwhile to do. Idling and moping around in the north of Scotland had to stop sometime.

He didn't know what he could do, but, irrationally, he powerfully wanted to be there for her. Maybe it would make up for the years of neglect? Maybe it would make him feel better? The relationship had got off to a decent start. It looked as if she trusted him, and he was sitting in the house, seemingly awarded the – largely undeserved – title of chief mourner.

"Tell me about yourself, Jack," Pam said.

He shrugged. "There's not much to tell. Scottish, fortyish. I went to university and then became a university lecturer."

"In what?"

"Economics and history."

"Do you enjoy that?"

"I like the subjects, but I didn't like the work. I gave it up a few years ago."

"To do what?"

"Nothing really."

"Can you afford to do that?"

"Yes, I inherited some money."

Her eyes fell. "Money's not everything."

"No, it's not," he agreed, "but it's better to have it than not."

"Aren't you bored?"

"Sometimes, I suppose" Jack admitted.

Summarised aloud, it was a disappointing CV, and he felt it. He really hadn't achieved that much. He had money and could do what he wanted these days, but the reality was that the last few years had been years of indulgence.

"So, is there a wife, a girlfriend, a boyfriend?"

Jack shook his head, hoping she would abandon this line of questioning.

Luckily, she had good manners and changed the subject. "How much have you heard about Dad's death?"

"Not much. A car accident. Driving fast and lost control."

"Well, that's the headline, but there's a bit more than that."

Jack waited.

She looked at him closely. "The police said he was high on drugs, cocaine. What do you think of that?"

"I never knew him to take drugs. But I don't know much about drugs. Isn't it pretty common in the City?"

Pam turned to him and looked at him fiercely. "Dad didn't do drugs. Never."

True or not, Jack didn't really care. Maybe they would find out? Either way, today she was entitled to frame her father's memory as she wanted.

"Look," she said, "I know he never took drugs. I mean, if he had done, well, that would have been up to him. But he didn't. It's not that important to me. I loved him and I don't care about how he lived." She paused, then delivered the punchline. "But I do care about how he died."

She was talking quickly now. "If we are being told that he was off his head on drugs and that's what caused him to lose control of the car, yet he didn't take drugs, where does that leave us?"

If Jack had been talking to his friend Amanda Barratt, whose stock-in-trade was death, the answer would have been clear and would have led to an unequivocal drive for more information. But Pam wasn't Amanda and he didn't want to fuel these thoughts. He said weakly, "I don't know. Accidents happen."

"Yes, they do. But what about this?" Pam reached across to a side table, picked up a brown A4 envelope and handed it to him.

He took it from her and immediately noted two things. Firstly, the seal had been broken, and secondly, and more intriguingly, the envelope was addressed in large bold characters. "Jack Edwards."

He dealt with the minor point first. "Did you open this, Pam?"

"Yes, but only after Dad died."

Jack delved into the envelope and retrieved a thick collection of papers, which, after a short review, consisted mostly of figures and charts, with some kind of financial report. Stapled to the front of the collection was a short covering note. It read:

Jack, I hope you are well. If you're reading this, you are in better shape than I am, and I need your help. I'll make this short

Over the last few weeks, I've become convinced that my company, Canisp, has been compromised. As you know, ours is a complex international business and getting things clear is difficult, but I'm getting close to being able to prove that many millions, maybe billions, of pounds are involved. Normally I would expect to get to the bottom of this but if I'm not here for any reason, see what you can do. My safety may be at risk; people get angry about this amount of money. I don't know what you are up to these days, but remember, you owe me a favour, so do what's best and, most of all, make sure Pam is okay.

Your friend, Paul.

Jack read this note twice. "When did Paul write this?"

"The day before he died."

"And he gave it to you?"

"Yes."

"Why did you open it?"

"Well, why not? There's just me now, and I don't know you. Why would Dad think that you could help? I've been through his study, checked all his documents. He's left some papers, but they contain nothing exceptional, as far as I can see. Do you know anything about hedge funds and the way they operate?"

"Not much," Jack admitted.

"So why would Dad think you can help?"

"Well, as you already said, Paul didn't have any other close friends."

She shook her head. "True enough, but there must be something else. I mean, he could have hired experts. There must be a reason that he chose you?"

Jack looked at her. He knew already that he was going to have to do something. He certainly did owe Riordan a favour. That alone would have been enough for him to act, but there was a more powerful reason. Her eyes were blazing with determination. If he didn't do something, *she* would. Jack didn't believe that Riordan's death was anything other than accidental, but if he ignored it and somehow Pam was hurt, he knew that he would have a lot of trouble forgiving himself.

She was waiting for an answer.

"I've got a friend who has quite a lot of connections in the City. Maybe that's what Paul had in mind?"

Pam considered this for a moment. "Maybe." She leant forward. "When do we get to meet this friend of yours?"

Jack raised his hand in admonition. "Hang on. I'll have a word with my friend as soon as I can, and afterwards I'll let you know what she thinks."

This bland proposal came nowhere close to the sort of action plan Pam apparently had in mind. Her expression was unchanged. She was going to get closure and then she would mourn.

Jack knew when he was beaten. "Okay, I'll phone her now and see if she's around." He took out his phone. He had no idea whether Amanda would be available. For once, he hoped that she wouldn't answer. And then she did, in that familiar rich voice that he knew and missed.

"Amanda," he said. "I'm in London."

"Hello, it's great to hear from you."

He smiled, then got rid of it when he caught sight of Pam's impatient face. "I need a bit of advice."

Her voice became a little more business-like. "Of course. What do you need?"

"I've been at a funeral today, an old friend of mine, and something came up. I need to pick your brains … maybe need a favour."

"Okay, I'm going to the theatre tonight, but I could come round to your flat before. Say half past six for half an hour?"

Jack wondered who she was going to the theatre with, but it was none of his business and this wasn't the time. "Half past six is fine. See you then."

He put his phone back in his pocket.

"So, who's this Amanda?"

"A friend, I've known her for years."

"A girlfriend?"

"A friend," Jack said firmly.

"Where are you meeting?" Pam asked.

"At my flat in Bloomsbury."

She looked at her watch and did some calculations. "Okay, it's one o'clock now. When do we leave?"

Jack said, "Don't you have things to do here?"

"No, not here, but there are a few things I could do in town. Let's head up there now, and I'll do my chores and then come round to yours at half past six."

Jack was going to have to read all these papers and maybe do some research of his own. At least he could have a cigarette in his own flat. He picked up the envelope and said, "Okay, let's go."

The middle of the day was about the only good time to drive into London, and the journey was over in less than an hour. As they got out of the car in the car park under the Bloomsbury flat, he said, "Well, do you want to come up or do you want to go into town straight away?"

"I'll come up, have a quick coffee, and see where the flat is."

After less than a day in residence, Jack had had no time to make a mess in the flat, so was relatively relaxed at admitting a visitor.

The kitchen was informal and home to a large, wooden central table. It was free of debris, and Pam sat down. He made coffees before joining her. From the envelope, he produced Riordan's papers, spread them over the table and began to scan them.

Jack was no expert, but he had some knowledge of financial markets. There were quite a few sheets, but sadly there appeared to be no overarching narrative, simply lists of clients, arranged by dates of sign-ups, introducing managers and a list of various cash movements. The clients bore names that meant nothing to Jack. "Do you recognise these clients?" he asked.

"No, none of them. I don't know anything about the business, although I do know a little bit about finance, academically of course."

"Is that what you did at university?"

"Not exactly. Physics and Mathematics, but that's the sort of qualifications they look for in hedge funds."

"Were you intending to join the company?"

"No, I wasn't, but now, who knows?"

"Well, we're going to need a lot more information to make anything of this. First step seems to be finding out more about these clients. Presumably they were the ones Paul was investigating."

He lit another cigarette, and Pam waved her hand to diffuse a plume of smoke. "Right, time for me to go. I'll be back in good time."

"Okay, take this key, just in case I'm out."

The door slammed behind her, and suddenly Jack was very tired and decided that he needed some sleep. He went through to his bedroom and flopped on his bed and, within minutes, fell asleep wondering where all this was heading.

Chapter 4

It was probably the opening of the front door by the returning Pam which roused Jack from his extended afternoon nap. He felt a bit refreshed, although slightly concerned that he should need an afternoon sleep. No doubt it was a one-off. It was six o'clock by the living room clock when he went back into the kitchen. Pam was there and made him a cup of coffee.

Annoyingly, she said, "Been sleeping?"

He felt old and defensive. "Oh," he said airily, "just dozing after all the driving."

She seemed to understand that, which was also annoying, but she gave up nursing him and got back to business.

"So, this friend of yours – tell me all about her."

"Well, her name is Amanda, Amanda Barratt. She works in the Home Office and we have done a bit of work together before."

"What sort of work?"

These short, direct questions were tough to avoid. "Oh this and that … just a bit of help with her investigations."

"What sort of investigations?"

"Some sort of police work. I'm not quite sure what her job is, but she might be able to help us get a bit of information."

Pam watched more television than Jack did. "So, is she an agent, a spook, like in *Killing Eve*?"

Jack had heard of *Killing Eve* but had never watched it. He laughed at the suggestion. "No, well, maybe, I'm not really certain, but I'm sure she'll be able to give us some advice. She's due soon."

Jack collected Riordan's papers and returned them to the envelope. The intercom buzzed and he directed the concierge to show Amanda up. As he waited at the front door, he was surprised to find himself putting his hands through his hair in a feeble attempt to look his best. Grooming concluded, he waited and listened.

The sound of a door swinging open was followed by clicking heels. Shoes for a night out. Then Amanda was beside him, smiling.

Her grooming had been a lot more successful than his. She was dressed casually, jeans and boots and a shirt, but it worked very well. Whoever she was going to the theatre with wasn't going to be disappointed. Jack was, but he smiled back. She linked her arms round his neck and looked up at him. "Nice to see you."

He looked at her bright blue eyes. "Great to see you." Without either of them initiating anything they kissed, then a long, comfortable hug.

She broke off and looked at him. "Let's go in." She took his hand and followed him into the kitchen.

Jack said, "This is Pam, my god-daughter."

Amanda shook Pam's hand and sat down.

"Drink?" Jack asked her.

"Yes, a small gin and tonic."

"Pam?"

"No, nothing."

Jack went out of the kitchen and returned with a drink for Amanda and one for himself.

Amanda looked at Jack. "Okay, what's up?"

"We were at Paul Riordan's funeral today. He was Pam's dad and my friend. He left this for me." He picked up the envelope and handed it to Amanda.

She lit a cigarette and they all sat in silence for ten minutes as she read the contents before slowly returning the documents to the envelope.

Pam was impatient. "So, can you help?"

Amanda said meditatively, "Perhaps, perhaps."

Jack knew from experience that Amanda wouldn't be hurried.

Pam didn't. "What are the next steps? What do we do now?"

Amanda looked at Pam closely. "Nothing at the moment." With this, she stubbed out her cigarette and got up. "I have to go to the theatre now. I need to think about this, maybe make a couple of calls. If it suits you both I'll be back here at half past ten, and we can talk then."

Pam opened her mouth to speak but closed it again.

"I'll see you both then. Don't bother to see me out."

The front door slammed and Jack looked at Pam. "Okay?"

"Yes, she seems very efficient. I think she is going to help." She looked to Jack for confirmation.

"Yes, I'm sure she will, but don't get your hopes up. There might be nothing to find out."

"We'll see."

Jack muttered a neutral response and wondered what to do now. He didn't know what to say. The next few hours would be long and difficult.

She helped him out. "I've got a university friend who lives nearby. I think I'll go and see her. I'll be back by ten."

Jack was relieved. "Yes, good idea."

After she left, he poured himself a largish brandy, put on some music and sank deeply into an armchair, wondering what he was getting into. He wondered about Pam. He liked her, but he didn't know her. She wanted help, but was that what she needed? Who knew? It was clear that she wanted an investigation, but why? Was it in place of mourning? Mourning would surely come, and if it was deferred it would come harder. Finding out your loved one had been murdered wasn't easy to deal with either, as Jack knew from bitter experience. It didn't soften the blow; instead, it added another layer, a layer of anger and, sometimes, an urge for revenge.

These were worrying thoughts and he didn't know how he could make it easier for her. Maybe Amanda would conclude that there was nothing to investigate, but would Pam accept that? Whatever else, he knew that he would have to see her through this. He owed Paul that much.

Jack turned his thoughts to Amanda. It had been good to see her, although, as ever, the circumstances were not ideal. It was all pretty ridiculous. He had endless opportunities to visit London or to call her. He had no idea why he hadn't. He ignored this question and spent a strangely anxious time wondering who Amanda was at the theatre with. He admitted that he hoped that it wasn't a serious date, and this wasn't a very comforting thought either, so he reached for the buff envelope and re-read Paul's note.

It was vague by his standards – probably scribbled in a hurry. Paul had been a rigorous academic and would have hated to pen a note such as this, but it was obviously all the information that he had to hand – or was prepared to share in writing. He re-read the note, the most compelling part of the improbable murder theory.

Paul had died the next day. Could that be a coincidence? Maybe, but there were other troubling issues. The manner of his death was superficially plausible. In middle age, Paul had become a convert to fast cars, but that didn't mean that he tore along on the public roads. Jack recalled vividly their last phone call. That was about six months ago, and a part of the conversation had focused on his purchase of this supercar. Paul had been enthusiastic, but his words came back clearly. He had joked about the risks of speeding and had insisted that he would never do that. The police were extremely keen to pull over cars like his, he had said. He would satisfy his urge for speed on track days. Jack could hear Paul saying these things. He had believed him then, and he believed it now.

And then there was cocaine. A devoted daughter insisting that her father was not a drug user was one thing, but Jack shared this view with near certainty, although he had said nothing so far. Neither he nor Paul had ever developed a taste for drugs and Paul, more than himself, was extremely illiberal and openly hostile to drug use. People changed and sometimes they didn't tell the truth, but in this case, it was going to take a lot to convince Jack that Paul Riordan was a cocaine user.

Chapter 5

The front door cracked open and Jack hauled himself from the depths of a comfortable armchair. It was after ten and he wondered where the time had gone. Both Pam and Amanda came into the sitting room. They were talking and looked relaxed and natural together. They made coffee and joined him in the lounge.

"How was the show?" Jack asked.

"Very good," Amanda said.

He couldn't bring himself to ask who she'd gone with and she volunteered no further information, which was annoying.

Instead, she got down to business. She looked at Pam and then switched to Jack. "Okay, I know Pam wants something done, but what about you, Jack? Time to be frank, please. Do you think we should look into this?"

"We've got the note."

"Is that it?"

"All I can say is that I knew Paul Riordan very well. The man I knew didn't do drugs and wasn't a reckless driver."

"Surely that's enough?" Pam interjected.

Amanda's face was hard now. "Maybe, maybe not. Let's be clear – this could be a painful process and might not work out the way you want. It's up to you, Jack?"

He looked at Pam, then nodded to Amanda.

"Okay," Amanda said, "I've had a think about this, and I might be able to help … or at least suggest something."

Jack waited and Pam leant forward in her seat.

Amanda took a cigarette from Jack. "The thing about hedge funds is that they are very hard to police. They operate all over the world and their methods are complex, sometimes impenetrable. Investigations can take years."

It was a bad start, but she balanced things up. "That's the bad news, but financial regulations, although tight, are largely ineffective. Regulators usually find out that a fund's in trouble when it goes bust. Then they'll point out that they have scrutinised the fund to the maximum extent allowed by the law. Ticked the boxes and conducted annual inspections."

Amanda raised a cynical eyebrow. "And then another regulation will be introduced as a response. Of course, that just covers the circumstances of the last blow-up and is of no use for the future. Really, no one cares if a single fund goes bust; it's all high-net-worth individuals, hot money and state money. As long as they don't bring down the entire financial system, it's simply dismissed as a high-risk venture that went wrong."

Amanda concluded her macroeconomic critique. "Anyway, what I'm saying is that the regulators, while ineffective, have a lot of powers, so there is very little difficulty in turning up at a hedge fund for an unannounced visit."

"So, you can arrange for the regulators to go in and dig around?" Jack asked.

Amanda laughed. "Yes, something like that." She looked at Jack in an all-too-familiar way and outlined a familiar plan. "Well, I could get *you* in, Jack. It's always a mistake to let more folks into an investigation than necessary."

"But surely you have contacts in the regulators?"

"Yes, obviously. That's how I can get you accredited and through the doors. But these groups are not trained for the sort of enquiry that we need. Besides, I trust you."

"I'm a bit short of experience myself," Jack protested.

She smiled. "True, but I can help a bit. If you get the information that I need, I'll get it analysed. While you do that, I'll have another look at Mr Riordan's accident."

For once, Jack didn't immediately protest at being involved in a scheme of Amanda's. A day or two in an office seemed less risky than most of her projects.

Pam chipped in. "What do I do?"

"Nothing," Amanda said. "Surely you know the people that work there?"

"No, I've never been in the office or met any of them."

"But didn't you say the funeral was today?"

"Yes, but I wasn't in the church, and I didn't see anyone."

"Hmm, it's still a risk, you can't be certain that no one knows you. Maybe your father had a picture on his desk?"

Pam's lips tightened. "I don't know."

"To be honest, it's difficult for anyone who is emotionally close to be involved with this sort of thing."

Pam's face fell and she made to speak, but Amanda cut across her. "Look, you can help us behind the scenes. I promise you."

Pam still looked dissatisfied with this proposal, but after a long sigh she nodded.

"All right, I'll call you tomorrow, Jack, and I'll arrange for you to get a briefing on how to become a regulator."

Amanda got up and crossed to Pam. She put her hand on her shoulder and said, "I'll do what I can."

Pam looked at Amanda and Jack looked at Pam. For the first time today, she looked young and vulnerable. She leant forward and put her hand softly on Amanda's. She was now on the point of tears. Jack braced himself, but mercifully Pam fought them back. Her voice was cracking and barely audible. "Thanks."

Amanda squeezed Pam's hand and got up, and Jack walked her to the door.

She turned and looked at him. "She's a nice kid."

"Seems so."

Amanda looked serious but she didn't say anything. She kissed him on the cheek. "See you tomorrow."

He shut the flat door slowly, deep in thought, and ambled back to the lounge.

Pam was deep in thought also.

"You want a drink?"

"Oh, okay, a gin and tonic."

He had one too. It was pushing midnight and there was little prospect of her getting back to her house tonight. "You'll stay here tonight?"

"If you don't mind."

"No, of course not. There's four bedrooms and I never use three of them. Take any one you want." He wasn't sure whether she wanted to talk, but for the first time, he did. He was beginning to feel anger about the injustice of Paul's loss, but his loss was nothing compared to hers. He looked at her. Just a normal teenager. God knows what she was feeling. "Are you okay?"

"No, but I'm trying hard not to show it."

"There's nothing wrong with letting go. It'll come out eventually."

"Yes, probably, but I don't feel ready. I just keep thinking that if I concentrate really hard on something else, maybe things will be easier."

Jack didn't really believe in this strategy, but maybe he was wrong.

"What else do you need to know?" Pam asked. "I want you to have all the information you need."

Jack sighed. "When did you notice a change in your father's behaviour?"

She considered. "Just in the last month. It wasn't unusual for him to be late at the office, but it was every night in the last month. He was tired and not really himself."

"Did he say anything?"

She shook her head. "No, just that things were hectic. I knew him and I thought it was probably more than that, you know, dealing with losses or something. But he told me nothing."

Jack uttered a mumble of agreement. That sounded like Paul. "When you told Amanda that you didn't know any of your father's colleagues, was that true, or did you just say that so you could be involved?"

"No, it was all true. Dad didn't mix home and work lives – at least as far as I know, although I've been at university for the last three years."

"And what about yesterday?"

She confirmed her earlier answer. "Quite honestly, I don't know whether they even know that Dad had a daughter."

"Do you know anything about the business?"

"Nothing, all I know is that I own about forty percent of it now."

"Surely you know some of the people that Paul worked with?"

"No no-one."

Jack reached over to his iPad and conducted a quick search. David Ferguson was listed as the managing director of the Canisp Hedge Fund; his photograph sat alongside those of a woman called Selena Thornton and of Paul. For a fast-moving financial operation, he considered it sloppy that they hadn't managed to remove Paul's photograph yet.

Ferguson was a good-looking modern man of about forty with dark hair, dark eyes and salt-and-pepper stubble on his chin. His good looks didn't impress Jack much, but he had to admit that the man's bio was impressive. His academic qualifications were stellar, and he had built and sold many businesses across the globe.

As for Thornton, she was about the same age. She was blonde and possessed the beaming smile and perfect teeth that screamed American. Her experience was mostly legal and corporate.

Jack passed the iPad to Pam. "Have you met either of them?"

"No, never."

He left it there. She failed to suppress a yawn and her eyes were heavy. It wasn't surprising. For both of them, it had been a very long day.

Chapter 6

Jack spent a wakeful night worrying about the next day. Over the years, he had written a few economic reports and he had some experience of working with companies in the financial sector. But he was a long time out of the PowerPoint culture and was not looking forward to returning, but now it was important to be professional. This time it wasn't just about him. This sense of responsibility was weighing heavily on Jack. It had been a very long time since he had had to think about someone else, and he hadn't done much of a job the last time.

He glanced at a bedside clock. Four-thirty. He didn't know for sure when Amanda would call, but he knew it would be early. He gave up the struggle for sleep and got out of bed. He went to the kitchen and made a strong coffee, which he drank with a couple of cigarettes. It wasn't the traditional means of inducing sleep, but it worked for Jack, and he went back to the bedroom and, at last, he slept.

Amanda was in a sympathetic mood and her call didn't come until 11 a.m. Jack was still in bed, but he caught the phone before it went to voicemail. She sounded busy, and her instructions were short and simple. He had to get to Lime Street in the City as soon as possible and ask for an official called Peter Smith, who would provide him with a full briefing.

He got up, showered and dressed. Pam was in the kitchen.

She looked up expectantly. "Has Amanda called?"

"Yes. I am to meet a guy in the financial regulators' office this afternoon. He'll give me a briefing and I expect we will work out a plan."

"Do you know him?"

"No, I've never heard of him, but Amanda must know him."

"Are you meeting today?"

"Yes. What will you do today?", Jack asked.

"Go home, I think. Doesn't look like there's anything else I can do."

Jack was glad she said that. She needed some rest in her own space and so did he. "I can give you a ring later and update you."

"Do you think Amanda would help me out with some information? I want to look at a few things, do a bit of background research. It's about time I knew a lot more about the Canisp Hedge Fund and its people." She looked at Jack, waiting for an answer.

He hadn't known her long and he felt he trusted her, but he wasn't ready yet to give out Amanda's private number. "I'll ring Amanda and ask her to speak to you."

"Okay, but remember to do it."

Jack stubbed out a last cigarette and promised.

The taxi driver did well and within fifteen minutes deposited Jack in the heart of the City of London. The regulator's office was modestly sized, but less modestly appointed, with wall-to-wall marble and high-end furniture.

A receptionist in an expensive suit flashed him an expensive smile.

"Jack Edwards. I'm here to see Peter Smith."

In a well-honed accent that might have been fake, he announced that he had never heard of his colleague, but his back-up computer had a better memory. "Yes, Mr Edwards, if you would have a seat, someone will be with you shortly."

Jack ambled to some suspiciously authentic occasional chairs and waited. Another man from an Armani catalogue arrived after a few minutes and, annoyingly, conducted a brief safety induction course.

Jack didn't listen to a word but apparently passed the test and was rewarded with a visitor's badge, which he hung around his neck. He posed for a photograph and waited again.

Five minutes later, a man in a standard but slightly ill-fitting blue pinstripe suit and a misaligned tie moved towards him. From Jack's point of view, this was more promising. He had a taste for maverick employees – he had been one himself.

He rose, shook Smith's hand and told him to call him Jack. Smith's office was on the first floor, so Jack was able to use the stairs, which he preferred. Smith led him past a few dozen leisurely workers in an open-plan area and a number of glass meeting rooms. Smith had an office of his own, something indicating high status in the increasingly egalitarian workplace. Smith's title was also quite strong – head of investigations. He invited Jack to take one of the seats surrounding a modest-sized meeting table and sat alongside.

Smith looked at Jack appraisingly. "Amanda called me yesterday. She said you needed an excuse to poke around at Canisp."

"That's about it."

"Why do you want to do that?"

"Didn't Amanda say?" Jack replied cautiously.

"She didn't say much."

Jack shrugged.

Smith waited a moment, but as Jack added nothing, he gave up. "We have nothing scheduled with Canisp, although we have visited them many times. However, as Amanda may have mentioned, we can pretty much go in at any time. How long do you think you need in there?"

"Not sure, maybe a couple of days."

Smith thought for a moment. "No problem, we can use our special investigation powers. They are pretty open-ended. Now, what we need is a headline justification."

"Our excuse?"

"Yes, but, don't worry, I can make up pretty much anything I like." Smith thought for a moment. "We'll call it a reserves and stress test review. I've got documents that cover this process and which I can go through with you." He started fiddling around on a laptop. "I've also got a standard PowerPoint presentation I'll show you."

Jack groaned and smiled weakly in response to Smith's offer. Well, it was going to be easier than doing it himself. "What can you tell me about Canisp?"

"Quite a lot. It's a major hedge fund, profitable, and has grown quite a bit in the last few years. We inspect it annually and interview key employees."

"Files on the key staff would be of interest to us."

Smith indicated a low pile on the desk.

"Thanks, I'm sure they'll prove useful. So, how did Canisp come out of your last investigation?"

Smith said, "Fine, no real concerns. There were the usual recommendations, of course, but it was all low-level housekeeping stuff. Canisp have been around about fifteen years. They started slowly and did okay for about five years, but about ten years ago they got into the big league. Now they've got a high-powered board with global contacts. They're one of the biggest in the City and still privately owned."

"How did they get into the big league?"

"I don't know, probably acquired a major client. Really it's all about getting the customers in that game."

"And who are their customers?" Jack asked.

"Billionaires, Middle Eastern clients, multi-national corporations … anything or anyone with a lot of money."

"Governments?"

"Yes, some, and, of course, a lot of clients that are government fronts from Russia, China, a lot of African states, that sort of thing."

"A representative sample of good, bad and ugly?" Jack suggested.

"I suppose so."

"What's your position on some of these customers?"

Smith laughed out loud. "Our position? Money and morality … that is an interesting discussion, Mr Edwards. However, our brief, beyond flagging up and reporting accounts in the names of proscribed terrorist organisations, and our responsibilities under money laundering legislation, does not extend to the morality of customers. We focus on mismanagement and threats to the global financial system. Other issues, moral or political, tend to be pursued by others – sometimes Amanda and her colleagues."

Jack nodded. The morality of international capital could wait. "So far as you are concerned, Canisp is financially strong and has no obvious problems or issues?"

Smith said cautiously, "As I say, we have no outstanding issues at the moment."

"Did you know Paul Riordan?"

"Not well, but I met him a few times. An impressive man. Quite ethical too. He built a good business."

"Did he talk to you about any issues he'd had in the last couple of months?"

Smith laughed. "No. Our customers don't often approach us if they have problems. What sort of problems?"

Jack ignored this question. "What about the other top executives? How well do you know them?"

"I know David Ferguson and Selena Thornton also, but again, not well, just through our annual audits." Smith got up, dimmed the office lights and returned to his laptop.

Jack endured about fifteen minutes of slides, and with an effort, acquired an unwanted and superficial knowledge of numerous directives, investor protection regulations and money laundering Acts.

"I'm hoping that my having detailed knowledge of these Acts will be assumed," Jack said.

"Don't worry. They won't ask you about the Acts. They never do – they'll just want you out of there as quickly as possible."

"Hmm."

"Honestly, they won't. So, what information does Amanda want?"

"Mostly the client records."

"Anyone in particular?"

"Don't think so."

"Let me make a few changes to this presentation." Smith bashed the keyboard expertly. "Okay, Jack, you will be formally undertaking an urgent, unannounced stability and liquidity review. It's our gold standard. It allows you access to any records and documents that you demand."

There was a knock at the door and a man came in and dropped what looked like a business card on the table. Smith picked it up and looked at it and then at Jack. "Not a bad likeness," he said and handed Jack his identity card. All too quickly, Jack was a fully-fledged financial inspector.

After escaping the regulator, he opened his investigation by going into a bar. He was in the city of London in the middle of the working day, so it was packed. He fought through the crowd, ordered a pint of Guinness and, with difficulty, secured a seat. Through the din, he called Amanda, who said she could join him shortly. She arrived in about half an hour, by which time the crowd had thinned as the lunchtime drinkers reluctantly headed back to their offices.

He got her a drink and secured a booth, which allowed for a bit of working space.

"How did you get on with Smith?" she asked.

"He was okay. He gave me files and a presentation to use. And this, my very own identity badge. Apparently, I'm ready to go."

Amanda looked at the badge. "Hmm, we'll say it's a bad picture of you," she said enigmatically.

"Best I can do."

"Yes," she said discouragingly. "Anyway, do you feel ready?"

"Why not? I'm never going to be ready, but I'll just keep things simple. Go in, have a look at the key folks and demand information, which you can review, and we'll take it from there. Apparently, with the powers I have we can go on until we find out something or whenever you think best. As far as the need for a report, we'll just say that some things came up and we will return later. No one's going to complain that a regulator's gone."

Amanda laughed. "You have an aptitude for this sort of thing. As you say, keep it simple. When were you thinking about starting?"

Jack took a sip of Guinness. "How about you come round tonight and we can sort things out, tell me what you want me to ask for? Then I suppose I can start tomorrow."

"What about Pam?"

"She's fine. I said I'd ring her later tonight."

"Has she gone home?"

"Yes."

"Where is that?" Amanda asked.

"Buckinghamshire, one of these posh medieval villages. St Simon, it's called. Do you know it?"

"Vaguely. We could go out to her and brief her in person if you like? I think we should keep her in the loop. I don't want her running off on her own. Besides, she's clever. She might be able to help."

"Okay, when?"

"I need a few minutes at my office. I'll pick you up in half an hour, outside the pub if you like?"

After another couple of pints, Jack was outside and waiting on the street for Amanda's arrival. She was on time and he climbed into her SUV, then they struggled through the heavy London traffic.

Amanda had been busy. "I have had a quick look at the police files on Riordan. At first glance, there's not much out of the ordinary. Guy in a sports car, going too fast and he missed a bend. Traces of cocaine in his system. Seems straightforward."

She paused. "He was unlucky – it couldn't have been a worse spot to go off the road. The road climbs for a mile or so. At the summit, there's a hundred-foot drop and it's steep sided."

"Is there no barrier?"

"There is, but he was going so fast the car just crashed through."

Jack pursed his lips and shook his head slightly. "It's just not the Paul that I knew."

"When did you last see him?"

"A few years ago," Jack conceded, "although I spoke to him on the phone last Christmas. But I'm not convinced. Cocaine … never knew him to take drugs."

"People change, Jack."

"True, but what about the reckless driving? That doesn't sound like Paul. And then the worst part of the road. That was very unlucky."

"There's a lot of luck in life – and in death."

"Did you find out where he been on the day of his death?" Jack asked.

"He was in his London office all day, and afterwards at a City wine bar for about an hour. Seems that someone was leaving. He popped in, apparently, just to show his face."

"Did he have a drink?"

"Just a couple of tonic waters."

Jack nodded. "That sounds more unsurprising. He was never a drinker. He used to scold me about my drinking."

"Also unsurprising," Amanda teased.

"I've cut down."

She snorted. "A sort of work in progress?"

"Something like that."

"I also had a look at the autopsy." She looked across at him. "Do you want to hear about that?"

"Yes, what did it say?"

"Well, the conclusions were hardly surprising. Basically, the impact killed him. I mean, he didn't have a heart attack at the wheel or anything like that."

"What about the cocaine?"

"Quite a high amount in his system. I'm told it wasn't enough to knock him out, although who knows, it affects people in different ways."

"Surely the doctors can tell if he was a regular user?"

"Maybe," Amanda said. "I'll ask, but really, does it matter?"

"Oh, I don't know, maybe not … but if not, why would he take drugs on this occasion?"

He took out a packet of cigarettes from his pocket and offered her a drug of his own.

"No, I'm trying to give up cigarettes."

"Oh, good for you," he said unenthusiastically. She was the last person he knew that still smoked. If she quit, he would be the last smoker. It was a dispiriting thought.

"Go ahead. It doesn't bother me. I'm taking it slowly. Another work in progress, you might say." At least she hadn't turned into a fanatic. "Now, about Pam. She seems a decent kid, but we need to protect her from all this."

"That's going to be difficult. She's headstrong, she knows her own mind and she wants the truth."

"Hmm, the truth. I wonder whether the truth is always the best thing for people. Sometimes it's better not to know things. I mean, she loved her father … she's got a certain image of him. Who knows what'll come out?"

"I think she'll be able to handle it, whatever comes out."

"You've only known her a couple of days. She's lost her father, her mother's dead and she's only twenty. We need to be careful, and, you might need to step up as a godparent."

Jeez … Jack was struggling to look after himself.

Amanda sped past a slow middle-lane driver and indicated to leave the motorway. "Is this the right way?"

"Yes."

"I think I know how to get to the village now."

She did, and with only a single wrong turn, headed through the village and in a few minutes halted outside the gates of Pam's house.

Jack texted Pam. The gates moved apart and Amanda drove in. They got out of the car. Pam stood framed in the front doorway, just a kid desperate for some good news.

Chapter 7

Jack got out of bed at about nine the next morning, which wasn't bad considering he and Amanda had returned to London at about 2 a.m. The meeting with Pam had gone well enough, he supposed. She had listened intently to Amanda's updates and asked a lot of questions. Despite Amanda's concerns, she had exhibited no squeamishness when it came to questions about her father's accident. It seemed that this project, and her drive for the truth, was her way of coping.

There had been some push-back when Amanda again ruled out any active role for Pam, but she had eventually accepted this in the face of Amanda's insistence that she was too close. If she wanted to get to the truth, a professional approach was essential. Mercifully, she had not queried Jack's status as a professional, but he supposed he was, at least, more experienced than she was.

He showered, reluctantly shaved and, even more reluctantly, struggled into a business suit. It had taken him years to retire that suit and he resented its reappearance, but it was for a few days only and it was for a good cause. He fiddled with his tie, then the buttons of his jacket, but nothing much helped, and the mirror reflected an unsatisfactory sight. He stopped wasting his time. It was as good as it was going to get.

A short taxi ride took him to the heart of the City of London. It was about ten o'clock and he had no fixed appointment, so he had plenty of time. He managed to gain a small standing area in one of the endless coffee bars. The coffee was hot and weaker than it should have been at this price. As he gazed across through the crowd at the uninviting entrance to the Canisp Hedge Fund across the road, he began to focus on what he thought was a familiar figure. He dismissed the thought, but a second look convinced him to abandon the watery coffee and leave the café.

The figure sat on a four-cornered wooden seating area on a concrete concourse in front of the entrance to the hedge fund. Halfway there, it was clear that Jack's eyes had not played him false.

He sat down next to Pam. She was dressed in a business suit. He looked at her.

She smiled at him, didn't apologise and said, "He was my father and I want to be involved."

Jack lit a cigarette. If she wanted to go in, there was really nothing he could do. Well, she was a major shareholder. Maybe it would be better if he kept her closer, as if he had a choice. "Are you absolutely certain that no one knows you in there?"

"Yes, I've already told you that."

He gave up. "Okay, but only if you just follow, back me up, say nothing at all."

"I promise."

"Honestly, Amanda's not going to like this."

"Do you always do what she says?"

He said firmly, "Yes, especially in investigations."

"When do we go in?"

Jack thought of a practical problem. "You don't have a badge."

Pam laughed. "If you can't get past that, we are going to have a real struggle with this enquiry."

Jack sighed. "Come on." She followed him into the building, and a moment later they stood before a receptionist, to whom Jack introduced himself.

It didn't impress the receptionist much and she insisted that the only route to admittance was to ask for a member of staff by name.

Jack said hopefully, "Let's try the manager?"

The receptionist remained unimpressed, but got to work. "Take a seat, please. Mr Common will be with you presently."

Presently took about ten minutes, time which Jack spent fretting over the many things that could go wrong with this venture. He had successfully generated a fair number of potentially dismal outcomes, before a well-suited, balding man of about fifty approached.

The office manager extended a hand. "Ray Common, general manager."

Jack flashed him his identity card, and said stiffly, "I and my colleague are here for the purpose of undertaking an unscheduled strength and reserves inspection."

Ray Common sat up a bit straighter. Unlike Jack, he looked like he understood what this all meant. "Of course, Mr Edwards. Will you need an office?"

"Yes, thank you, Mr Common."

"If you wait here, I'll arrange that. Can I get you coffee or something?"

"Yes coffee, thank you." Jack added, "And perhaps a list of all staff and job titles?"

"Yes, of course, Mr Edwards." Common got up and had a word with the receptionist before disappearing up the stairs.

"Nice work, that seems to have got their attention," Pam said.

"Yes," Jack agreed, "but let's not get carried away. Say nothing, and we keep things simple."

He looked across at the formerly disinterested receptionist. Pam was quite right. These few magic words of introduction had certainly got her attention, and she was busy now, making a series of calls. A moment later, a young, perfectly dressed assistant arrived with coffee.

Ray Common returned and announced that an office had been set aside for them. He led them up the stairs and then into a frosted-glass office. It was home to a couple of desks and a decent-sized conference table. "Thank you, Mr Common, this will be fine. Could I have a set of keys please?"

Common had anticipated this and produced them from his pocket. "And here is our staff listing, Mr Edwards. I've indicated who's in and who's out today."

Jack started weakly, possibly misquoting the relevant act, but Common nodded so he figured he had gotten away with it. He blustered on. "I will want to speak to, let me see, David Ferguson, Selena Thornton, yourself, of course, Mr Common. Also, Ali Cairns, and, perhaps, other senior managers. In the first place, all together if possible."

He then added casually, quickly adjusting to possession of absolute power. "I would also like to interview your board members."

Common was acting like a man who favoured being on the right side of a regulatory investigation. "Let me go and check diaries and I'll get right back to you."

He left the office at a purposeful pace and Jack sat back, satisfied that his opening bluffs had not been called. Pam, meantime, had extracted the laptop from Jack's bag and was firing it up. Perhaps this would be an area where she could assist? He hadn't booted up a computer in years, and although Amanda last night and Smith yesterday had walked him through the presentation, he was not confident. "Are you any good with computers?"

"Yes, very," she said immodestly.

This self-assessment proved accurate as she located his presentation in seconds and conducted a rapid review. "We need to ask for personnel files, monthly management accounts and customer lists."

Jack did this when Common returned with the news that a management meeting was scheduled for 11 a.m. and, if it suited them, the top team would receive them at its conclusion, around noon.

"Fine," Jack said. "If you can supply us with these records in the meantime it would help, and we will need access to a printer."

"Yes, leave it with me."

Business as Usual

Within minutes, a succession of staff arrived and deposited paperwork and hooked up a printer. It was just after eleven now, so they had an hour to make a start.

Jack was already exhausted, but Pam wasn't, and now he was glad she was here. "Have a look through that presentation," he said. "That's basically what we're pretending to do. Get in about these files and, er, make some kind of a start."

It wasn't much of a brief, but Pam was full of energy and enthusiasm. Jack pulled over the individual personnel files and conducted a desultory review.

"There's a problem with these lists," she said.

"What is it?"

"Well, it seems that clients favour obscure and exotic trading names. They tell us nothing. Who are they?"

Jack shrugged. "We can ask, and Amanda should be able to help."

Pam was still hammering on the keyboard. She stopped and exclaimed. "Wow, have you any idea how much money is under management here?"

"A few billion?"

"Hundreds of billions, actually. Where on earth does it come from?"

"That's what we're trying to find out," Jack said unhelpfully.

"We need more details on these clients, and we need these lists electronically."

Jack nodded and reached for his mobile. He phoned Common, who promised action.

A few minutes later, a young, well-dressed man with a close-cropped beard knocked and entered. "I'm Rob. Mr Common has asked me to assist you."

Pam said, "We need electronic versions of these files."

Rob looked through the papers. "Yes, fine. I will arrange it."

He left the room. "Being a regulator certainly opens a few doors," Pam said. "Amanda had the right idea."

Adam Parish

Jack spent the available time before the noon meeting familiarising himself with the key people they were about to meet. David Ferguson, he had already encountered from Canisp's website. He was forty-two and possessed an overwhelming number of educational achievements and business triumphs. Could anyone be this good? Not stated on the website was his basic salary of one million pounds annually. That was eyewatering enough, yet was dwarfed by his bonus payments, which for each of the previous five years had ranged between seven to fifteen million pounds.

Jack had got his money for nothing – a legacy from his aunt – but nonetheless he found himself, unreasonably, wondering how such sums could ever be justified. These musings could wait. He was here to investigate a death – the death of a friend. As for Ferguson, Jack could conclude only that he was a powerful individual with global experience.

Similar conclusions could be drawn regarding Selena Thornton, the third member of the top management team. She was American and a more recent arrival at Canisp, and her salary and bonuses were smaller than those of Ferguson, but not so much as to provoke a discrimination action. Thornton was thirty-nine and her expertise appeared to be more legal and corporate than that of Ferguson, although her global reach was at least as long.

Whatever else, Canisp certainly were running a tight ship with the top executive team: formerly three, and now reduced to two following Paul's death. This lean structure continued down the organisational chart with only a further two personnel listed as senior managers. Ray Common they had already met. The title of office manager wasn't very exciting, but he was very well rewarded, albeit at an order of magnitude below the top team. He was an accountant by trade and had made a career in that role across the various City firms.

The file of Ali Cairns – who, it turned out, was female – was more interesting. Aged only twenty-nine, her title implied a technical role. So, *she* was the rocket scientist. It took such a person to manage and, at least partially, understand modern finance. Jack had run a few

Business as Usual

courses, years ago, on options and portfolio theory and he hadn't believed in it then. Some of the mathematics were elegant, but in his view, it just didn't work in practice. It was likely that the industry agreed with him, but nobody could admit that or the whole gravy train would hit the buffers.

This debate could wait, however, and he threw down the files and rehearsed his opening lines for the upcoming meeting.

Ray Common was prompt, and a few minutes before noon, he led Jack and Pam past a busy, open office area and through to what, presumably, was the main boardroom.

Under the circumstances it was only modestly opulent, with a highly polished table and accompanying chairs. The modern art on the wall looked suspiciously original and by sought after artists.

They were offered sandwiches, which Jack and Pam declined, and they sat down on one side of the table opposite four faces: Ferguson, Thornton, Cairns, and Common. An obligatory few minutes were wasted connecting the laptop to a large screen before Jack started.

In a sociopathic tone, typical of investigating bureaucrats, he started by making a superficial reference to the Acts he could remember, assured them that the company had been selected randomly and stated that, typically, such an investigation lasted for two or three days. Drunk with his eloquence, Jack added a rider that such an investigation could, of course, last indefinitely depending upon the findings.

These remarks were received without comment, so Jack went straight to the formal presentation, which was also received in silence.

"We can, hopefully, let you get on soon," he said. "As you are all together, perhaps you can give me a bit of background on the company. Management, financial strength and controls are a key part of our report."

The first thing they learnt was that Ferguson was in charge. He was impressive and handsome and highly articulate. Jack noted that the others continually looked to him.

Jack's first impression was a good one. Ferguson exuded authority and competence. He was a man who was in full control of himself and his audience. His voice was relaxing, his accent neutral and his words measured. "I'm David Ferguson, acting CEO. Mr Edwards, thanks for your brief introduction. All of us are fully aware of the work of our regulators and we are very happy to assist you in any way we can. As far as the executive team is concerned, we are confident that Canisp is in a strong position. Let me introduce our team."

Ferguson introduced Selena Thornton, Ray Common, and Ali Cairns.

"We are, of course, missing our founding partner Paul Riordan, who unfortunately died last month. He is a great loss, but he built a great company and has left us with a very strong team. Now, is there anything more we can do for you at the moment?"

"Thanks," Jack said. "I'd only ask that you make yourselves available for short individual meetings, not more than thirty minutes. Other than that, I think we have all we need for now."

"We are all available this afternoon," Ferguson said.

Jack thanked him and he and Pam returned to their office.

The meeting had lasted about twenty-five minutes but Jack threw his feet over a nearby seat and yawned loudly.

Pam allowed herself a laugh and said, "Shock to the system?"

"Yes, I haven't been in an office for about five years. But what did you make of them?"

Pam considered. "Ferguson was impressive, a smooth operator. If anyone knows what's going on, he seems to. As for the others, nothing. I mean, they didn't open their mouths."

"Have we got electronic versions of these client lists now?"

"Yes, nearly all of them, and I've got quite a lot of the information on this template." She flung across an A4 sheet which had been pre-completed with metrics comparing the figures against the last inspection. It was now three quarters completed. This far, all the so-called vital indicators were in the green zone, and all at least as good as in the last period.

"Well, we've learned pretty much nothing," Jack said. "Damn stupid idea this."

"Maybe these one-to-one meeting will be better?"

"Only if we ask the right questions."

"And what are the right questions?"

"I really don't know, to be honest."

Pam didn't seem discouraged. "At least we got the information Amanda asked for."

"Yes, that's all we can do at this stage."

Further discussions were cut short by the arrival of Ray Common. "When do you want to start these meetings? Do you need lunch?"

Jack looked at Pam. She shook her head. "No, we are fine. Is someone ready now?"

"I can be," said Common.

Chapter 8

"Okay, Mr Common," Jack said. "Here's the sheet we are compiling."

Common reviewed the numbers and nodded confidently. "Yes, as I expected. We are very satisfied with our progress and performance since the last statutory returns. Obviously, you want to finalise this. If you need background, let me know."

"I understand that you lost your CEO recently?"

"Yes, as David mentioned, Paul will be a big loss."

"How significant will this be going forward?"

Common considered. "Paul was the founder of Canisp, but one of the reasons for our growth was that Paul recruited great people. You've met some of them already. So, it's a big loss, but all the work's covered going forward."

"David Ferguson seems very able."

"Yes, I think he was Paul's first hire. He knows the business and the City very well."

"Since the last inspection, is there anything that you know of that is material or potentially might be harmful to the smooth running of Canisp?"

"Nothing at all, Mr Edwards."

"Okay, I'll leave it at that. We will, of course, want to go through all the figures with you when we have completed them."

"Of course. Do you want me to arrange your next meeting?"

"Yes, please."

They didn't have to wait long. Within a few minutes, Selena Thornton came into the small office. A good-looking woman with an on trend short blonde hairstyle. Her eyes were blue and bright and her teeth perfect. She was approaching forty but hadn't quite accepted this fact. Elegantly dressed, she sat down gracefully and looked at Jack.

"Thanks for seeing us Miss, er *Mrs* Thornton?"

"Miss."

"Perhaps you can talk us through the performance of the company over the last six months?"

Thornton retrieved a pair of spectacles from the top pocket of a well-cut suit. She looked carefully at Jack and started to talk in a low authoritative voice. It was a short and well-structured reply. Everything was just great at Canisp.

"You've been at Canisp for about five years. What were you doing before?"

"I'm American, and a lawyer originally."

"East coast?" Jack ventured.

"Yes, Amherst."

"Nice place."

"You been there?"

"No, but I knew someone from there. A long time ago."

"Who?"

"An old girlfriend. We haven't kept up."

Selena said, "Our family have been there for a long time. We came over on the Mayflower." She looked skyward, seemingly distracted, and then re-focussed on Jack.

Jack decided that this was no time for a chat about his old girlfriends. "Your background is mostly corporate. Do you know a lot about international finance?"

She flashed him a wintry smile. "I am not a financial expert to trade, but I know the business pretty well, I would say."

"What about clients? Who gets them and who manages them?"

"Every senior manager has a responsibility to secure new clients, and each major client is managed by an individual senior member of staff. Naturally, the most important clients are managed at the highest level."

Naturally. "So, with Mr Riordan's death, there'll be a few clients to reassign?"

"Yes, but there will certainly be no disruption."

"How do you acquire new clients?"

"Word of mouth, referrals, hanging around with the right people."

"And who are the right people. Anyone with money?"

Selena's mouth tightened a bit, and she stared at Jack. "Our ethical standards are as high as any other financial institution. It's very important to us. There are so many challenges: plastic in the oceans, climate change, global human rights to name just a few."

While she was talking, Jack watched her intently. There could be no other corporate line, but Jack always doubted corporate commitment. But he didn't detect any cynicism in Selena Thornton. Her face was mildly flushed, and either she was a consummate actress or she really *did* believe in these issues. A professional inspector might have left it there, but Jack couldn't help himself. He challenged her again in a tone designed to irritate. "And do all your clients share these values?"

She refused this invitation to be irritated and said coldly, "Many do. In fact, I would say most, but with a few we are happy to provide education and support."

Jack managed to suppress a laugh. "Are all the partners committed to these issues?"

"Of course. We select our partners very carefully."

Jack gave up and decided to suspend his disbelief, and after Selena Thornton again opined confidently that there were no negative developments in the company operations since their last investigation, she left.

Jack said to Pam, "And if you believe all that, you'll believe anything."

Business as Usual

Pam said credulously, "You're out of date, Jack, and far too cynical. A modern corporation has to take these issues seriously."

Jack failed to suppress a laugh this time. Pam looked annoyed.

"Sorry, let's not prejudge this issue," he said. "Perhaps when we get into the client list we'll find out."

Pam made to answer, but further political disagreement was avoided with the arrival of Ali Cairns, a fresh freckled-faced young woman originally from New Zealand. She wore large glasses. Her hair was packed into an untidy bun and she was make-up-free. Her seniority while still in her twenties could be for one reason only: that she could do something very much better than almost anyone else. She outlined her background, which confirmed this. A first-class degree, a Masters from Oxford, a PhD at twenty-four and a fellowship at twenty-six. Stellar indeed. Her areas of expertise were extensive: mathematics, astrophysics and a bit of natural science. She skipped over these routine accomplishments and described her two years at Canisp.

"I never really saw myself working in the City, to be honest."

"So why did you come here?" Jack couldn't resist asking.

"I was headhunted. They chased me pretty hard, and eventually I thought, why not?"

Jack knew what she meant. Very few twenty-nine-year-olds earned a million pounds a year. A few years in the City would set her up for life.

She confirmed as much. "Yes, the money was an attraction, but there are things to learn in the City and ..." A flash of emotion crossed her features but she suppressed it. "Paul Riordan was a real pioneer in his field. Working with him was an attraction."

As he looked at Cairns, a thought occurred to Jack. Paul had lost his wife many years ago and was devoted to his work, but there had surely been women in his life. He looked again at Ali Cairns, and thought of Paul and she working together. She looked young to him, but he supposed the age gap wasn't that much. "Will Mr Riordan's death create a problem for Canisp?"

She wore a professional mask and uttered a stock answer, but Jack wasn't listening to her words. He was watching her hands, shaking at first, then clasped tightly together, and concluded that Ali Cairns was experiencing emotions far deeper than those usually associated with the loss of a work colleague.

"Have there been any significant changes or particular difficulties with Canisp since our last inspection?" he asked.

Cairns shook her head. "No, our balance sheet remains strong and, if anything, as we have grown, we've been able to spread risk more satisfactorily."

"The world economy's pretty volatile."

"Of course, that's how we make our money."

"And your trading strategies?"

"It varies depending on client requirements, obviously supplemented by our advice."

Jack wasn't yet out of his depth, but he was getting close. "So, as far as you are concerned, there are no current trading or operational difficulties that we need to know about?"

"Absolutely not."

"Okay, thanks very much, Miss Cairns. It might be that we have some detailed questions later."

"Of course, I'll be happy to help."

After Cairns had left the room, Jack turned to Pam. "Did Paul ever mention Ali Cairns?"

"No, no, he didn't, but he rarely talked about work."

"I wasn't really thinking about work, to be honest."

"Oh, a girlfriend?"

"Something like that."

"Oh. She's nice," Pam said. "A bit young maybe, but the sort Dad might have gone for. Brainy and understated."

"Did he have other girlfriends?"

"As far as I know, there was no one special. After Mum died, well, it was pretty much all work for him, along with looking after me. Then

Business as Usual

I was away at boarding school and then university. He probably had girlfriends, but I'm sure nothing serious otherwise I'd have met them."

Jack nodded. He knew better than most that it was quite possible for middle-aged straight men with advantages to forgo the company of women for a long time. Especially after a grievous loss. He looked at his watch. It was after two now, and in terms of meeting key people and obtaining documents without being rumbled, he supposed they had done well.

Chapter 9

There was a knock at the door. One was never alone when conducting a surprise inspection. This time it was the top man, David Ferguson, the managing director. Being a financial inspector certainly opened doors. "The board are ready now if you are," he said.

Ferguson was tall and had a strong, fit body. He was as good-looking as his online photograph suggested. They followed him to the conference room.

There were three people already in the room sitting around the bottom end of the table in a semicircle. It looked like a Star Chamber.

Jack again reminded himself that, while in character, he was in charge. He and Pam sat at the near end of the table and Ferguson resumed his seat at the other end.

"I appreciate you making yourself available," Jack began. "Mr Ferguson will have briefed you about our investigation."

He looked down to the far end of the table. Sir George Black sat facing him. Now in his seventies, but looking ten years younger, the chairman of Canisp and veteran corporate raider evaluated Jack in return. His rugged but still taut jawline betrayed no emotion. Jack asked him if he would introduce his board and outline its role.

Sir George removed his spectacles, glanced at his colleagues and began to speak in a deep, pleasant and compelling tone. On his right he indicated Katherine Carver, yet another American lawyer of about fifty who had served both Republican and Democratic Presidential administrations. On her right, Leo King, the chairman and CEO of a private bank favoured by the aristocracy and, according to the press, rumoured to be favourite as the next governor of the Bank of England.

Alongside the banker sat a man that Jack recognised. Lord Jeremy Steel wore a well-cut suit and no tie. He must have been pushing seventy but his attire admitted only to mid-forties. Steel had been a senior figure in British politics for about twenty years. He had represented a "left of centre" party, but as far as Jack was concerned, Steel was a committed globalist, a multi-millionaire and now sat on the board of a hedge fund. Maybe that was socialism?

Sir George concluded these abridged introductions, and handed over to Katherine Carver. Her clothes looked straight from Milan, and they made her look older. She had a hard face, which seemed to be a work in progress. Her voice was well bred and transatlantic, and after listening to her for a second or two, Jack was sure that, at least in her own mind, everyone else was lucky to be listening. Mercifully, she didn't talk for long. To someone who had prosecuted American presidents, providing a five-minute overview of the role and competences of a hedge fund board was a simple task, and she closed by giving a personal assurance that the board had carried out all of its duties perfectly.

Maybe that was true; maybe Jack should leave now. But he decided to stick around, being reasonably certain that no member of this Board had the slightest idea of how a hedge fund worked. He decided not to share these thoughts at the moment and confined his remarks to seeking an oral confirmation that the board were satisfied that no material concerns had been noted since the last audit.

"If we had concerns, I would have said so," Katherine Carver replied.

There was no answer to that, so Jack thanked them and excused himself and Pam, vaguely muttering that he might have to speak to them again. He hoped that he would not have to.

He and Pam rose and the managing director, David Ferguson, again escorted them back to their office.

"Can we have a quick word with you, Mr Ferguson?" Jack asked.

Ferguson looked left, then right. He slid into the office and closed the door behind him without relinquishing his hold on the handle.

He was a big man and seemed to fill the office. His neutral expression became more benign. An explanation was required. "Sorry about this, Mr Edwards. I do want to speak to you, but not here."

"An irregular request, Mr Ferguson. Why would we need to speak elsewhere?"

"Can we speak in private?"

Jack looked at Pam. This was no time for debate. She smiled sweetly at both of them and left the office.

"Will you sit?"

Ferguson preferred to stand. "I'll be brief. Can we speak off the record?"

"I cannot promise that, Mr Ferguson."

"No, of course not, I understand, but I can assure you what I am going to say is not directly material to Canisp's solvency. We are in good financial shape. I can guarantee that."

"Well, what's the problem, Mr Ferguson?"

"I've been reviewing client accounts recently. It's very important that we have no dubious connections, ethically speaking. We undertake reviews like this regularly."

"And how can I help?"

"I want to have a chat about one of them. Off the record."

"Why off the record?"

"The client was introduced by someone at a high level in our company. There are potential political sensitivities. I'd like your opinion."

"Can't you send me something by email?"

"I'd rather talk it through. I keep the papers at home."

Jack had a million questions but was pretty sure that he would get nothing more out of Ferguson here and now. His heart was beating faster. This was an exciting development, but he remembered that, to a financial inspector, it would sound highly irregular. He summoned up an astonished expression, then a pause which he didn't need. This done, he said, "I don't usually do this, but perhaps under the circumstances."

Ferguson looked relieved. He delved into his pocket. "Here's my home address and mobile number. Could we say 7.30 tonight?"

"Why not?"

Ferguson thanked him and left the office.

For the first time, Jack reckoned he was making some progress.

Chapter 10

Pam returned to the office. "What was all that about?"

"Ferguson wants a bit of advice on one of his clients."

"Maybe he was working with Dad?"

"He didn't say so, but he says he has more papers at his home. I'm going to meet with him later."

She was eager for details but Jack cut her short. "Let's get out of here. We've made a good start, but I want to speak to Amanda."

He called her and, without detailing their progress for the day, asked for an early meeting.

She agreed and proposed a nearby wine bar.

"See you there in half an hour."

"Where to?" Pam said.

"A wine bar near Leadenhall in about twenty minutes. Let's go."

They arrived at the busy bar in good time. After a short struggle, Jack procured a couple of soft drinks. A search for a seat failed, however, and they stood uncomfortably for a few minutes.

Jack's phone rang.

"Are you in the wine bar yet?" Amanda asked.

"Yes, just arrived."

"Good. I want you to leave there now and head west for about five minutes until you get to Smith Court. Turn right and the St George pub is about a hundred yards down the lane. You can't miss it. I'll see you there."

Business as Usual

Jack said to Pam, "Come on, change of venue."

Amanda's directions were good enough, and after the promised five or so minutes they arrived at the St George. It was a traditional public house, and it looked as if it had been there since the Great Fire. Inside the interior was a little more modern, dating from about the nineteenth century.

Unlike the wine bars in the heart of the City, the St George was very lightly patronised – specifically by a barman and Amanda.

She jumped off her bar stool as they entered and led them through a door marked "Private" and up a narrow staircase. The first-floor landing was home to a single door, through which was a large office-cum-lounge whose purpose was hinted at by a collection of computing and telecoms equipment.

Amanda indicated a sofa. "Have a seat. Coffee?"

Jack said, "Can I smoke?"

"If you must."

He lit up. "Was this subterfuge really necessary?"

Amanda said playfully, "I favour caution," and added, "which is just as well, because you were followed."

Jack was disbelieving. "By who?"

Amanda moved behind a desk and typed on a keyboard. "Have a look at the screen."

On a large monitor affixed to the wall, a crystal-clear picture of Ali Cairns was displayed.

"How do you know she followed us?" Pam asked. "I mean, she might have just gone for a drink."

"Well, she left the building at the same time as you and waited outside the wine bar for the five or so minutes as you did, then followed you inside. She then left the wine bar when you did and followed you along the street."

"She followed us here?" Jack said.

"No, she lost you, I saw to that."

"How do you know all this?" Pam asked.

Amanda handed them both a coffee and said, "The same way I knew that you were with Jack, despite what I told you last night."

She sat down alongside them on a sofa and added, "The City of London has more surveillance cameras per square mile than anywhere in the world, and I had a trainee who was in need of some counter-surveillance experience. Whatever she wanted, it's important that we're not seen together. If they get wind of your unofficial status, there'll be a hell of a row. Their board is very well connected." Amanda took a mouthful of coffee. "How did you do today?"

Pam handed Amanda the laptop and Jack provided some commentary. Amanda reviewed the files on the laptop; Jack waited until he felt Amanda was going to express disappointment with his efforts and then dropped the Ferguson bombshell. She took the news in her stride.

"When and where's the meeting?"

"Hirston at 7:30. That's in Surrey, yes?"

Amanda said, "Yes, about forty or fifty miles, an hour and a bit driving at that time of night."

Jack nodded. "Okay, I'll leave about six."

"And me?" Pam asked.

Jack looked at Amanda.

"Ferguson will expect me – or at least not be surprised if I'm there."

Amanda looked unconvinced. "I think a better idea would be if you stayed here, Pam."

Pam made to protest, but Amanda cut her short. "I was going to say that we would make more progress this way. I've got one of my guys coming round. He's an IT and finance expert and can start looking into those client accounts, but it'll be quicker if you help him."

Pam's expression cleared. "Okay, when is your man coming?"

"He's due now."

For a blissful few minutes, no one had anything to say, and Jack poured himself another coffee, settled into the sofa and gently shut his eyes. It was a long time since he had done anything close to a full day's work. A half-day was a small sample, but it had provided him with conclusive evidence that it was no longer for him. He glanced over to the far side of the room, where Pam and Amanda were sitting in front of several computers, sorting out a pile of papers. His watch showed five and Jack figured he had about another hour of perfect peace before they would head for Surrey. He leant back heavily into the sofa.

Annoyingly, the perfect peace was broken in just a few minutes by the noisy entrance of a badly dressed teenager who nodded to Amanda and made for the coffee. Spies were certainly getting younger these days, Jack reflected, as he was reintroduced to Max Harris. The youngster shook Jack's hand, laid down his backpack and rid himself of his earphones.

Harris conducted a brief audit of the available equipment, then switched on all three of the wall-mounted monitors. He produced a keyboard, to which he attached a strap, and then, improbably, suspended the keyboard from his neck. This done, he opened a can of energy drink and gulped some down.

Then the performance began. "Okay, read out the first one."

Amanda said, "Mountain Stream, address: Ludgate Hill, London."

This limited information proved enough for Harris to make a start. His fingers were a blur on the keyboard and the monitors constantly changed views. After about thirty seconds, he stopped and, reading the screen, shouted, "London to Liechtenstein to Cayman. Associated with Idaho Construction. Possible CIA link; mark it as 1." This performance was repeated many times at the same frantic pace.

Jack wasn't completely clear on the precise classification system, and the pace of the investigation precluded asking questions. Quite quickly Amanda, also perhaps exhausted, relinquished control of the laptop and handed it over to Pam.

She poured herself a drink and fell heavily beside Jack on the sofa.

"Wow," Jack said.

"Yes, impressive, isn't it?"

"Where did you get him?"

She laughed. "It's quite an interesting story. Max dropped out of school and has never been to university. But he's got an IQ of about

200 and a photographic memory. He was working in our call centre. They were about to sack him, actually. I happened to be there and, I don't know why, I talked to him. There was something about him and I had a vacancy for an office junior, so I took him on. It turned out to be a good decision."

That was the understatement of the year. By the time that Amanda had explained her unconventional recruitment policy, Max and Pam had completed an initial sweep of client accounts and Harris was now going deeper.

Suddenly he let out a loud expletive. "Sorry, boss," he said to Amanda, who appeared unconcerned.

Jack looked enquiringly.

"I think he's just hacked the CIA's website," she said. "He'll have to wipe away what they call the digital footprint."

There was no real answer to that.

"I'll come with you to see Ferguson tonight. Those two seem to be working well together."

Jack said, "Yes, that's a better idea, although how will I explain you to Ferguson?"

"We'll talk about that in the car."

Chapter 11

Amanda had a car parked at the side of the pub. Jack reviewed his phone. "Samson Farm, Hirston sorry, no postcode."

"Never mind, I know that area slightly, and if we get lost you can call him." The satnav predicted a fifty-five-minute journey time. It was ten past six now, so they had plenty of time. That, at least, was the theory, but at seven o'clock they were still on the M25 and, with half an hour until the meeting, the satnav now forecast them to be late. This deficit was never recovered, and at seven-thirty with some dozen miles to go, Jack reached for his phone. No answer.

He tried again without success when they had eventually left the motorway and progressed smoothly to the village of Hirston. Amanda halted outside an old coaching inn and despatched Jack inside to enquire about Samson Farm. This worked, and he returned with good news. "About a mile out of the village. It's signposted."

This proved true; the route indicated led to a crossroads, but again Amanda got it right and eventually a sign indicated a track which led only to the house.

It was 7:45 now. The light was fading, but the evening visibility was still reasonable. The track was uneven and potholed and went gently uphill. At the summit they were finally afforded a view of the property. Quite clearly it was no longer a working farm, and although there were a couple of outbuildings, the scene was dominated by a large, modern two-storey house. It wasn't unattractive, and the house was situated on a local high spot. Behind it, there were distant views over the Weald of England, tinged orange by the setting sun which sat just over the house.

About a quarter of a mile from the house the track improved, morphing into a smooth tarred surface. The road dipped mildly and for a second the light dimmed as the structure blocked the setting sun, but for only an instant before being replaced by a blinding white light and, a second later, an ear-splitting explosion.

Amanda reacted quickly; first violently braking and then reversing wildly whilst some low-level debris thudded against the car. She controlled the vehicle admirably, but it was a bumpy ride before she finally stopped back at the crest of the track.

They sat in silence for a moment, staring ahead, both once again compelled by the beauty of the setting summer sun, this time with the view unhindered by Ferguson's former home.

Chapter 12

The silence that followed lasted for what felt like a long time before Amanda reached under the steering wheel and produced some kind of radio. A short conversation consisted of some English and some code, but it proved better than the standard 999 call. A few minutes later, an unmarked Land Rover pulled up behind them.

A knock on the window signalled the arrival of a fit-looking man in military fatigues. He opened the door and announced himself in crisp, refined tones as Captain Parker. Amanda flashed him a card.

"Evening, ma'am." He stood back a little and purposefully sniffed the air, then, bending down, flashed a torch around the Range Rover and picked up what looked like mud. He sniffed it. These crude tests concluded, he said, "A big bomb, ma'am."

"Yes, and a single explosion, I think." She looked to Jack.

"Yes, one only."

Parker said, "Do you want to come with us, ma'am?"

"No, I'll leave it to the experts first. Give me a shout when you're clear."

At this, the captain returned to his vehicle, which moved with another past them and onto the ground where Ferguson's home had been. There was only waiting now.

Jack offered Amanda a cigarette and she hesitated before accepting. Jack looked down at his own hand. It was shaking. "Thank goodness we weren't on time," he said, then followed with his principal concern. His voice faltered as he said, "And thank goodness I didn't bring Pam."

She looked at him and squeezed his arm. "We need to get her well away from this now. This is big league stuff."

"Yes, maybe not surprising when there's so much money involved."

"Hmm. What I'm interested in is whether they were just after Ferguson."

"What do you mean?"

"It's Ferguson's house, so that he is a target is obvious. The question is whether they knew that you, or you and Pam, were meant to be there?"

"Seems unlikely. What did we know?"

"Nothing, but Ferguson was going to talk to you tonight. Far better to get rid of all of you. Make sure that no one talked."

"Maybe, but what we *do* know is that Ferguson knew something and Paul knew something. And they're both dead."

"Yes."

Jack drew on his cigarette and started shifting on his seat.

Amanda said, "Are you okay?"

"Not really. I'm thinking about Pam. I'm angry with myself. You told me not to involve her and I didn't listen. I came down here determined to make up for the last twenty years. Never being there for her. I've been here two days and nearly got her killed. Fuck, if I really want to help her, I should leave her alone for another twenty years."

"Is this where I take your arm and tell you it's not your fault?" Amanda asked.

Jack laughed. "Why don't you take my arm for a minute? That would be nice. You don't have to say anything."

She reached across and gently clasped and rubbed his arm.

"That's nice, keep doing that. It's helping me think. Maybe it was an accident, a gas explosion or something?"

"No, I don't think so."

"You sure?"

Business as Usual

"Not 100% but I have some experience in this sort of thing."

"So, who uses bombs?"

"Terrorists, governments, terrorist governments. Not usually hedge fund employees," she added dryly.

During these inconclusive deliberations, many vehicles passed. Night had fallen now, but powerful spotlighting at the scene allowed Jack sight of many silhouetted operators working in what appeared to be a depression of variable depth. "How long do these things usually take?"

"Who can tell. Maybe a day or so, but we'll get a provisional update soon enough. I can see Captain Parker heading this way."

She dropped the car window.

"All safe now, ma'am."

"And the explosion?"

"Provisionally C4 with maybe a fertiliser blend."

"Northern Irish?" she asked.

"Not sure, ma'am. That's a bit before my time."

"How many bodies?"

"Too early to be certain. One dead for sure, although it's only a trace."

Trace wasn't an offensive word but it hung in the air, powerfully emphasising the inevitable outcome of a contest between a human body and a devastating explosion.

"Can I have a look?" Amanda asked.

"Yes, it's quite safe now."

"I'll come across in a few minutes."

"So you were right," Jack said.

"Seems so. You coming?"

Jack started to speak but was interrupted. The back door of the car opened and a man in a heavy coat sat down without speaking.

Amanda looked round. "Evening, sir."

The man said in a slow, commanding voice, "Who is your companion?"

"Jack Edwards, a part-time resource in my department. He's fully cleared."

Jack glanced in the rear-view mirror. A hard face.

"I didn't know we had part-timers. Anyway, tell me why I've got a bomb explosion in Surrey."

"We were heading out to have a chat with David Ferguson, MD of the Canisp hedge fund," she said.

"Why?"

"I've been checking them out. Last month their former MD, Paul Riordan, died."

"I read that in the *FT*," the man said. "Surely a car accident?"

"Maybe."

"What have you got?"

Amanda said, "Just a few bits and pieces. Riordan had some suspicions about dodgy accounts. His daughter contacted us."

"How?"

"Riordan was a friend of Mr Edwards."

"Hmm, so worst case is murder, money laundering, fraud, economic crime and corruption."

"Maybe an international dimension, sir," Amanda added. "Up until now, we had nothing. This bomb changes things."

"And this is Ferguson's house?" the man asked.

"It was."

"What were you going to talk to Ferguson about tonight?"

"No idea. He asked us to come over."

"Unusual."

"A bit."

"And no idea what he was going to tell you?"

"No. He didn't want to talk at his office. We might have been inside if it hadn't been for the traffic. We were late."

"Not too late, thank goodness."

It was a sobering thought.

The man continued, "A dodgy hedge fund, two killings – at least one for sure – and a bomb explosion in Surrey. Do you want the case?"

Business as Usual

"Yes," Amanda said.

"Fine. I'm going to call this a gas explosion for the press, and I need deniability at this stage. Use McMahon as liaison. He'll give your people any support if you need it. Do you need surveillance authorisations for mobiles?"

"Yes, I will."

"Go ahead. This counts as an emergency under the Act."

"What about other agencies?" Amanda asked.

"Contact National Crime and ask for a quick cyber audit. Make sure Canisp's not under attack and that this is a local problem. If that's all clear, keep National Crime and MI6 out of this until we know more. You can move quicker on your own, at least until we know for sure. Keep me up to date. Christ, a bomb in Surrey, what next?"

This question went unanswered, and the man left the car.

"Your boss?" Jack asked.

"Everyone's boss."

"What now?"

"Let's go and see the captain."

A short, unpleasant walk took them to what was left of Ferguson's house. Debris littered the approach road and a decapitated metal lion's head that had once guarded the gates lay on the ground, defeated and with an apologetic expression.

At the first of the standing spotlights, Amanda flashed her card to a young man in military fatigues and asked for Parker.

He led them to the edge of what proved to be a very large crater which, in the centre, looked about ten feet deep. Very little obvious evidence that a house had occupied the space now existed. Outside the crater, light shone on further granulated debris and the whole scene buzzed with small teams carrying out activities the purpose of which were not clear to Jack.

Parker had an update. "Definitely a bomb, ma'am, and one death confirmed. Maybe more, but we'll need to test that. I'll know tomorrow."

"Is that all?"

"Officially, yes."

"Unofficially?"

"I haven't confirmed this for certain, but part of a detonator looks to us like British Army."

"Fuck, that's all we need." Amanda added, "I'm OC now. For the moment, this is a gas explosion. Who else knows about this detonator?"

"Me and one other," Parker said.

"Fine but no-one else is to know. Anything else?

"No."

"Do you need more people?"

"No, ma'am, not at the moment."

"I'll have someone over within the hour as liaison. Talk to him and only him."

"Understood, ma'am."

Amanda and Jack went back to the car. "British Army detonators?" he asked.

Amanda said, "Don't be too quick to judge. A foreign agency would hardly use their own equipment."

"A foreign agency?"

"It seems possible."

"Why does your boss want MI6 kept out? Don't they deal with foreign stuff?"

"I'll talk to them if necessary," she said, "but in the meantime, I don't want to listen to their platitudes about diplomatic niceties."

"We need to make sure Pam's safe."

"Yes, I'll call."

In the summer night, the insistent tone of the mobile pulsed once, then again. Jack's heart rate rose. On the third ring it was answered. A man's voice.

"All okay?" Amanda asked.

It seemed so.

"We'll be back in an hour. Stay there until we get back." She rang off but remained silent for a moment. Then she made another call.

"I've sent two more guys round. Pam will be quite safe until we get back."

"You sure?"

"It'll be fine."

Despite this assurance, Amanda drove fast back to London, and they talked little throughout the journey. It seemed longer, but they made good time and arrived back at the pub before midnight.

Their knocks were answered by a tall, powerful man in a suit who addressed Amanda as "ma'am," which calmed Jack a bit. He led the way up the stairs, and everything was good. The work of the day was evidently complete, and Harris and Pam sat lounging on either side of a corner sofa, both absorbed with their mobile phones.

Pam looked up. "Well, how did you get on?"

Amanda poured coffee for herself and Jack and they both sat down.

Amanda ignored Pam's question. "Right, Max, where are we at?"

Harris clicked a few buttons on his phone and reluctantly laid it aside. "Nothing for certain. We've been through every client. It's the usual mix of sheikhs, government money from third world, government money through contractors, all sorts really. However, we've run a few models looking for links around client size, country of origin, type of business – let me show you."

Harris rose and picked up his keyboard. His speed was impressive as ever, but the images on the screen were truly bewildering. He teased his audience by flashing past unconventional charts and dynamic Monte Carlo simulations before freezing the screen on a simple bar chart. "This is the high-level position of Canisp's portfolio." He didn't allow much time for them to digest this, preferring instead to concentrate on something he considered more interesting.

"Now, this is something that Pam suggested." One of the wall screens flashed into life. A pie chart and a lot of colour and writing.

"We've classified clients by 'the number of stations before final destination'."

"What does that mean?" Jack asked.

Harris looked at him with sympathy. "The total number of different financial institutions that touch the money as it moves from the hedge fund and, eventually, back to the client."

"Is that important?"

"It can be if you want to rinse money. Basically, we have about a dozen clients whose money has more than half a dozen stopovers. That's high, and we need to look further at these clients."

"What do we know about these clients? Any common features?"

"Not so far. Different trades, different locations, different sizes and different account handlers in Canisp. Let me show you." Harris presented the clients on the screen in tabular form, then clicked on the first name. "No significant banking overlaps, but still a lot of movements. I'm going to need a little time to look into this. Some of these institutions are tough to get information on. As far as I can see, at this stage the only common thing is that they are all American."

Jack looked at Amanda. She took this news in her stride, but he could see that this was an unwelcome development.

"Can you penetrate these banks; get the information you need?" she asked.

Harris was confident. "I reckon that Pam and I—"

Amanda cut him short. "No. Pamela needs to take a back seat now."

Pam's voice was shrill. "I don't want to take a back seat. I started this. It's my father who's dead."

"And it's up to me to make sure that *you* don't end up dead."

"Why would I be at any risk?" Pam's casual tone fooled no one.

"Maybe for what you know, or maybe for what people *think* you know."

"But I don't know anything – you know that."

"Yes, I know that. I wonder if David Ferguson knew anything?"

Pam asked irritably, "Well, did he?"

"We don't know," Amanda said. "You see, he's dead too."

Pam gave an audible gasp. "What do you mean dead? Didn't you just see him?"

"No, we didn't see him. I'm afraid there was very little of him to see. There was an explosion at his house."

"When you were there?"

"No, just before we arrived. Look, we don't know all the details yet, but in the meantime it's too dangerous for you to be involved in any way."

Pam said slowly. "So does this mean Dad was murdered then?"

"We don't know that. We don't know anything yet, except that it's not safe for you to be involved."

This ended the discussion and Amanda turned to Jack. "Call Canisp tomorrow. Tell them you have been redeployed – some financial emergency or something. Say the investigation's postponed until further notice. Now take Pam home and wait there until I contact you."

She looked at Pam, as if inviting her to dissent, but command sat easily on Amanda and her orders were accepted.

"I'll do what I'm told," Pam said.

"Good. Max, you keep working on these clients. Go test your hunches as fast as you can. As for me, I'm going to Canisp tomorrow. We no longer need a cover story."

"So, when will we hear from you?" Jack asked.

"I'll ring you tomorrow, early evening, and I'll update you both." She had a further thought. "Maybe you'd both be better staying in London."

"I'd rather go home," Pam said.

Amanda said, "Yes, all right, but I'm sending someone with you." She picked up her phone, and a moment later the suited man who had admitted them entered. "This is Mike. He will go with you. Have you room to put him up?"

"Yes, no problem."

Amanda whispered something to Mike and he left and returned with a small briefcase. He sat beside Jack and displayed its contents.

"This is a Glock 17, Mr Edwards."

Jack sighed, "Yes, I know how it works."

Chapter 13

Amanda managed about three hours' sleep before her phone alarm interrupted her at 5 a.m. This would be a busy day. She showered and dressed casually in jeans, boots and a shirt. The mirror awarded her morning face pass marks, so she tied her hair back. They would be here in ten minutes.

She made coffee, lit a cigarette that she wasn't meant to have and spent the remaining time checking her gun. It felt heavy, although it never did when she used it, which had been too often. It wasn't that difficult to kill someone, but it was difficult to forget that you had. Amanda didn't have nightmares, but she had perfect recall of everyone whose life she had ended. Not just the details, but vivid images of every single scene. On the whole, she was glad about that. To forget would be inhuman. She worked hard not to censor or sanitise the horror of these recollections. When you killed someone, there was blood and torn flesh, and you took away everything they had. Only God knew if she had the right to kill someone. She thought that she had a decent defence case, but when the time came, she was going to be up against a tough judge.

The loud knock on the door cut short these deliberations, and she holstered her gun and picked up her jacket.

After a short drive, the south London suburb was beginning to wake up when Amanda, sitting in the rear seat of the Jaguar, instructed her driver to stop. "Tell them to go now."

Business as Usual

She waited, and a few minutes later the rear door opened and a balding man of about fifty fell into the car. He had been allowed to partially dress with shoes and trousers, but he was still battling with his unbuttoned white shirt. "Just drive," Amanda barked, and the Jaguar pulled away.

Peter Smith wasn't at his best at this time of the morning, and having now buttoned his shirt, began to utter incoherent profanities.

"Shut up, Peter."

Meekly, he complied.

Amanda came straight to the point. "Peter, I sent a man to you yesterday. Jack Edwards."

"Yes, what of it?"

"Someone tried to kill him last night. Now, attempting the life of a financial services regulator is pretty much unheard of. However, I live in a more dangerous and fantastic world where anything is possible." She looked at him hard. "Now, only you and I knew what and who Mr Edwards was, and I didn't mention it to anyone, so that just leaves you."

Peter Smith stared at her open-mouthed. "No, no, I didn't say a word. Why would I do that?"

"I don't know," Amanda admitted, and pressed on airily, "I forgot to mention that Mr Edwards is safe, but someone was killed last night and at the moment you're the only lead I've got."

Smith began to mumble a further protest, but Amanda cut him short. "I've got a death and my boss all over me. So, here's what's going to happen."

Smith looked scared. "Who's dead?"

"Never mind that. I'm in a hurry, so you can tell me who you told, or I'll hold you until I've got to the bottom of things. You've got five minutes."

Amanda knew he would crack.

Smith summoned all his strength and determination and managed to hold out for about twenty seconds. His voice rose an octave as he said, "All right, all right, I had a call from Canisp yesterday."

"Go on."

"Look, these sorts of companies get edgy when we move in unannounced. Reputation's everything in the city. I didn't really say anything, just that they had nothing to worry about. That we had no financial concerns about them."

"I told you, not a word. Who called you?"

"David Ferguson," Smith said.

"You know David Ferguson well?"

"We've both been in the City a long time."

"So, a friend?"

Smith shrugged.

"And what did Ferguson say when you told him that?"

Smith said, "Not much, he took it in his stride."

"Did you tell him about me?"

"No, not exactly."

"What does that mean?"

"I said it was another department, but only that."

"Surely he asked you for clarification?"

"Well yes, but I swear I said nothing."

"And he didn't press you further?"

"No, it was a very quick call. I mean I couldn't hang up or refuse to speak to him. That would have been even more suspicious."

"Surprising that he left it at that."

Smith said, "Well, he did. He seemed relaxed, almost like he understood why that might happen."

"Why do you say that?"

"No reason. He didn't comment, just took it in his stride."

"A cool customer indeed. Hard to believe. Is there anything else?"

Smith's voice was shriller than ever. "Nothing else, nothing at all. It was less than a minute, I told you."

"Now I have to decide whether you're someone who should be of interest to me or you are just a fucking idiot."

It wasn't an easy question for Smith to answer so he didn't try.

Amanda looked at him hard, then shook her head. "Stop the car."

Business as Usual

The jaguar pulled up at the side of a busy road.

She looked at Smith. "I'm going to settle for fucking idiot for now. Mr Edwards will not be back at Canisp anytime soon. If you get any more calls, please say that Mr Edwards has been redeployed. That's all, nothing more."

Smith nodded frantically.

"One word from you, one whisper, anything I hear about you, then …"

She didn't need to finish. Smith was muttering agreement.

"Hopefully I'll not be seeing you anytime soon, Peter. Now get out of my sight."

He left the car and turned back towards her. "But who's dead?"

"Your friend, David Ferguson."

Chapter 14

Amanda had offices in a town house in Bloomsbury and was dropped off there. Her small directorate numbered no more than thirty permanent staff and their work patterns were irregular, so it was unsurprising to find the office busy at this early hour.

Amanda occupied an office that took up most of the attic floor alongside an ill-defined conference space. She threw her coat and her holster and gun onto a sofa and sat at her desk.

She sent Mike a text and received an instant reply. Jack and Pam were fine. At least one thing under control.

Through the open door, she noticed Max Harris switching on computer equipment. She picked up her phone. "Get me Doctor Jamieson."

On the second ring a voice shouted "Yes, what is it?"

"Hello, Ian, anything new?"

"Ah, Miss Barratt, my favourite spy. No, nothing at all."

"Nothing?"

"No. I don't know why I indulge these wild theories of yours."

"Because sometimes I'm right."

"Hmm."

Amanda said, "If we work on the assumption that he was murdered, would that change the things you would investigate?"

Jamieson said, "Not really. Unless you would like to be more specific."

"I can't at the minute. Just keep looking. It seems unlikely that a careful driver in good health just drives straight off the road."

"Very thin, Amanda," Jamieson reasonably countered. "It happens every day, if you haven't noticed."

"Very true, Ian, but have another look. I'll make it up to you."

Jamieson laughed loudly and the line went dead.

Amanda shouted for Max. He walked into her office. "Morning, boss."

"Have the cyber team looked at Canisp yet?"

"Yes, nothing amiss. No other alerts in the City."

"That's something. Now I want to talk to you about a car accident." She briefed him on Riordan's death. "If you wanted to arrange an accident, what would you do?"

"Shoot out a tyre? Shoot the driver?" Then he had another thought. "What sort of car?"

Amanda said. "Some kind of supercar." She reached into a file and threw it across.

Max scanned the document, thought for a moment, then reached across to her computer, through which he soon obtained detailed technical specifications of the vehicle. After a few minutes of flicking between screens, he stopped and said, "Interesting."

"What's interesting?"

"I'd need to look into this a bit more, but I'm sure I could hack that car."

Amanda was sceptical. "Hack a *car*?"

"Why not? Modern cars are full of computers and computers can be hacked. That's the rule."

Amanda suspended her disbelief. "Okay, how do we test your theory?"

"This is a supercar, but it's built by a relatively small company. There's no way their firewall will be robust."

Harris began to give a potted history of driverless and remote vehicle technology. "Basically, the technology exists, and, if it exists, you know who'll have developed it first."

Amanda knew the answer to this one. "Military?"

"Spot on, boss."

"Are you telling me you could, somehow, take remote control of a vehicle like this?"

"Pretty much, although you might need something physically attached to the vehicle. Maybe, maybe not with this car."

"So can you establish whether or not Riordan's car was hacked?"

Max said, "I'd need to inspect it, get some parts and do a little more digging. The parts may all be destroyed. Do you want me to look into this?"

"Yes, and also I want more information on Canisp's client accounts."

"Where is the car?"

"In Croydon, at the recovery centre."

Max said, "If you get me a driver, I can go down there and keep working on these accounts in the car."

"Yes, do that."

Harris left a few minutes later, leaving Amanda feeling old and nostalgic for good old-fashioned murder.

Chapter 15

In Buckinghamshire, Jack slept late, and, when he descended the stairs, Pam was sitting in the lounge staring into space, while Mike, the bodyguard, sat reading a newspaper in the kitchen. Mike managed to mutter "good morning" but was otherwise a man of few words, which suited Jack fine. Muscle was more important than loquacity in a bodyguard, and Mike had plenty of muscle on his lean, six-foot frame. He lit a cigarette.

"Is that allowed?" Jack asked.

"Yes, I asked Miss Riordan. It was raining and she took pity on me."

Jack lit a cigarette as well and they sat smoking in silence. He reflected on last night. He hadn't known Ferguson, so he wasn't entitled to mourn. He wondered whether he had a family. Probably. If he did, they had just lost out on thirty or forty years. It didn't seem fair, but since when did fairness have anything to do with destiny?

He stubbed out his cigarette and went into the lounge. "Morning, how are you today?"

"Bored and impatient," Pam said. "I called Canisp and told them our investigation was deferred."

Jack had completely forgotten Amanda's instructions from the night before. "Oh good, thanks, er – sorry. I overslept."

She accepted this miserable excuse and said, "I wonder what Amanda's doing?"

"I don't know, but she'll be busy."

"How long do we have to stay here doing nothing?"

Jack answered her sharply. "Look, this time we're going to do what we're told." His voice cracked a little and he said softly, "Sorry, but this isn't a game. If you had been with me last night you might have been killed." He added, almost in a whisper, "and I don't want that to happen."

She looked benevolently at him and touched him on the arm. This time she looked sorry. "I know that." While she wasn't crying, tears didn't seem far away, but her determination was stronger. "We have to find out what happened to Dad."

"We will, but we must let Amanda lead."

Pam got back to practicalities. "Yes, fine. I expect she will call us later. She said that she would and I think Amanda's the sort that does what she says."

"She always has," Jack said.

They sat together in silence for a minute or so before the peace was broken by a sharp sound from a buzzer.

"What's that?" Jack asked.

"The intercom at the gates."

Jack leapt from his chair, but Mike had beaten him to it and was carefully studying a grainy closed-circuit monitor.

He pressed a button. A voice came through loud and clear. "I'm looking for Pamela Riordan. Is she in?"

Mike said nothing and looked at Pam, who had now joined them.

She squinted at the image on the screen and said to Jack. "It's that girl we met yesterday."

"Which girl?"

"Ali something or other."

Jack supplied the surname. "Cairns."

"Yes, that's it. What's she doing here?" That question was mostly rhetorical and was followed by a more interesting question. "How does she know I live here?"

Jack shrugged. "Let's find out." He said to Mike. "Ask what she wants her for, then say she's out at the moment."

This approach conceded that this was Pam's house, but Jack figured that that ship had sailed. A routine enquiry to a neighbour would be all it would take to confirm this.

All three huddled round the intercom system, waiting for her reply.

The visitor was either a good actress or she was genuinely upset. She admitted, "I don't know Pamela, but I knew her father well. I really need to see her. How long will she be?" Her voice was breaking up now. "I can wait," she added desperately.

Jack's first instinct was to tell Mike to get rid of her. However confused Ali Cairns might be, the sight of Pam and him, yesterday's inspectors, would confuse her further and completely blow their cover.

As he processed these rational thoughts, he countered them with two less certain considerations. The first was the impression that he had formed yesterday that Ali Cairns had been close to Paul, and the second was that, unless they let her in, maybe she also would end up dead. Set against this was the small question of what part Cairns had played in this affair thus far. That might prove trickier to establish, but if they let her in, they could at least make a start. He looked at Pam. "Do you want to let her in?"

"Why not?"

"There are many reasons, but …" He looked at Mike and decided. "Let her in."

Mike had his say now. "You sure?"

Jack wasn't, but said "Yes."

"Okay." Mike flicked through a series of screen views of the lane outside. "It looks clear, I'm going outside. Open the gates."

Jack watched through the screen as Ali Cairns tentatively made her way towards the house. Mike was taking no chances, and as she reached the front door, he emerged from behind the car and shouted, "Stop." He then welcomed her by conducting a full-body frisk.

This done, he followed her to the front door. Being frisked for a weapon when making a house call in Buckinghamshire must have been a surprise for Cairns, but when she stood at the front door confronted by Jack and Pam, it was a bigger surprise.

It took Cairns a second or two to match the faces with these unfamiliar surroundings. Then her eyes widened. She stammered, "Oh-hello again. I'm looking for Pamela Riordan. Is she with you?"

Pam took a step forward. "I'm Pam Riordan, come in." She led Ali and Jack through to the lounge and invited her to sit down.

She then sent Jack to the kitchen to make coffee. When he returned, the conversation hadn't started.

Out of the office, Ali Cairns was a pleasant but unexceptional-looking woman. Her sandy red hair was bordering on unkempt and her green eyes were dulled by heavy, round glasses. It was possible she had a good figure, but it was tough to be sure what lay beneath her thick woollen jumper and baggy jeans. She cupped the coffee mug with both hands and sat deep and passively in a sofa. Eventually she said to Pam, "Do you work for the regulators?"

"No."

Ali Cairns had the IQ of a genius. "Oh."

Pam said, "I just tagged along with Mr Edwards. As I own about half of the company, I thought that would be alright."

Ali looked at Jack. "So why are you here today, Mr Edwards?"

Jack decided that he was due some information first. "Let's leave that for now. I think we need to know why *you* are here?"

Glancing at Pam, Cairns replied, "Well, obviously I worked closely with your father but," she added almost shamefacedly, "we were also quite close outside work." As she let slip this admission, she looked at her feet.

It felt strange. In a world where almost anything went, what was wrong with a man and a woman being in a relationship? No doubt the company frowned on that sort of thing, but they were surely past the point that it mattered?

Ali Cairns had used up most of her available energy now, and with a fading voice said, "I miss him so much."

Business as Usual

"So do I," Pam said softly. She got up and sat beside Cairns on the sofa and took her hand.

Jack decided to leave them to their shared grief, and he returned to the kitchen to join Mike. As he drew on a cigarette, he began to think of what he should ask Ali Cairns. He hoped that she would have something important to contribute, otherwise, yet again, Amanda was going to be very unhappy.

Chapter 16

Amanda had no need of a cover story when she, accompanied by a detective inspector, visited the headquarters of the Canisp Hedge Fund. If the cause of Riordan's death was unclear, the death of Ferguson was unambiguous. She had made arrangements earlier to ensure that the main board was assembled. At reception they were informed that, while Selena Thornton was in the building, both senior managers, Ray Common and Ali Cairns, were on annual leave.

Amanda decided to start at the top. As befitted the new senior executive, Thornton had an office about the size of a warehouse. Expensively furnished, it was designed in three distinct areas: a conference section, an informal meeting area and (backed by floor to ceiling windows) a desk and personal work area. They were directed to sit in the informal area and, after a long walk, Selena Thornton joined them.

The police inspector spoke first, introducing himself and Amanda without indicating her rank. He then, unnecessarily, explained why they were here. Thornton had already been informed by phone about Ferguson's demise.

The inspector continued on about identification challenges. This was a delicate subject. Amanda looked carefully at Thornton, but she took it well and nodded without reaction. Quite impressive. Thornton was older than Amanda, but better presented. Her blue eyes complemented her short cut blonde hair – natural, probably. She continually looked over her thick black spectacles, suggesting that they were more of a fashion accessory than an ocular necessity. Her highly bred and cultured voice held only a slight American trace, and told of East Coast money.

Amanda said, "Thank you for getting your board together at such short notice."

Thornton accepted her thanks.

"I understand that you've been here about five years? Who hired you?"

"Paul and David." Selena said. "They always made the important decisions together."

Amanda rattled off a few of Selena's career highlights and asked, "Why finance and why London?"

If the object of these questions was unclear, Selena didn't comment. "No specific reason. I just fancied a change."

"And your work here, who did you work more closely with, Paul or David?"

Thornton reflected. "Paul was more technical than David, but really we worked together. We were a small executive team."

A lot smaller now, Amanda thought. "And the executive team's just you now. Will the business be in safe hands going forward?"

Thornton tightened her lips and forced a smile. "Yes, we have a lot of talent in our management team."

Amanda suspected that Selena was talking mostly about herself, but to be fair, she was impressive and every answer was delivered with confidence and assurance. But Amanda wasn't thinking about answers; she was wondering about the questions that Thornton *wasn't* asking.

Amanda was more used to violence and death than Thornton, but even she would surely have had a thought about her own safety given the fact that two of her colleagues were already dead.

"We must consider the possibility that you are in danger, Miss Thornton."

Thornton looked puzzled. "Why should I be concerned, Miss Barratt? Paul had a car accident and I understand that David died in a gas explosion. Both tragic accidents."

"These are preliminary findings. Nothing has been confirmed yet."

"What else could it have been?"

Amanda decided not to fuel any speculations. She looked hard at Thornton and stated an obvious truth instead. "The fact is that two out of three Canisp managing partners have unexpectedly died in the last fortnight. We have to be sure that this is just bad luck."

Thornton stared at Amanda. "Are you a police officer, Miss Barratt?"

"No, I'm with the Home Office. I take an interest in the financial services industry."

"I am surprised, Miss Barratt. I would have expected to encounter you before. Are you in charge of these investigations?"

"Yes." Amanda resumed asking the questions. "Don't you find the hedge fund business challenging, ethically speaking?"

At last, Amanda detected a chink in Thornton's professional exterior. Quite clearly Thornton considered that this was none of Amanda's business. She said stiffly, "Canisp leads the industry in ethical investments." Just for a second, her eyes blazed as she went on, "Climate change, third world development, women's rights."

Amanda was as cynical as Jack and doubted this was true, but she thought she had at last learned something unusual. Selena Thornton really did believe in these things. She decided to stop poking her in the ribs and said, "Thank you. When will we be able to speak to the board?"

On safer ground now, Selena got up and talked to someone on her desk phone. "They are ready now if that suits you."

"Yes, perfectly."

As they walked, Amanda said, "Just for the record, where were you yesterday, Miss Thornton?"

Business as Usual

Thornton's tone was ice cold. "A normal day in the office, nine to just after six thirty, followed by a takeaway meal in my Knightsbridge flat. Alone."

She opened a door into a large well-appointed room, dominated by a highly polished traditional boardroom table. Selena joined her board at one side of the table and Amanda and the inspector were allocated the deserted near side.

The board of Canisp looked at them with fixed expressions.

"I'm Amanda Barratt of the Home Office. I'm here because two of your partners have been killed in the last few weeks. The police will, of course, be proceeding with their enquiries; however, the Home Office always takes an interest in major City institutions."

Sir George Black said testily, "The board is also concerned, Miss Barratt."

"Canisp is a major hedge fund. We must be sure that any problems do not represent a systemic risk to the financial system."

The board members all nodded, now comfortable that the Home Office had its priorities right and was now focused on money.

Amanda continued blandly, "We have to ensure that there are no problems or threats to Canisp."

Sir George Black said, "I see, yes, I can see that," but he was in no doubt. "As far as the board is concerned, Canisp is in a strong position."

"Thank you, Sir George. Nonetheless, the Home Office would be grateful if the board could undertake a short, discreet due-diligence exercise to verify just that."

Sir George looked at Selena Thornton, who shrugged in weary acceptance. He looked round at his board. There were no objections. "Of course, Miss Barratt, we will do so." He gestured towards Carver. "Katherine, could you lead this with Selena?"

It was a well-judged nomination, Amanda thought. Katherine Carver had investigated – and probably buried – as many investigations as anyone through her American Justice connections. She was able and experienced, but Amanda didn't like the look of her. An insider in the

Western global order. To be fair, neither Leo King nor Lord Jeremy Steel were much different. Well, what did she expect of the board of a major City of London financial institution?

The formidable Katherine Carver indicated her acceptance of the role and Sir George looked over at Amanda for her reaction.

"Yes, that would be helpful, Sir George. When should we arrange our next meeting?"

Carver responded, "I would imagine that we can satisfy ourselves and, of course, the Home Office soon ... a few days." She looked at Selena, who didn't demur.

The return date was set and Amanda made to leave. Before she did, Lord Jeremy Steel had a question.

Amanda knew who he was: a twenty-year veteran of British politics. She had never met him, but she didn't care for him. She resented that Steel had prospered from his years of what he liked to call *public service*.

Amanda pushed away these unhelpful pre-judgements and decided to give him a fair hearing.

"Is it quite usual for the Home Office to take an interest in these things?" He continued, predictably, "When I was at the Home Office—"

Amanda gently cut across him. "Policy has changed. We now pay closer attention to the City of London."

Then he name-dropped, as she knew he would. "Yes, I'm aware that Mr Devoy takes a close interest in the City. Is there anything else we need to know at this stage?"

If Amanda was looking to confirm her view of Steel, this speech helped. If Steel thought that name-dropping Devoy, her ultimate boss and Britain's top spy, would impress her, he was wrong. Apart from anything else, Amanda knew that Devoy shared her low opinion of Steel. "No, nothing at this stage. We simply wish to ensure that everything is in order."

This time, she and the inspector did leave. He declined a lift, preferring to walk, and Amanda returned to her office, wondering why none of the board of Canisp had mentioned their own personal safety.

Chapter 17

Amanda hoped that Max would be back from Croydon, and she was in luck. The open conference and meeting area outside her office was untidy, the floor strewn with cables and unfamiliar electronic components. Harris was smiling and singing tunelessly, which was a good sign. He loudly acknowledged her while she charted a course through the debris. She dumped her coat in her office and went back to join him.

"What have you got?"

Harris rattled out a few further keystrokes, reviewed the wall-mounted monitor and addressed the question. He pointed at the items on the floor. "These are all parts from Riordan's car – most of the key electronics." He quoted the names and function of the various parts. Amanda didn't know any of these and tuned out, figuring that Max would eventually get to the point. When he reached it, about a minute on, it proved worth the wait.

"The most interesting thing is this." He held aloft a tiny card that looked very similar to a sim card from a mobile phone.

"Why is that interesting?"

Max replied triumphantly, "Well, it's completely blank."

Amanda might have been able to deduce the implications of this finding eventually, but it had been a long day, so she asked him to explain.

"You see, it should be full of data. This little card – all the machine code goes through it. It has a memory – or more accurately a storage capability. But I've checked and there's nothing on it."

Amanda was catching up now. "Is it faulty?"

"No, there's nothing wrong with it." He hit the keyboard again and recommended her attention to a monitor. "You see?"

A mass of random alpha-numeric characters danced across the screen. "Yes, I see."

"I just sent it some code and you can see it," Harris explained. "So, the question is, why is it blank?"

Amanda came up with what Harris considered the correct response. "Someone wiped it?"

"Yes exactly, now, the question is, *who* wiped it?" He answered his own question. "Unless someone in the vehicle recovery shop did it, and why would they?"

"Why not?"

"Well, unless they are somehow involved in whatever is going on … I suppose it's possible." He rejected this hypothesis on practical grounds with a few shakes of his head. "The trouble is, it's not a very easy thing to do. Unless there's an IT genius working in the recovery garage."

"Is it really that difficult?"

Max said without arrogance, "It took me a couple of hours to work it out."

"So, the hacker theory's not impossible?"

"Someone's gone to a great deal of trouble to wipe the car's brain and there's got to be a reason."

"Have we any clue as to who might have done this?" Amanda asked.

Harris was clear on this point. "Sorry, boss."

"Will you be able to find out?"

"I'll try, but I don't think so. You're going to have to settle for the fact that someone blanked it."

"That's something, I suppose. It was a long shot anyway. Keep at it. Now, what about Canisp, these client accounts?"

"Yes, I'll get to that, but here's my party piece."

A virtual vehicle appeared on the monitor, which he was able to control as it raced round a simple circular track. He uttered loud expressions of self-satisfaction. "Not bad, boss?"

The vehicle moved mesmerically round and round the little track. A simple computer game, but it made Amanda shiver.

"Now, if I just make a few changes …"

The car managed another circuit and then slowly drifted outside the grid lines. Max had a last trick up his sleeve. The vehicle disappeared, and the word "Boom" appeared.

It was just a word – insensitive perhaps, but it worked for all that. Even Max wasn't smiling now.

Amanda stared at the word until he slowly wiped it from the screen. "Can you do this?"

"I can create a simple simulation but, yes, the principle's the same."

"Could you perfect it for the field?"

"I think so, but it's a complicated project, and I'd need a lot of equipment. How's the budget?"

"Stretched. What sort of equipment?"

"The sort of stuff that you need to drive a car. Steering wheel, brakes, pedals, lots of screens. Bespoke software and hardware. You need to smooth out the connection – smooth connection is vital. Actually, it might not be possible, other than in certain locations. I mean if you are trying to drive remotely." He stopped and shut his eyes. "Then there's the car. It's a difficult project, even for me."

Amanda said, "Keep thinking about it and ring around. There must be someone who's looking at this technology. Now, what about these client accounts?"

He refreshed the screen and replaced the car crash with a chart. He retrieved a pen from behind his ear and used it as a pointer.

"More progress here, boss. These are the client accounts we mentioned yesterday. I took out a couple and added a few." He paused for a second, which was encouraging. Max always did that when he had discovered something interesting.

"As I said yesterday, all of these accounts have a few things in common. The money takes a long journey before arriving at its ultimate destination. The final destinations are all different, but there is one common link." He refreshed the screen again and pulled up a list of names that looked like banks.

"They're all different," Amanda said.

"They have different *names*, but some are trading names, and besides, they're all banks that do a lot of work with our American allies. In an hour or two, I'll have this nailed."

As Max talked, a casually dressed middle-aged man arrived. He nodded to Max and flopped onto the sofa beside Amanda. He accepted a drink and ticked her off for smoking.

Devoy was an old friend and, as the UK's top spy, was Amanda's boss. He asked, "How are you getting on at Canisp?"

"Progressing. We're just going through the client list now. It's complicated."

Devoy added to the complications. "These army detonators, they were stolen from an army base. Last year."

"Which one?"

He told her.

"Isn't that base a shared facility with the Americans?"

"Yes."

"That ties in with what we're finding."

"Treading carefully would be good."

"Yes … but we carry on?"

"Of course. Allies or not, I'm not having anybody letting off bombs in Surrey." He gulped down his drink and got up.

A thought occurred to Amanda. "Did Jeremy Steel get in touch with you?"

Devoy laughed. "No, but one of his friends mentioned something at lunch yesterday. I just nodded, but don't worry about Steel. Just do your job."

Chapter 18

Since the arrival of Ali Cairns, Jack had spent many idle hours smoking and, from time to time, attempting to amuse a disinterested tabby cat. Once, he had sidled up to the lounge door and eavesdropped for a few minutes. He had chosen a good time, for it had been a moment when Ali had been stutteringly describing her relationship with Paul Riordan. They had been best friends and they had been lovers. It wasn't difficult to believe this. Jack was now quite certain that Ali Cairns would have been Paul's type. She was an attractive woman, although not necessarily in a conventional sense, but would, he felt sure, scrub up well. More importantly, she was brainy and seemed to be interested in the same things as Paul. They would have been good together.

Jack was keen to talk to her about Paul again, about what he had been doing before his death. Maybe she had forgotten something? He decided to defer that discussion. One look at Pam's face was enough. Before Ali Cairns arrived, she had been alone with her thoughts. Now she had someone to talk to about her father, someone who might have loved him. She looked happier. It was part of the mourning process and she had a lot of catching up to do.

He returned to the kitchen and decided to talk to the cat. Formerly Jack's best friend when seeking food, it wandered past his outstretched hand with its head in the air.

His mobile rang. At least Amanda wanted to talk to him.

"Hi, I'm heading over. Just leaving. I'll be there in an hour or so, traffic permitting. How's Pam?"

Jack decided not to mention Ali Cairns. That might need careful timing. "All good here."

"See you soon."

Pam came into the kitchen. "Was that Amanda?"

"Yes, she's coming over."

"Has she found out anything?"

"She didn't say."

"We can ask her when she arrives. Do you guys want coffee?" Pam put a mug in front of Mike but held onto Jack's. "Come on, come through."

Both Ali Cairns and Pam might have shed a few tears but they were both better for it. Pam was business-like now. "Jack, Ali's having **difficulty believing in Dad's accident as well.**"

Jack sighed inwardly. Clearly Pam had shared her suspicions with Ali. In truth, he might have done this; how else was he to get Ali Cairns to do likewise? But could she be trusted?

It was a bit late for that, so Jack jumped in. "Do you know what Paul was working on?"

"Yes," Cairns said. "He was investigating what he thought was a major fraud – money laundering, that sort of thing."

"And?" Jack was in a hurry. He wanted something to tell Amanda.

"He hadn't arrived at any final conclusions, but he said he was getting closer. He had reduced his enquiry to a small number of clients. He said …" Her voice faltered. "He said a few days before the accident that it was time for a detailed forensic look at some of them."

"Do you have the list?"

He got a break at last.

"Yes."

Cross-referencing her list with Harris's analysis was an obvious next step, but Jack wanted more. "Did he say anything about who was involved?"

"No. that wasn't his way, he was intellectually rigorous. He wouldn't say anything he couldn't prove."

This, annoyingly, rang true, but it wasn't helpful. Jack persisted. "What about the people at Canisp? I mean, who was he investigating?"

"Well, everyone. One thing he did say was that it had to be controlled high up, which is kind of obvious, I suppose."

Jack was annoyed with Paul now. For all his rigour, he had failed to factor in the risk of his dying and most of his unfinished analysis dying with him.

"Surely Paul said something. What did he think of the board members, partner, senior managers?"

"As for the board, he got on okay with most of them. Sir George Black and Leo King, he liked. They were with him at the start when the business was small. They believed in him, and at the beginning they were a big help. They had status and contacts. Paul was always grateful. Lord Steel was the next board member."

Jack asked, "How did that come about?"

Ali Cairns had a cynical streak. "He was touting for directorships in the City and we needed more political connections."

"Did Paul like Steel?"

"No, not personally. It wasn't his politics. I think he thought that he was just a high-class grifter, to be honest. David Ferguson did most to recruit him. Paul knew that the board had to grow and accepted the logic of his appointment."

"And Katherine Carver?"

Cairns said, "Katherine's a force of nature. Very able. As to her appointment, well, it was natural enough to go for an American and, of course, we needed a woman."

"Do you like her?"

"Yes. I mean, she's a bit full-on at times, and she's not always right, even though she thinks she is. But what high-powered figure isn't?"

"Does she know about finance?"

"Oh no, she just knows important people and what they want. We've got plenty folks who understand finance."

"What about Paul and David, were they close?" Jack asked.

"They were very different, both brilliant in their own way. Workwise they were very close. David was the first person Paul brought in, and to be fair, they both built the business."

"How were they different?"

"Paul liked the work more, saw it as an end in itself. David was more … balanced. I mean, he was good, very good technically, but maybe he saw the work as a means to an end. He liked the status and he liked the money." Cairns added, "Actually, it worked well. Paul was better in the background and David liked to be out front."

"Did Paul involve him in his enquiry?" Jack asked.

"I'm not sure. They had quite a few after-hours meetings over the last few months, but that wasn't unusual. Paul liked to work alone mostly."

Ali Cairns had a question of her own. "Was David murdered?"

Jack skirted on the edge of the truth. "We don't know for sure at the moment."

"So not necessarily a gas explosion?"

"Not necessarily."

Everyone had run out of energy and they sat in silence. Jack had learned a bit but was still concerned that Amanda would be more annoyed than pleased at his decision to confide in Ali Cairns.

On cue, they were interrupted by the sound of movement in the hall. Instinctively, Jack got up and joined Mike at the front door. He was staring hard at the small screens. An SUV was parked outside the gates.

"Amanda's early." Jack made to press the button to open the gates, but Mike pulled his hand away roughly. "Wait, that's not Miss Barratt. The car's been sitting there for a few minutes."

"Maybe she's on the phone."

"Let's just wait a minute." A minute turned out to be two or three seconds. Mike uttered an audible expletive.

Business as Usual

Jack moved forward to share the view. From the roof of the SUV, first one then three figures leapt over the iron gate and into the grounds. They were masked and armed.

Mike shouted, "Get the women out of here!"

Where he was going to take them was not clear, but Jack's first step was easy enough. After retrieving his Glock from the kitchen, he raced through to the lounge and roughly pulled both of them up from their seats.

Mike was already halfway out of the front door and gun shots were cracking outside.

If Jack went outside, it would help Mike, but it wouldn't help Pam or Ali Cairns if he was killed, so he led them up the stairs. They reached the landing. "Wait here a minute."

At first, his choice was which of the rooms it would be best to die in. He looked up and tried a better option. "How do we open that?"

Pam was admirably calm. With steady hands, the long metal rod found the hook, and a second later a folding metal ladder dropped down.

There were fewer gunshots now, and that wasn't necessarily a good thing. "Hurry up," he demanded. Ali followed Pam. Jack wondered if he should risk going downstairs, but now there were only loud voices and the sound of many footsteps down the stairs. This was discouraging, and he followed them up.

The ladder was heavy, and retracting it from above wasn't easy, but he managed it. As he replaced the hatch, he caught sight of a man with a gun striding up the last few stairs.

Clearly the frontal assault had now succeeded. He wondered whether Mike was alive or dead.

Pam and Ali had moved to the far corner of the attic, huddled together but calm. Jack joined them by means of a run and a dive. This precaution proved wise, as an instant later, the attic floor was penetrated by blasts that Jack knew were from a shotgun. Apart from the risk of being shot outright, the gunmen would be up there in a minute. His only advantage was the bottleneck that was the narrow attic hatch, but perhaps they would just keep shooting through the flimsy attic floor.

Jack was thinking furiously about how he would prepare for a possible last stand when he spotted the skylight. "Where does that go?" he yelled at Pam.

"Onto the roof," she said.

Two deafening shotgun blasts penetrated the floor very near them, which made the decision an easy one. A couple of storage boxes made a secure step and, after a bit of fettling, the catch on the skylight gave way. A thump with the heel of his hand released the window and it crashed violently back onto the roof slates.

Pam shouted, "Let me go first. I know the way." Jack got out of the way, and after a couple of elegant moves, Pam was perched on the roof, reaching down with her hand. Ali took hold of it and was soon alongside her. Jack had to wait a few seconds. The loft hatch shifted. His hand was steady and he waited until the hatch was part open before firing two rounds from his Glock. There were curses and the sound of an awkward descent from the ladder. This slowed them down and allowed Jack time to struggle up and onto the roof.

Pam and Ali seemed to be able to retain their balance on the slate roof, although Jack had to keep one hand on the sill of the skylight. He looked across several pitched roofs. "How do we get down from here?"

Pam knew. "Follow me." Using the roof tiles as a slide, a few seconds took her safely onto a small, flat felt section of the roof. Ali and Jack followed. The area was small, a gap between several pitched roofing areas of varying heights. "What now? Stay here or try to go down?"

Jack looked up. There was no way to keep out of sight of the skylight. "Down. Do you know how?"

"Yes, I used to play here when I was a kid." She led them through a series of easy descents before emerging on to another flat-roofed area which sat only about six feet above the rear lawns. The lawns were extensive and there wasn't much cover. There might be gunmen there. It was a risk that they had to take.

Jack descended first and helped the women down.

Pam pointed ahead. "There's more cover over there."

Jack looked around quickly. "Let's go. Fast as you can"

They set off in a sprint over the lawns, Pam and Ali out-pacing Jack by several lengths, and arrived at a line of beech hedging. It was dense, but there was a gap and they followed Pam through it and into a swimming pool area.

Jack ran across to the far side. "What's down there?"

"Woods."

"And then?"

"A few open fields and the village."

Jack was already breathing hard. He doubted that they could outrun highly trained professionals, and he didn't like the sound of open fields.

A quick decision was needed. Voices. Very close. "Take Ali down there, into the woods. And stay there."

"What about you?"

"I'll stay here, and slow them down. I'll catch up with you soon, I promise." It was a careless promise – one that he had no confidence in fulfilling.

Pam spotted that too. She looked at him, stared at him hard. Her blue eyes were full of doubt. She threw her arms around him and held him. "We'll see you soon. Don't you fucking die."

With this order, Pam took Ali's hand and they ran until they reached the wooded area.

The voices from the house were louder now. Yards away. Jack needed cover.

There were two huts beside the swimming pool and the door of the second one was unlocked. He ducked inside. There were a few loungers and other assorted junk, but there was a decent amount of space left and a small, grimy window allowed for a hazy view of the entrance gap in the beech hedge.

Jack looked at his watch. Almost seven. Amanda was due any minute. He took out his mobile. It was a risk but maybe he could warn her to be careful. With trembling fingers, he rang her. Two rings, three. Through the gap in the hedge, a light flickered from a head-torch.

The phone was answered. Amanda said, "Hi, Jack."

Jack didn't have time for even a greeting. All his attention was now on the light and the masked figure.

"Jack? Hello? Are you alright?"

He whispered, "No," then killed the call and turned off the ringtone.

The gunman was alone, moving slowly round the head of the pool. He stopped at the first of the huts, kicked in the door and discharged the shotgun.

Inside a small wooden hut was no place to be against a shotgun, and as the man sprayed shot into the first hut, Jack was already outside. Peering round the gable end of the hut, Jack withdrew a pace as the man turned and headed his way. There was just enough space for Jack to wriggle behind the back of the hut, although the close beech branches crackled loudly as he did so. His heart pounded just as loudly.

Jack counted on the man making a similar assault on the second shed. Only light, sure footsteps broke the silence. They stopped. It took an agonising amount of time before the man repeated his routine. The hut shuddered under the twin assaults of the man's boot and shotgun. Then more footsteps, louder now, on the flimsy wooden floor told Jack it was time. He needed only two strides: one to the corner of the shed, the other to the front of the door.

Jack pointed the Glock into the shed and the man turned, but he never left the shed, as three rounds from Jack's Glock thundered into his chest.

Chapter 19

Amanda wondered why Jack wasn't answering his phone. When the car pulled up at the entrance to Pam's house, she also wondered why the gates were open. There were two cars parked near the house and the front door was open. She decided she had seen enough and pulled out a gun. She said to the driver, "Stop the car here and bring the shotgun."

They approached the front door cautiously. In the hall, two prone bodies came into view. One was masked and wore a military suit. The other dead body wore a regulation business suit and used to work for Amanda. Mike couldn't be helped now, so Amanda and her driver stood either side of the front door. He covered her and she moved into the hall. There was no one there, nor in in the lounge or kitchen.

Where was everyone? She conducted an analysis. There was one rogue car in the driveway, so that meant four or possibly five hostiles. One was dead, but that left three or maybe four.

She was very worried about Jack and Pam now. They had a small chance, she told herself. Jack wasn't that bad with a gun, and usually he showed a bit of courage when pushed. But her cursory examination of the dead assailant at the front door was not encouraging. The equipment and clothing were modern and professional.

Her driver joined her in the kitchen. "It's all clear downstairs, ma'am."

Adam Parish

Amanda said, "Okay, follow me upstairs." In textbook form, Amanda and partner cleared the rooms quickly, then she stood beside the metal ladder to the attic. She looked up. Shotgun and automatic rifle fire had not improved the ceiling. She listened intently. Why was there no sound? She put her foot on the bottom rung of the metal ladder.

Her driver pulled her back, "I'll go, ma'am."

He was up and back quickly. "No one up there, but there's a skylight open. I had a look outside, but there's no one on the roof."

"Let's try outside."

They moved quickly down the stairs, through the kitchen and into a conservatory. The French doors were open. Outside, the light was fading, but two figures were silhouetted clearly on the lawn. Amanda had a few toys of her own, and the night binoculars left no doubt as to their identities. What was in doubt was how best to get to them. A late evening stroll across about a hundred yards of lawn followed by a Wild West gunfight didn't represent good odds.

That said, she had no idea where Jack and Pam were. The casual way the gunmen were talking wasn't encouraging, but the fact they were still here was. Professionals didn't usually hang around for a chat once the mission was complete, especially when there were dead bodies lying in the hallway. This assessment was justified; when the men split, one disappeared from sight, heading further down the grounds and the other, helpfully, sprinted back towards the house.

Amanda withdrew into the conservatory and waited. The assassin was out of luck because he was heading straight for the conservatory. It was all over in a few seconds. Crouching behind a wicker sofa, she gave him a chance. At about the "P" in "Armed Police" she fired and he dropped. Amanda was a professional. She knew she had killed him.

The lawn was now clear, and Amanda and her driver sprinted frantically to where the other man had been.

The lawn ran out into the beech hedge, solid at first, but then broken in a zigzag shape. She edged through it gingerly and squinted through the last light of the day into an enclosed area with a swimming pool and a couple of huts. All was quiet and she moved forward slowly, flashing a torch into the first hut, which was empty, then the second, which was home to the dead body of another hooded man. Good for Jack.

Over the hedge, dense woodlands. In the fading light, the tightly packed trees were mostly bad news for her and, in terms of concealment, good news for those already there.

A flash of light from the forest made up her mind. She sprinted across the clearing and collapsed at the base of a voluminous oak tree. She listened and heard nothing above her racing heart. She wondered how long back-up would take. Back-up or not, there were now lights and voices coming from the house and nearing. They were at the pool now. Their commands could be clearly heard.

"Clear – one hostile dead, clear," were reassuring messages. Three, then four, points of light broke cover from the pool area, and an instant later a man stood beside her.

He was about a foot taller than her. Heavily armed but friendly, and so were the others who joined him.

Amanda said, "We have two friendlies, I hope, in these woods. One man, about forty, Jack Edwards, He's armed and, hopefully, with an unarmed woman, aged about twenty."

"Wait there, ma'am," the first man whispered and turned to brief his men, but his instructions were never to be heard.

A crack of automatic gunfire rang out. Amanda froze. An instant later, from not far away, three evenly spaced and rapid responses from what she recognised as a Glock rang out. She sprinted into the trees, her senses on overdrive. She halted and ran again. Her eyes were now working better in the half light, and in a clearing, she was certain, quite certain, that the silhouetted shape on the ground was a body. Her heart leapt as she arrived at the body. It wore a black military suit like the other dead men, and she let out a sigh of relief.

She turned in response to a footstep behind her. Jack stood inches from her. "Getting slow, Miss Barratt."

"Where is Pamela?"

Jack took her hand. "Over here." Behind another tree, Pam and Ali Cairns were huddled in each other's arms like babes in the woods. Amanda picked up Pam and gave her a hug. "You alright?"

"I think so."

She turned to Jack and pointed at Ali Cairns. "Who's this?"

"A friend. I'll explain later."

"How many gunmen?"

"I saw four. Is Mike okay?"

"No, he's dead." She had flicked a switch and was back in full professional mode. Turning to the men beside her, she barked out a number of instructions. This done, she cast a perplexed glance at Ali Cairns and led them all back to the house.

It was bustling with people, all of whom worked for Amanda. She led Pam and Ali to the lounge and shut the door. She kept Jack by her side as she conducted further meetings, the last one outside the front door, where a short and emotional exchange confirmed Mike's death.

A couple of space-suited individuals were swarming over the attackers' SUV.

They walked over. Amanda asked, "What have you got?"

"Car stolen three hours ago from Central London. All clean, no weapons." The spaceman added a crime scene joke. "No prints, but as all four are littering the grounds, that hardly matters."

A short discussion with a technical type who had studied the CCTV system confirmed the attackers' strength as four men.

In the kitchen, Amanda freshened two coffees with a liberal amount of brandy and asked Jack for a quick recap of events. Unusually, Amanda awarded him a little praise. "Mike was a good man, very experienced, and he couldn't stop them."

"Who were they?" Jack asked.

She tightened her lips and cocked her head. "We don't know anything for sure at this stage. Professional, certainly. Top grade equipment. Can't tell any more than that at this moment."

Jack nodded, lit a cigarette and took a mouthful of coffee.

"Who's the girl in the lounge with Pamela?"

Business as Usual

He doubted he was going to get much praise this time. "Ali Cairns," he said. "She's one of the senior managers at Canisp."

Amanda didn't criticise him immediately. Instead, she asked, "What the fuck is she doing here?"

Jack shrugged. "She came to see Pam. It seems she and Paul were an item. Well, so she says, and Pam believes her."

Amanda snorted derisively. "How do you know she's not involved in this?"

"I don't for sure, but I think she's okay."

"Not great, Sherlock."

Jack had a thought. "She's got some of Paul Riordan's analysis – his list of suspect accounts and maybe more."

Amanda still seemed unimpressed "Is she technically skilled?"

"I think so – that's what she is, academic rocket scientist type."

"Well, maybe I can use her, get her in a room with Max and see what they can come up with. That's if she is what she says she is. Let's go and see them."

In the lounge, Pam and Ali were sitting quietly, which wasn't bad under the circumstances. By any standards they had both been through an experience that nobody should have, far less a twenty-year-old who had just buried her father.

In a composed voice, Pam said to Amanda, "What's happening now? Is everything cleared up?"

"For now."

"What now?"

Jack wondered how open Amanda would be in front of Ali Cairns. She appeared untroubled by this. "Well, Pam, you can't stay here at the moment – that much is clear."

This assessment was unarguable. "Where can I go?"

Amanda said, "We'll talk about that later." She looked hard at Ali Cairns. "And Miss Cairns, you will come with me. Jack tells me that you have knowledge of Mr Riordan's investigations."

Ali didn't have any fight in her. She managed to check her tears and, in an emotional whisper, asked, "Where am I going?"

"Somewhere quiet, so we can have a proper chat. I need to find out what else you know about this business."

Pam looked hard at Amanda, in apparent criticism of this plan. She leant over and patted Ali's arm and issued some words of comfort. This met with limited success and an arm round the shoulders was soon needed.

Amanda said nothing to break the uncomfortable silence and lit a cigarette without regard for house rules, all the time staring at Ali Cairns.

Chapter 20

For the second day in a row, Amanda was up at five in the morning, having managed about four hours' sleep. Today, the bathroom mirror suggested that it wasn't enough. She ignored its unwanted opinion and dressed quickly. Normally, when you were the boss, fieldwork was light, but not this time. A few days ago, she had been vaguely investigating a road accident. Now she had six or seven deaths, including a colleague, corruption in the City of London with the potential involvement of many high-connected personalities and, maybe even, the involvement of a friendly foreign power.

All in all, it justified her personal attention. Devoy was supportive but she was a realist. He had deniability, and she knew that if things got worse, he would play that card. Whatever else, a quick resolution to this mess was needed.

At least she could get on with things now. There were no such things as normal hours in her business. Sir Jasper Reed, the capital's leading forensic pathologist, was no exception. Sir Jasper loved his work, but he also loved to play golf. For this reason, he started work at 2 a.m., leaving afternoons free. His office consisted of a large annex to a City hospital and included a morgue and a collection of rooms and apparatus which, combined, made up an unconventional research facility. He answered her knock at the door himself.

Sir Jasper was a man of about sixty, maybe even seventy, but he loved his work and this enthusiasm made him look young.

Adam Parish

On seeing Amanda, he smiled and, in a booming voice, welcomed her. "What a pleasure, Miss Barratt. Come in, come in." He led her down a typical endless, deathly hospital corridor, past a few laboratories and eventually into a large, cold, tiled room. At his invitation she sat on an uncomfortable plastic seat beside a metal table with a few suspicious stains. She accepted a mug of stewed black tea without enthusiasm.

As a mortuary, it was disturbingly well-designed for its purpose. The floor was part rubber-tiled and part steel-lined, and three of the four walls were lined with pale blue 1960s tiles. That was depressing but not as bad as the fourth wall, which consisted of a five-by-four arrangement of metal drawers which were home to Sir Jasper's customers.

He scraped some unknown detritus from his index finger and then enjoyed a gulp of tea. "Right, you'll want to know about the four you sent me last night? Over here, I'll show you."

With enthusiasm close to relish, he pulled back four adjacent drawers which, as expected, revealed four dead men. Amanda had checked them over last night, but their overnight stay with Sir Jasper had done nothing for their appearance.

"Died from gunshots," the world expert stated. "All from handguns. Glock 9mm." While stating this, he had indicated each corpse in turn. He halted at the last. "This one is most interesting. Thank goodness it was a head shot," he noted with professional satisfaction. He explained, withdrawing the covering sheet further. "Because it leaves us with this."

Pointing to a couple of stars tattooed on the chest, he looked at Amanda, awaiting her guess.

"Eastern European?"

Sir Jasper nodded. "Not bad, not bad. I think that would cover all of these fellows, but these tattoos are Russian prison tattoos. These stars show very high status."

Amanda noted this with interest but it didn't take her much further forward. "Can we identify any of them?"

Business as Usual

Sir Jasper was discouraging. "No, sorry, nothing on our or the European records for DNA, dental or fingerprints. CIA have nothing either." He tried his hand as detective. "Maybe they were imported for this job."

"I'm afraid that I've struck out with Customs and we're not on great terms with our Russian friends."

Sir Jasper said, "Yes, but they have been in the country for a little time."

"How do you know that?"

He went over to a side table, returned with a pair of boots and demonstrated a surprising range of practical expertise for a scientist. "These boots have only been available for about two or three weeks and they're only sold in Britain. In fact, all the clothes were bought here." Discouragingly, he continued, "But they are widely available, so not much point in chasing them down."

Amanda asked, "Anything else?"

"Sorry, nothing."

"What about Mike?"

Sir Jasper showed he had a heart. "I was sorry to hear about that. Good man."

"Yes, he was."

Sir Jasper reached for a file. "He's not here, but I made a phone call. Numerous gunshot wounds, 9mm parabellums. Uzi pistols?"

"Yes, we picked them up at the scene."

"Most common gun in the world."

"And in Buckinghamshire."

"Well, Amanda, unless I can tempt you with another cup of tea, I don't think there's much more I can tell you."

Amanda looked at the filthy mug. "No, I think I'll pass. Let me know if you have any brainwaves."

"I will."

"Thanks. I'll see myself out."

She retraced her steps on an even more depressing return journey. She was thinking about Mike. It wasn't her fault, but that didn't help.

Adam Parish

It was still early, just past six, but only work was going to help here. She thought about walking the fifteen minutes to her office in the morning London air, but she really didn't have time. If she had been in Buckinghamshire fifteen minutes earlier last night, Mike would probably still be alive.

The taxi ride took about fifteen minutes also, but at least when she arrived at her office Max Harris was already there, hammering on a keyboard.

"Morning, boss," he chirped.

This encouraging tone usually meant that he was pleased with himself.

"Have you got something for me?"

He indicated with a jerk of his head. "That phone over there."

"Yes?"

"They picked it up last night at your shoot-out."

Amanda said, "Hmm, they didn't tell me that."

"Oh, they didn't find it until much later. Seems it had fallen out of someone's pocket and it was under the car so they didn't see it at first. They dropped it in early this morning."

"Does it help us?"

"Naturally, it's a disposable. A burner. There were no incoming calls or messages."

"Outgoing calls?"

"Yes, one. I can't break into it but I've got the number."

Amanda knew better than to interrupt Harris when he was showing off. He handed her a single sheet of paper over his shoulder. It said "Prism, 24 Malcolm Street, EC3" and then what looked like a telephone number.

"And Prism are?"

"Private military contractors, based a few miles from here."

"Promising," said Amanda. "Get as much background as you can. I'll pay them a visit."

"On it, boss."

Business as Usual

Harris went back to his keyboard and Amanda went to her office. She made herself a decent cup of tea in a slightly cleaner mug and summoned her next appointment by text. Ten minutes of perfect peace, save for some birdsong from the park over the road, and a discreet cigarette through the open window was enjoyable, and Amanda was ready and refreshed when Ali Cairns was shown into her office by two tall men.

Ali Cairns wasn't under arrest but she wasn't free either. Her hair was disordered, the freckles on her cheeks pronounced and she was wearing the clothes she had had on yesterday. Despite this, she was composed and looked good. Youth could overpower anything in the looks department, but it wasn't much use when you were sitting in front of a director in British Military Intelligence.

Amanda could be gentle and understanding, but today she didn't have time for that. She thought that Cairns' part as a distraught lover seemed plausible enough, but she was going to shake the tree hard before confirming this assumption.

"Right," she said. "I've got about seven dead and a possible fraud in the City so under these circumstances I can do pretty much anything I want." She looked at Cairns, who was already showing signs of stress.

"That includes holding any person for questioning for initially up to 72 hours, and then further by application if necessary." Amanda, in truth, felt nothing for Cairns at this point. She was remembering the dead people – not the four shooters from last night, but Riordan and Ferguson and, again, mostly Mike. There wasn't much time for mourning in her business. She would do that later. At present she was focused on closing this case, and if Cairns had any part in that at all, she would crush her.

Amanda said, "So you say you were in a relationship with Paul Riordan, he suspected a fraud and you have details of some of the client accounts which he was investigating." She paused for a moment but when nothing came back, added, "Is that right?"

Cairns had to speak this time. She looked vulnerable and cowed and her voice was thin but sounded truthful. "Yes, that is pretty much it. He didn't confide in me with all the details."

"So, you were his lover and you're a senior manager in Canisp. Strange that he didn't take you into his confidence."

Ali Cairns looked sad. "Yes, I can see why you would say that. I wish he had ..." She paused, obviously searching for a better word than trusted. "... confided in me, but that was just the way Paul worked."

Amanda wasn't so careful with her words. "Maybe he didn't trust you or maybe he thought you were involved?"

Cairns shook her head vigorously and summoned some defiance. "No, he didn't think that. And I'm not involved, not in any way."

Amanda looked at her hard. Cairns had regained some strength and now held her gaze in return. Amanda said, "Right, you are going to help me, and I expect you to do that voluntarily."

"Yes, of course. I've got nothing to hide. I want to find out what happened to Paul."

"Follow me." Amanda led Cairns out of her office and introduced her to Max. "Max, Ali has some knowledge of the client accounts at Canisp." They exchanged a bit of what Amanda imagined was IT-speak and Harris said, "Fine, let's see what you've got." He pushed his chair aside and invited Cairns to use the keyboard. She was impressive. Amanda exchanged glances with Max and could see that he also was impressed.

Many keystrokes followed as Harris and Cairns alternately operated the keyboard. Their short-term objective was rapidly achieved, and both leant back and reviewed two columns of names juxtaposed on the monitor.

Amanda moved forward for a better look, and it didn't take any expertise to see that there were three or four names which were common to the respective lists.

Harris and Cairns both looked at Amanda.

"Get on with it."

Chapter 21

A five-minute walk took Amanda to the Colonial Club. By Whitehall standards it was a progressive establishment and Amanda was one of the pioneering women members. It was comfortable and convenient and it never closed, save for one day a year, the 31st of December, as a nod to the founding of the East India company in 1600.

A top-hatted concierge nodded and admitted her. Although it was only just past seven in the morning, the club was busy and the marble foyer was packed with breakfasting and overnighting members. A junior member of staff in a modern business suit approached her. "Mr Devoy is in the library, ma'am." He escorted her there, although she knew the way, and opened the door.

The library was warm and sumptuous. It was a high-ceilinged room enwrapped with books on several levels. The seating was informal and divided into arrangements of twin-facing armchairs designed for discreet tête-à-tête discussions. Sunk deep within one such chair, Nick Devoy greeted her and ordered fresh coffee.

"I had a busy time last night." He continued slowly, "I was having a quiet spot of dinner, then guess who joined me?" He looked at her playfully.

She shrugged. "The prime minister?"

"Actually, I did run into the PM, but I was thinking more about Leo King and Sir George Black. They're old friends of mine, known them for years." He looked at her. "Are they in the clear?"

"It's early days. So far, I've got nothing on them." She trusted Devoy and knew he trusted her. An appeal over her head wouldn't work.

True to form, he said, "I told them I didn't know anything and they should speak to you." He reflected, "It's funny, though, no one ever believes that, so they kept talking."

He gave her the headlines. "King's worried that any scandal will cost him a chance at the Bank of England governorship, and George, well, he's just worried that he'll lose a comfy billet." Devoy pursed his lips. "I wonder why they didn't ask about their personal safety? I think I would have."

"I've wondered that myself. Maybe they all buy into the accident theories. I mean, who kills hedge fund managers?"

"Probably many would like to, but are they really in danger?"

Amanda said, "They might be. Anyone who's involved in this, or knows something about it, is in danger. Everything points to a major fraud, but no one on the board has any technical skills. Frankly, I doubt whether any of them have the slightest understanding of how a hedge fund works."

"I'm certain they don't," Devoy agreed.

"But you know, I can't help thinking it's more than a fraud. I mean, after all this, there can't be any chance of the fraud continuing and all this just makes it certain that we will investigate. What do you know about the board members?"

"As I say, I know King and George Black. Neither one is officially connected with us, but from time to time they have been useful. As far as I'm concerned, they are sound enough – no other dubious connections as far as we know."

Devoy moved on to more promising material. "On the other hand, Katherine Carver has strong connections with our American opposite numbers, right up to the top. She was on the shortlist for my equivalent in the States last time. She's a spy in plain sight."

At least something was clear.

Devoy saved the worst for last. "Now, Lord Jeremy Steel …" He grimaced. "Steel's got friends, or at least *connections*, all over the world through the business he runs. It's called the Progressive Global Alliance."

Devoy was the top British spy in a progressive era, but he was no progressive. In fairness, he was no reactionary either. It was impossible to maintain any sort of political partisanship after thirty years in his business, when you had seen every lie and endless cynical messages pushed onto a disinterested and gullible public. What Devoy shared with Amanda was a dislike of people who used politics as a route to personal wealth. Steel fitted perfectly within that bracket.

Devoy said, "Steel will work for anyone, anywhere – despots, dictators, fascists, communists – basically anyone who pays. All in the name of progressive politics, of course." He allowed himself a humourless laugh before summing up. "I wouldn't trust him as far as I could throw him."

Amanda had met Steel only once but was inclined to accept this assessment. "Is he a loyal subject?"

"Loyal to himself, but no real threat in my judgement. Oh, he's got some rotten contacts, but nobody I know would trust him with anything important."

Amanda's telephone rang. It was a moot point as to whether mobile phones were allowed in the library, but she answered anyway. It was Max. He was talking rapidly and told her that he and Cairns had made progress. Forty billion pounds of progress.

Chapter 22

In a long life, Sir George Black had made a lot of friends and quite a few enemies. Personal hostilities and abiding enmity weren't uncommon in public life, but this typically stopped short of guns, bombs and murder. His confidence was low and he was miles out of his comfort zone. The board – on paper a high-powered mix of talent and experience (at least, according to the Fund's annual report) – suddenly seemed to him quite useless.

In any emergency the board usually had a couple of tried-and-tested approaches to problem solving, but it seemed too late now. Worryingly, Sir George was running out of management to blame, and the window for a dignified resignation had closed.

He was early for the meeting and thus far only Leo King had arrived. Always a man of few words, he sat alongside, silent, fidgeting with a pen.

King was at least ten years younger than Sir George but he didn't look it. His tie knot was too big and was sitting untidily off-centre. His thick blue pin-striped suit was shiny. Once, it might have fitted him. Despite that, King was considered a serious, credible man – some said the next governor of the Bank of England – but as Black looked at him, he saw only a tired, time-served career bureaucrat, way out of his depth. At least he believed King was trustworthy, which was something.

Business as Usual

The uncomfortable silence was broken by the arrival of Lord Jeremy Steel, who strode confidently across the plush carpet and casually laid down an impressive collection of papers on the table. He nodded to King, who struggled but just about managed a response. Black managed an audible greeting, but his heart wasn't really in it. It took a crisis for the truth to emerge, and now Black knew for sure that he despised Steel.

In better days, he had managed to convince himself that they were just different, but now he was struggling to summon any respect for Steel. That he couldn't be trusted was a given, and his self-regard was unrivalled and nauseating.

Steel was leafing through his papers but would be engaged in thoughts only about himself – Black was sure about that. Could Steel be involved in this?

He wondered if Steel had courage. He doubted it. Steel had connections, many of whom were of dubious standing. He specialised in providing cover for the world's bad guys. For a fee (a large one), Steel would reposition you as a champion of progressive policies across the globe. A charitable foundation here, the funding of a good cause there was usually all one needed.

***

Steel, tired of pretending to read the documents in front of him, looked across at his colleagues. King looked a broken man and Black was completely out of his depth. Only he and perhaps Katherine Carver had the ability to safely steer the company out of this mess. It was a mystery to Steel how people like King and Black had reached their respective positions. Uninspirational, tedious and without original thoughts. He shook his head.

He supposed that at least King and Black provided a contrast to his own abilities. They gave him a chance to shine by comparison, and Steel credited himself hugely with the growth of Canisp. He had introduced so many new clients – important international players.

Certainly a few had dubious histories, but Steel felt sure that with his guidance and experience, he was making a contribution to the building of a better world.

As for the current difficulties, he was unconcerned. Certainly some of his clients operated at the political and legal frontiers, but that was nothing to do with him. He compared his well-cut Savile Row suit to the others, and having declared himself the winner in the sartorial stakes, he mused comfortably on his lot and yawned. Would Black ever start this meeting?

***

Outside the board room, Katherine Carver waited in a small, adjacent office, fine-tuning her upcoming presentation. After a day of investigations she had, in truth, made little progress, the task being made more difficult by the absence of most of the executive staff. She excused Riordan and Ferguson since they were both dead; however, both Ray Common and Cairns were also absent, apparently on holiday. Selena Thornton had been impressive, however, and her unexpected acting chief executive role suited her very well.

Elsewhere, the company was well-served with high-quality staff, and both Common and Cairns had talented deputies.

All her enquiries pointed to a clean bill of health. The deaths of Ferguson and Riordan were surely what they appeared to be: accidents. Time to move on. So why was she still sitting outside the boardroom at ten past nine?

It wasn't an overwhelming thought, but it kept coming back, no matter how often she expelled it.

She got off her seat. Get this meeting over. This was ridiculous. She was Katherine Carver. When did she ever fail?

Chapter 23

Katherine left the boardroom and went back to her small office without wasting any time with the board members and their trivial post-meeting small talk.

Her report had been received in silence with relieved approval. This had been no surprise to her. She had neither liking nor respect for her fellow board members. You could only really judge people when things were going badly, and they had, as anticipated, come up way short. Anyway, she had given them what they wanted: the illusion of command and control. It was a fix that millions, maybe even billions, needed every day and people like her provided it. They were lucky that there were people like her, people that knew sincerely and unshakeably the right thing to do.

Her mobile rang. An uncomfortable call. She wasn't used to that. Annoying.

Katherine knew Selena Thornton a little better than the other staff at Canisp. That was natural enough – both modern American women with, superficially, similar values. Katherine knew that Selena regarded her as some sort of a role model. Why not?

This admiration wasn't reciprocated. Selena was useful, and although not an idiot, she had reached the peak of her ability, if not her ambition. Good enough for Canisp, but not part of Katherine's grand plans. Selena had a flaw. She really believed what she said and never changed her opinions. Katherine knew that couldn't work.

Political positioning was far too important to be based upon what you privately thought. There were winning positions and losing positions, and only a fool knowingly championed a losing position. Katherine never did.

It took time and intelligence to understand the absurdity of the public positioning of the world's richest people and corporations, but, once you realised it was all nonsense, then almost everything made sense. The world needed leadership, not debate. Simple.

Selena Thornton smiled broadly when welcoming Katherine into her spacious office.

"Nice office," Katherine said.

"I could get used to it I think."

"Yes, it rather suits you."

Selena said, "How did the board meeting go?"

"Easily." Katherine added confidentially, "They don't know what to do, just need a bit of reassurance. I was able to do that."

"Of course. Then again, there's really nothing to report. The funds are strong, no irregularities at all. I hosted the weekly conference call with our major clients first thing. They are all very supportive."

"Good. Do we need to do anything else?"

"No. I am sure we are good, but it's always expected that a couple of new initiatives come out of any review. I've been thinking about doing a bit of a restructure, and there are a couple of vacancies anyway," she added without irony.

"Are you going to move people up to the executive team?"

"Maybe one," Selena said.

"Common, Cairns?"

Selena shook her head. "Maybe we could do with some fresh blood."

"By the way, where are those two?"

"Holidays. Arranged a while ago. I saw no reason to recall them, besides …"

The sentence was left hanging but Carver knew what she meant. Investigations were often better conducted by outsiders, especially if you couldn't trust the insiders. Why that might be true was an interesting side-line, but Katherine let it go. Instead, she reached into her case and produced a single sheet of paper and handed it across to Selena.

She scanned it and looked at Katherine quizzically.

Katherine explained, "The board specifically asked about these four accounts – apparently they are new clients, Middle Eastern clients. Very large connections. Can you just check that everything's all right with them? I understand opening deposits were made last week."

"Yes, fine. I can do that now if you want."

"Why not?"

Selena returned to her desk and Katherine followed. Two or three keystrokes was all it took to review the short list. Selena made a couple of notes on the paper. "Yes, they all seem in order. David did mention them to me a few weeks ago. He was quite excited about securing these clients."

"Yes, it's an exciting new connection, so let's get it right."

"Of course, I'll keep a special eye on them, but at the moment, all the initial deposits have gone through and the agreed investment allocations are in progress."

"How long does that take?"

"It's all done at our end. It usually takes a day or two to get confirmation."

"Good. I'll feed that back to the board." A further thought occurred to her, "And who is handling those accounts going forward? I understood that David was taking the lead."

"I'm happy to do that, Katherine."

"Yes, make sure that you do, Selena."

"Of course."

Katherine got up and headed out of the office. Thornton, she trusted. She would do what she was told. That large office suited her and she didn't want to give it up.

All was well. Katherine had command and control.

Chapter 24

Nick Devoy had seen and heard a lot of things in his life, but even he was impressed by forty billion dollars. He whistled audibly.

Amanda said, "That's provisional. They're still looking at some big currency movements, so it's not conclusive yet. Maybe everything's fine. Hedge funds always move large amounts of money. However, Max is nearly always right."

Devoy produced his phone and spoke a few words into it. He snapped it shut and said, "Have another coffee. Bob Frost is coming over."

Amanda poured two cups and they sat in a comfortable silence until Frost arrived.

Amanda had met Frost a few times and she liked him. He was a round man with a booming voice and the look of a typical American tourist in London. He nodded to Devoy, said, "Hi, Amanda," and poured himself a coffee, which he reviewed unfavourably after a single mouthful.

"How's things, Bob?" Devoy asked routinely.

Frost was only about fifty but exhibited, and enjoyed, a weary "seen-it-all" attitude. Probably he had seen it all – he had been the CIA's top agent in London for at least a decade. He took off a pair of thick-framed spectacles and wiped them carelessly on his shirt sleeve. "Oh, just the usual, Nick. Arguing with the Young Turks about their crazy plans and schemes. They think they have all the answers."

Devoy agreed. "Yes, I've got a lot of that sort as well. Anyway, thanks for popping over, Bob. We have a small issue and wondered if you could help us out."

Frost leant back in his armchair. "Shoot."

In response to an indication from Devoy, Amanda led with a question. "I'm looking at a hedge fund in the City – Canisp. Do you know it?"

"No."

Amanda helped him. "Katherine Carver's on the board."

Frost said, "Oh, Katherine, yes, I know her."

"Is she one of yours?" Amanda continued undiplomatically.

"I know her, Amanda."

"George Black, Leo King, Jeremy Steel. What about them?"

"I know the names, but I don't know them."

"Canisp – that's the hedge fund. They have had a run of bad luck."

"Well, the market goes up and down," Frost said reasonably enough.

"Maybe, but it's not that. They've been unfortunate enough to lose both of their managing partners recently."

Frost looked quizzically.

"Two men both in their forties."

"Unfortunate indeed," Frost said.

"One crashed a car. Maybe it was an accident."

"And the other?"

"Blown up. In Surrey."

"Unusual."

Amanda said blandly, "I had a bit of bad luck myself. A run-in with four gunmen trying to kill some civilians. That was in Buckinghamshire."

Frost's job was to work closely with his British counterparts and ensure a harmonious relationship, so, irrespective, he was going to deny any knowledge or, indeed, involvement. Routinely he did both.

Devoy said, "Yes, fine, Bob, but we would appreciate any help you could give us. I mean, we can't have these sorts of things going on in the Home Counties."

Frost said, "No, of course not, but I've heard nothing about it." He took a mouthful of coffee. "I'll ask around and see if I can find out anything."

"Discreetly, Bob. I don't want other agencies poking their noses in."

"Of course."

Amanda said, "Bob, do you know a company called Prism? They're military contractors in the City."

"Yes, we've used Sebastian Mann once or twice."

"Are you using him now?"

"I think we have a few of his contractors in the Middle East; that's all. He doesn't take on projects for us, as far as I know. But I don't know him well. Surely you know him better than me?"

"Not as well as we should."

"Anything else, Amanda?" Devoy asked.

Amanda shook her head.

"Thanks for dropping in, Bob. If anything comes up, you'll let me know?"

"Of course."

Frost left and Devoy said, "What do you make of that?"

"A pack of lies, sir."

Chapter 25

After a scratch lunch at the club, Amanda summoned a driver. The traffic was heavy, and it took a long time to reach Park Road in the south of Croydon. Number 45 was a two-storey red-roofed villa which sat a little back from a busy thoroughfare. It was an attractive design from the 1930s with a few art deco features. Park Road would have been a semi-rural area at that time, but as the suburb had sprawled outwards, the road had become heavily trafficked and now the house was too good for the area.

The front garden had been given over to gravel and was free of cars, and they drove in. At the second ring of the doorbell a slow, shuffling sound could be heard from within. As could be predicted from the approaching footfall, the door was opened by a woman of at least eighty years. She was small and slender. A pleasant face behind ancient spectacles greeted Amanda.

Amanda smiled back. "Hello, madam. I'm Amanda, Amanda Barratt, and I'm looking for Mr Ray Common." She added a white lie. "The office gave me his address."

The lady, who Amanda had correctly inferred was Mrs Common, smiled again but expressed mild confusion. "Oh, I thought he was at work." This went unanswered and Mrs Common said, "Oh well, you'd better come in for a minute."

Adam Parish

She led Amanda into a bay-windowed sitting room, which Amanda suspected was used sparingly. She accepted a seat in a high-backed armchair and also the offer of a cup of tea.

Mrs Common shuffled out to the kitchen and Amanda spent the next ten or so minutes looking at some tired ornaments and lamenting how easy it was for confidence tricksters to ply their trade.

It would have been inhospitable to serve tea without cake and biscuits and Mrs Common didn't disappoint. Amanda thanked her and accepted tea and a piece of cake before it was forced upon her. She ate it quickly, as balancing a side plate on the arm of the ancient chair proved awkward. This done, she was better placed to resist Mrs Common's further entreaties and considered how best to begin this conversation.

She was still deliberating when the old lady started. "I don't understand why you didn't see Ray at work. I thought he would be back there today." She continued, "He was away last night on business, but he told me he'd be back tonight." Mrs Common looked unconcerned. She beamed throughout. She was proud of her son.

Amanda's heart was sinking.

Mrs Common continued, "He has a good job, you know. He left school with no qualifications and he's worked hard." She drifted back in time. "He had to work, you see, his father died when he was very young."

A flash of melancholy broke through the old lady's face and then it was gone. Amanda had got it wrong. This little old lady was tough. She had handled the bad times and she was still smiling.

"How long have you lived here?"

"Oh, not long, only about twenty-five years. Ray bought it … so much nicer than the south of London."

That, of course, depended upon which part of South London you lived in, but Amanda thought she could narrow it down to a few of the least fashionable areas.

Mrs Common had not yet asked what Amanda wanted, but she was getting to it. "Is Ray in trouble?"

Business as Usual

"I hope not. I don't know yet. There have been a couple of issues at work, but I have no evidence that it's anything to do with Mr Common."

Mrs Common was unfazed. "Evidence ... that's an interesting word, Amanda. Are you from the police?"

"No, not the police, but I do similar work with the Home Office and I have been doing some work with Canisp."

Mrs Common considered this information. "Does that mean you are a spy, Amanda? I mean, does the Home Office usually investigate financial matters?"

"Sometimes it does, Mrs Common." She added with a resigned laugh, "But yes, I am what you might call a spy."

"Well, that's good because you've got a lot more power than the police. So, you'll be able to sort things out quickly."

It was about the best vote of confidence Amanda had received this week.

Mrs Common again anticipated her. "I hope that Raymond will be back this evening, but if not, will you be looking for him?"

"I am keen to have a word."

Mrs Common got out of her chair with an effort and from the mantelpiece selected a photograph, which she presented to Amanda with some pride.

It was a group shot of four men decked out in football colours. Amanda wasn't much interested in football. She had heard of Glasgow Rangers (Jack sometimes mentioned them) and, racking her brains, she had heard of Chelsea. She thought they were a London team. "Chelsea?" she said hopefully.

Mrs Common knew her football. "No, Chelsea are west London. These are Crystal Palace colours. Anyway, you see, that's why I know he'll be back tomorrow. He'd never miss a match."

Amanda had a good look at the photograph. Ray Common looked happy – he and his three friends going to the match. They were all smiles and, as she looked across, Mrs Common was again smiling.

Adam Parish

Amanda was a professional and it was her job to smile back, but, try as she might, that proved beyond her.

Chapter 26

The traffic was lighter and the going easier back into town. Amanda was angry now. Despite trying to rid herself of unwelcome thoughts, the meeting with Mrs Common had forced her into thoughts of the fundamentals of life. It was easy to forget about this in her business, but right now high finance and intergovernmental intrigues seemed a lot less important.

What really mattered was that Pam Riordan had lost her father. He had left her money, enough for a full life, but what good was that? Amanda thought about her own parents, both dead now. There had been ups and downs but there had been love. She wondered how much she would pay for five more minutes with either of them.

Not just Pam Riordan but Mike, her former colleague. He knew the rules and died taking on four gunmen. In putting himself on the front line he had almost certainly saved Jack, Pam and Ali Cairns. It was an honourable way to die, and she knew Mike would have approved but, in the short visit she had made to Mike's partner, Amanda knew for sure that she hadn't cared about any of that.

At least Ferguson had no family. It was unusual for a man of his means, appearance and status, but at least his death had left no one mourning. Whether the four gunmen had left distraught relatives was a step too far for Amanda's current concern for humanity. She refocused on the living.

Adam Parish

Amanda had now managed to persuade Jack to take Pam to her own holiday home in Norfolk. It was where Amanda went when she wanted to disappear. It was only a couple of hours from London but there was nowhere quite like it to experience total isolation and recuperation. She was confident that they were safe, at least for now.

It wasn't simple to concentrate on the living in Amanda's business. These investigations weren't like that. All you could do was chase it down and hope that only the bad guys got killed. So, who were the bad guys? Her head hurt, so she lit a cigarette and concentrated upon what she was paid to do.

Max Harris answered her call on the second ring, and with characteristic enthusiasm, embarked upon an unstructured and highly technical update. She let him go on and sank back into the soft rear seat of the Jaguar. Harris was experiencing no such challenges on humanity and moral philosophy and continued to talk in technical terms, only some of which she understood.

Amanda relaxed her eyes and let his enthusiasm re-energise her for a full five minutes. Then he stopped talking.

She congratulated him on what sounded like progress, although she was forced to ask him for a shorter, non-technical summary. He was happy to do this. "I'm sorry, I made a mistake. It seems that my earlier estimate of 40 billion dollars was a bit bullish, it's now just over 38 billion."

"Thank goodness for that. I was thinking that things were serious."

Harris managed a rare laugh. "Yes, but I don't like to be wrong."

"You're forgiven. What else?"

"I've been working with Ali and we've drilled down into a few of the accounts. All of them were on Mr Riordan's initial list. They're all new accounts and set up quickly. Not much diligence."

"Is that unusual?"

"Yes, a little for accounts of this size. I would have thought these would get a lot of attention. A lot of sign-offs."

Amanda said. "Who authorised them?"

"Paul Riordan."

It wasn't the answer she expected. "When?"

"Three days ago."

"Interesting. Now, can you tell me who set them up, given Paul Riordan's been dead for weeks?"

Max said disapprovingly, "Afraid not, boss. It seems that IT security is a bit lax at Canisp. In fact, at least four or five people knew Riordan's sign-on details." He listed them. "Ferguson, Thornton, Ali herself and maybe Ray Common – oh, and there's a PA who might know."

Amanda had a brainwave. "What about the machine?"

She struck out again.

"It was Riordan's machine."

Amanda had a last go. "So, there's no way of telling who used it?"

"Afraid not. Sorry, boss."

"Okay, what else have you got?"

"Quite a bit, actually. Each of the four accounts had opening deposits in excess of nine billion dollars, all credited a couple of days ago and today" – he paused for effect – "all gone."

"Gone? Gone where? Returned?"

Max laughed. "Returned, I don't think so but I'm chasing the money as we speak. Quite a challenge."

Amanda, quite reasonably, asked, "Isn't it quite normal for the opening capital to be distributed into different investment vehicles?"

Max agreed but said, "However, it's not usual for the journey to be so complicated with so many stop-overs. This is what happens with dirty money. It's a complicated journey. Whoever programmed this knew what they were doing."

"So, all we have to do is establish where the money came from, where it's going and who's moving it."

Max laughed again. "That about covers it, boss. If you give me another hour or so, I'll be close to knowing all these things."

Amanda's driver was entering the outskirts of the City of London.

"What about Ali Cairns?"

"Shit-hot on computers," Max enthused.

"Do you trust her?"

"Yes, I think so. She seems genuine to me."

Amanda asked, "Are you better than her? With computers, I mean?"

"Yes, better overall, but she is good in her area."

"So, *she* could have got in about these funds?"

"Oh yes, easily. I mean, it's quite tough to hack. It took me nearly an hour to break into it."

"Fair enough. Just be careful what you say to her. We'll look like fools if she's perpetrating a fraud while working with us."

"Yes, I can see that, but don't worry. I'll know what she's doing."

"Just keep an eye on her. What about Prism?"

Again, Max didn't disappoint. "Yes, got a bit for you. It's run by a Sebastian Mann, forty something, ex para, ladies' man, well-connected."

Amanda said, "Ladies man, how do you know that?"

"Social media boss. It's all there. Although he seems to have calmed down over the last few months. Maybe he's in love. Anyway, he'll be in his London office this afternoon."

"Ok, thanks. I'll talk to you in a few hours."

"No problem boss," Max answered playfully and rang off.

Amanda shouted an address in the City.

"Ten minutes, ma'am."

Amanda yawned and straightened up slowly from her slouched position.

Harris was afflicted with the overconfidence of youth, but it was supplying the energy she needed right now. She yawned. Thirty-eight wasn't old, but it was about twice the age of Max. Damned statistics.

Chapter 27

Amanda pressed a button and the dividing glass in the car rolled up. It served well enough as a rude mirror, and she spruced herself up a bit with a little make-up and some rough hair-brushing. Well, it couldn't hurt, she figured. Max had said that Sebastian Mann was a ladies' man. When she wanted to, Amanda could put on a show. She wasn't going to sugar Sebastian Mann, quite the reverse, but every edge counted.

Her driver said, "We're here. Do you want me to stop outside the front door?"

"Yes, near as you can get. And wait for me."

He edged the car on to the busy pavement, attracting numerous hostile looks from passing City workers. Amanda got out of the car and was rewarded with a few more looks, and a "What the fuck do you think you're doing?" from a well-dressed lady – a question which she ignored and pressed on towards a glass-fronted double door, which was firmly shut. Inside a receptionist avoided her gaze.

She pressed a few buttons on an intercom. After what seemed like a long time, a well-spoken female voice enquired what her business was.

"I want to see Mr Mann."

"Do you have an appointment?"

"No."

"Sorry, meetings are by appointment only," the receptionist stated triumphantly.

Amanda sighed. "Look, please tell Mr Mann that it's Amanda Barratt from the Home Office and that I need to see him now."

A short silence. "I'll see if he is available."

The receptionist picked up the phone and listened. Without a word to Amanda, she reached for a button. A rasping sound unfroze a door. The receptionist pointed, and Amanda entered into a small, modern reception area. There was another desk, but there was no one behind it. She looked around, but there was no obvious exit or route to elsewhere. The door closed behind her. One of the old-fashioned desk phones rang. Amanda picked it up. It was a man's voice, cultured and controlled. "Miss Barratt?"

"Yes?"

"You have a gun."

Prism's security was impressive.

"Yes, of course I've got a gun." She was in the spying business but was tiring of this cloak-and-dagger approach. She said, "Look, Mr Mann, either you can let me in or I can come back with a dozen men."

"Come right up, Miss Barratt."

Low whistling engineering noises came from somewhere and then a lift door opened ahead of her. She stepped into the steel-lined box, and without her doing anything the door closed and she headed upwards.

The doors of the lift opened to reveal a powerfully built man of at least six feet. He was handsome and had a strong jaw and short, fashionably styled black hair, all of which made it easy to imagine him as a charmer of "ladies". A single step out of the lift took her very close to him. He looked her over with a trace of licentious approval and extended his hand. She held his gaze and shook his hand.

He broke off and said suavely, "This way, Miss Barratt." He guided her along a doorless corridor, which eventually opened into a circular area, home to three unmarked doors. He led her through the central door, which was opened by a fingerprint recognition pad.

Business as Usual

Sebastian Mann's office didn't disappoint either. It was large and colourful. All the furniture was modern and the technology was extensive and impressive. Mann indicated a seat beside a low, smoked-glass table and invited her to sit opposite.

He smiled at her and she smiled back a bit. Yes, he was handsome, but he was one of those men where each succeeding glance highlighted small imperfections, like the nose that, despite surgery, couldn't deny that it had been broken. His teeth were too perfect – perhaps all right for American clients - but far too suspicious for the UK.

Despite all this, he was a superior specimen. Amanda wasn't thinking much about men these days, but if she had been, Mann might have had a chance. He was **better-looking** and in better shape than Jack, but Amanda liked Jack better. Maybe she would tell him that?

Mann had an appealing deep voice and spoke slowly. She turned down a drink. He pressed a button on his desk. Ostentatiously, he spoke to an invisible assistant. "Hi, it's Seb. Redirect all my calls until I get back to you."

He turned back to Amanda. "What can I do for you, Miss Barratt?"

"How's business, Mr Mann?"

He stretched out his arms, indicating the opulence of his office, which told its own story. The private sector was evidently thriving and had come a long way in the last twenty years. No longer relying on nifty photographic work to capture cheating spouses, and the line between government agencies and privateers was blurring by the day. War felt permanent, part-privatised, and it was, as it had always been, the biggest business. The privateers were no pushovers these days and had plenty of money, but Amanda had the power of the State behind her and still held a few cards.

"I'm investigating a shooting incident. Last night in Buckinghamshire."

His face remained neutral. "Hmm, last night. I didn't hear or read anything about that."

"No, of course not. There's been nothing in the press."

"Where about in Buckinghamshire?"

"One of the Chalfonts."

"Unusual."

"Yes, I've got four dead bodies in the mortuary, hired guns, probably Eastern European or Russian."

Mann leant forward involuntarily. "Very unusual."

"Have you got any Eastern European personnel on your books?"

Mann replied, "Well, that's not much of a description, Amanda, but to be honest, I don't have great connections in that part of the world. I always found them a bit ill-disciplined and unreliable. My clients tend to prefer steadier types – ex-British military, American professionals, you know."

Amanda shrugged off her annoyance at his using her first name. "Are you a steady type, Mr Mann?"

Mann leant back and smiled at her, showing a lot of white teeth. "I would say so, Amanda."

Damn, he used her first name again. "What's your background?"

Mann put his hand through his black hair. "Sandhurst, then the Paras for twenty years, then I started working for myself."

"What rank?"

"Major."

"Did you get around much?"

"I saw the world."

"Let's go back to these Eastern Europeans. I'm told that at least one of them contacted your company a couple of days ago."

Mann was unfazed. "Well, we have about a dozen or so associates and many more clients. Lots of people contact us looking for a position. If you've got names or more information, I'll be happy to check it out for you."

Amanda was learning nothing other than the fact that she was developing a dislike for Sebastian Mann. She said sweetly, "Can you check it out now? I've got four dead bodies." She delved into her pocket and produced a mobile phone. "The call was made from this phone. Can you check your phone records, time and duration? Maybe you have a recording of the call?"

He regarded the unfashionable phone with disdain and said, "I can try. What's the number?"

Amanda handed him the note Max had prepared.

Sebastian Mann shrugged. "Give me a few minutes, Miss Barratt."

Amanda thought about making a quick search around the office after he left but rejected the opportunity, which turned out to be a good decision as Mann returned in less than a minute.

"I'm told that we can do a quick analysis in five or so minutes. How about a drink?"

Amanda didn't want one but decided to see if informal might work better. "A small one, please."

Mann returned with two large crystal glasses and handed her one.

"I was wondering why I hadn't heard more about you until now?"

Mann looked pleased. "We try to keep as low a profile as possible."

"Where are you working at the moment?"

"Well, I can hardly say."

"You can tell me. I don't think that we'll have any secrets between us, going forward."

Mann laughed. "The Middle East keeps us busy. So many problems."

Amanda looked at him. A good actor. A slight downturn of the mouth and a wistful expression. Many would have believed that he cared. "You know the area well?"

"A few tours."

She was interrupted when a twenty-something woman dressed for an evening in the West End returned with the mobile. She reached across to Sebastian Mann and handed it to him. Appearances could certainly deceive, and the bimbo gave Mann an impressive technical analysis with thirty seconds of well-chosen words.

"Okay, thanks," said Mann.

"Well?"

"There was a call from that number to one that was ours."

"When?"

"Last night, 5.35 p.m., duration about 18 seconds."

"Have you a recording?"

"No, we go through many mobile numbers. Most are replaced on a weekly basis. You know the drill?"

"But the call was yesterday."

"Sorry, the number was retired this morning and the phone broken up. We do this every week at the same time."

Another coincidence. Amanda was getting sick of them. "I guess it's just not my day?"

Mann had the sense to say nothing to this and let his story stand, improbable as it might appear.

Amanda could only move on. "Do you know the Canisp Hedge Fund or any of the partners?"

Mann considered. "The name is vaguely familiar. Maybe I read about it in the *FT*." He indicated a copy of that periodical at the far end of his desk.

Amanda persisted. "Paul Riordan, David Ferguson, Selena Thornton – do you know any of them?"

"No, never heard of them."

Amanda took a sip of what turned out to be good malt whisky and changed the subject. "I was talking to Bob Frost this morning."

Mann couldn't help himself, and this time sat up straighter in his chair.

"I talked to him about my problem and he agreed with me that this is a high priority. In fact, he assured me that you would be helpful." She looked at him. He was more uneasy now, which was good.

"Of course, happy to help, but as I've said, I'm not sure what else I can tell you."

Amanda said, "You need to be sure that you've told me all that you know, Mr Mann, and you need to be sure right now." She was in full flow now. "You see, when I close this case, which I will" – she let this sink in – "and Prism has any connection, anything at all, you'll be looking for a new office, Mr Mann."

Amanda wasn't bluffing. The truth was that businesses like Mann's didn't really have any rights and were allowed to exist because they were sometimes of use to the official forces, particularly when arm's length operations were needed. But ultimately, they were disposable. In Prism's case, Amanda had plenty leverage. They weren't a preferred UK contractor, so she could run them out of town any time. A smear here and a nod and a wink that Mann and his firm were unsound would be all it would take. Mann lived by his reputation for discretion and reliability, and falling foul of the UK government would be disastrous for his business.

He looked at Amanda, pursed his lips and swept a slow hand across his chin. She knew he was going to tell her something, but what?

"Okay, Miss Barratt. You understand that our business is based on confidence, but if, as you say, such big interests are at stake then obviously I would want to help."

Amanda waited.

Mann leant back and reached for a packet of cigarettes which lay on his desk. He lit one and, as an afterthought, offered one to Amanda.

"No, I'm trying to give them up."

"I don't know anything about what you have told me, but I *have* heard of Canisp. I don't have business with them, but I have a friend – well, more of an acquaintance – who works there."

"Who?"

"Ray Common."

"How do you know him?"

"I've known him for years, we're both from South London. We used to go to football together."

"What team?"

"You follow football?"

"A bit", Amanda lied.

"The Eagles, of course." He looked at Amanda, but this time she had done her homework

"Oh, Crystal Palace."

"Yes."

"So, you know Ray Common. Is that all?"

"Not quite, although I can't imagine that it's important."

"I'll decide that."

"He called me last week and said he had a problem – something about being harassed by a local bookmaker over money. He said he had been threatened and did I know anyone who could provide him with a bit of support. Naturally that's not our business, but of course, we do get to know a lot of people."

"Go on."

"I mentioned his problem to some friends. In the pub, not officially. Someone gave me a number and I gave it to Ray. That's it."

"And who was the enforcer?"

"No idea."

"Wasn't that a bit careless?"

"Maybe, but it felt so trivial. It can't have anything to do with your enquiries."

"Maybe not, but the fact remains that we've picked up a mobile phone at a murder scene. That phone made a single call to Prism."

Mann shrugged. "I've told you all I know. If you've got any more details about the dead guys, then it would help."

That wasn't unfair but it was annoying, and Amanda felt for the first time that the interview had run its course. "I'm going to need a list of all your associates, Mr Mann."

"Of course."

Mann made another call, and his efficient assistant emerged with some papers.

Amanda looked them over. "That will do for now. Thank you."

With this, the interview closed, and it was time to leave. She insisted that he direct her to stairs rather than enduring the claustrophobic lift. In the abandoned reception area, he extended his hand, which she accepted with a few valedictory words to the effect that he had better have told her the truth and the whole story.

Outside, the London public had become accustomed to the black Jaguar on the broad pavement, and her driver sat unmolested in his seat. She got into the rear seat and leant back.

"Where to, ma'am?"

Business as Usual

Amanda fell back into the soft rear seat, lit a cigarette and closed her eyes. "Nowhere. Just drive. I'm thinking." Her thoughts were unpleasant. Whatever hopes that she had had of restoring Mrs Common's son to her were fading fast. Sebastian Mann told lies for a living, but maybe he was telling the truth this time.

Mann, she was pretty sure, would sell his grandmother for money, so it would be easy for him to give her Common. Did she believe that Mann had such limited exposure in this whole affair? Like everything in this case, she didn't really know. Theoretically, she could have taken him in for further questioning, but what did she have? Nothing really.

Ray Common, on the other hand, was suddenly right at the centre of her enquiries.

Chapter 28

At five o'clock Amanda cut a weary figure when returning to her Bloomsbury office. Max Harris and Ali Cairns were showing no signs of exhaustion and were sitting close together, still working and rifling through a mountain of paperwork which covered a large meeting table. She uttered a low acknowledgement to them both, which Harris returned without turning round. Amanda was glad of that for the moment. She threw off her wax jacket and flicked on the kettle. It felt good to be in her office. Without doubt, it was the scruffiest and worst-appointed place she had visited today, but she liked it that way.

Her office was spacious and cluttered with cheap eclectic items of furniture which she had saved from being scrapped when moving in. She mixed a strong instant coffee and slumped into a threadbare but comfortable armchair. Her instinct was to rest and think, but she had a couple of things to do before that.

Devoy's man answered his phone promptly and Amanda put him to work. A tail and phone tap were arranged for Sebastian Mann and a full-scale hunt for Ray Common was instigated. Then she phoned Jack.

Suddenly the thought of Jack was comforting. He was a mess in many ways, infuriating sometimes and not yet fully grown up. But there were times when she felt that she needed him. Right now was one of those times, but it wasn't going to happen, as Jack and Pam were now safely hidden away in the Norfolk fens.

Amanda loved that house. It had been the holiday home of her late parents and she had spent many happy summers there. She dialled the number and he answered.

He sounded relaxed and pleased to hear from her. "Yes, all good," he said. "Mind you, I took a few wrong turnings finding the house."

"That's why it's a safe house. The satnav doesn't work there either. How's Pam?"

Jack hesitated a bit. "Fine, fine I think, although she's had a bit of a reaction. She's quiet."

"Not surprising. It's been a tough few weeks."

"How are you doing?"

She gave him an update on her busy day and told him about Common. "What do you think?"

"Quite honestly, it's tough to believe. I mean, yes, he's been there a long time so I guess he knows a lot but, well, he wasn't all that impressive. About fifty, a bit fat and balding," Jack continued honestly but unkindly. "I just can't see him as a criminal mastermind."

"Well, I'm not saying that he's the only person involved."

"So, what's it all about? Fraud?"

Amanda said, "There's a lot of money involved certainly, but it strikes me as a bit more than that. We're getting closer … hopefully Max will be able to cut through things."

"What do you want me to do?"

"Nothing at the moment, just stay safe. I'll hopefully make progress over this weekend and I'll give you a ring on Monday or before if something comes up."

Jack sounded disappointed. "If that's what you want." He paused for a moment and said, "I was kind of hoping that you would come up at the weekend."

This cheered her up and she said, "I'd like to but I can't."

"I thought you might need or deserve a day off."

Amanda said, "Well, I definitely *deserve* a day off, but it's not going to happen until we get this closed. Anyway, just keep yourself and Pam safe."

He rang off, and she closed her eyes and sank deeper into the armchair. She vaguely began to have thoughts of Jack's arms around her. Nice.

The moment didn't last. Max Harris hammered on her half-open door and with glinting eyes and a booming voice said that, if it suited her, he could give her an update.

She yawned, but there was no time like the present, and a moment later Max, joined by Ali Cairns, returned to her office. Harris nudged Cairns. She looked nervous, reasonable enough given her equivocal status in this enquiry – part detective, part suspect – but she began confidently. Financial analysis was, after all, her business.

"Right, in summary, three days ago thirty-eight billion dollars was deposited evenly in four new client accounts. These clients are based in the Middle East, but ultimately, our working assumption is that they are American controlled. The money has moved to various places but the full trail isn't important at the moment, just where the money ended up."

She handed Amanda a sheet of paper. The names meant nothing to Amanda and she said so.

"That's unsurprising. The first thing to say is what they are *not*. They're not investments in any sense, just bank accounts."

"Whose bank accounts?"

Max jumped in with the spy stuff. "We've only assessed two of them, but I think they are CIA accounts."

"How do you know that?" asked Amanda.

"Er, well, we managed to get into the accounts and were able to work out who controlled them. All roads lead to Langley."

Amanda lit a cigarette. "Jeez, is nothing safe?"

"Normally these accounts would be more secure, but these are also new. They were set up only a few days ago, so they haven't got round to it yet. Probably they intended to close them when the transactions were complete."

"So, the CIA are moving dirty money from the Gulf – is that it? Why didn't they just transfer it direct?"

"Obviously to cover their tracks," Max said.

Cairns piped up. "It's one program and it was created at Canisp."

Amanda was getting the hang of this now. "By who, Paul Riordan?"

"It was done with his log-in and his machine."

"Not conclusive."

"No."

Amanda thought about Bob Frost now. He had to know about this. He must be lying. It was a lot of money. She looked up at Ali and Max. "How sure are you about this?"

Max said, "Pretty confident, boss."

"We're going to have to be certain. Christ, that's all we need. Could the Americans not have laundered their money somewhere else?" She looked at Max. "Nothing to say?"

"Never interrupt your boss when she's having a rant."

"Is there more?"

"A bit."

"Okay. Rant over."

Max said, "We think that what you described was the original plan, but that something has gone wrong. You see, the money didn't sit in these accounts for long. There was another program, hidden very deep in the main program."

"And this program did what?"

"It distributed the money to a lot more accounts, about ten from each account, forty in total." Max handed her a sheet of paper. "We're not finished yet, but we have identified about thirty of them."

Amanda scanned the page and slowly lit another cigarette. The sheet had four columns: bank account number; bank account name; bank account owner; and amount credited.

In a crisis, people reacted in different ways. Amanda was always the same. The short, light hairs on her forearms rose and goosebumps broke out all over her body.

Many of the names on this list were familiar to her – sickeningly familiar. As Max had said, the list was incomplete but, after a careful line by line calculation, it was clear that by design - or more likely by accident – the CIA had, so far, disbursed about thirty billion dollars to some of the most dangerous and active global terrorist groups.

She put the A4 sheet carefully down on the low table. This revelation was worth another cigarette.

Max and Ali sat silently.

"Can we retrieve the money?"

Max shook his head. "No chance, ma'am."

This was worth an expletive. "Fuck." She looked at them. "How long to finish off the list?"

"Couple of hours," Max ventured.

He made to rise, but she stopped him. She picked up her mobile. Nick Devoy answered immediately.

"Sorry, Nick, but this can't wait. I need you over here immediately, if possible, with a couple of men who I want to keep." She added, "Field men."

The call ended. "I'm going to need both of you to keep going with this exercise. Get the list finished. I've got the Head of MI5 coming here in half an hour."

They both nodded and got up.

"Just a minute. Miss Cairns, wait here. Max, go and get an Official Secrets form."

He got up and returned with a short document, which he placed in front of Ali Cairns.

Amanda said formally, "I am going to need you to sign this, Miss Cairns." She outlined the absolute obligations contained therein. "Please read it through."

Ali Cairns did and signed.

"Okay. Let's get this done," said Max.

Chapter 29

In her West End flat, Katherine Carver was also working late. She poured herself a decent-sized bourbon and sat uncomfortably in her large and expensive drawing room. He was late. How like him.

The doorbell rang.

Bob Frost accepted a drink. Sitting opposite, she regarded him. He was heavier than he should have been and his face was becoming jowly. He looked like a middle-ranking clerk, and his suit was starting to shine, not in a good way. His tie knot was too big and his multi-coloured striped shirt had been out of fashion for more than twenty-five years. Frost's views had, similarly, been out of fashion for a long time, but somehow, he had clung on. Maybe the British liked him. Fuck them. Katherine didn't like the British and she didn't like Frost.

Katherine had been, nominally, working alongside Frost for six months, a sort of handover period. She had hated every minute. She didn't rate him one bit, and there was absolutely nothing that he could teach her.

There were things to do in the world – important things – and Bob Frost just didn't see that. He was a dinosaur. Maybe he was cleverer than he looked, but Katherine rejected that as impossible. He had achieved next to nothing in the last few years, and now she was about to show him up completely.

After a couple of long mouthfuls of bourbon, Frost said, "How are we doing your end?"

"Fine, I think, although there have been a few bumps along the road."

That was the understatement of the year but Frost didn't challenge it. He cut to the chase. "When will the money be through?"

Katherine was nothing if not efficient. She reached into her designer briefcase and produced a single sheet of paper, which she handed to him.

Deliberately, he placed the paper on his knee and reviewed it vaguely. "Can I keep this copy?"

"Yes."

He folded the sheet and slipped into a jacket pocket. "That seems fine. It'll be a major feather in your cap."

She didn't demur.

"Can I help you with anything?"

"No, I've got this."

"I'll let you get on."

Frost necked his bourbon and, without pleasantries, Katherine walked him to the door. It shut without him looking back, and she returned to the drawing room.

She pulled out more papers from her briefcase and reviewed them again and again. That didn't help. The numbers just wouldn't lie.

The United States was the wealthiest country in all of human history and its military branches were lavishly funded. Even so, they would still miss thirty-eight billion dollars.

***

Frost took a long time to navigate his way out of the plush London block of flats where Katherine Carver held court. It sure beat his two-bedroomed flat, annoyingly near to Kings Cross. He couldn't stand Carver. She had no understanding of the world outside her head. In his business, that was dangerous. But what could he do? He had offered to help.

Business as Usual

Frost had a feeling that Carver might be about to fall to earth. He was walking on air.

Chapter 30

Nick Devoy was the boss you wanted when you faced a crisis. Without demur or asking for the details, he accepted Amanda's invitation to come to her unpretentious top-floor office. In a nod to his status, he breezed in with his overcoat flying open, accompanied by six enormous besuited men.

"Wait outside," he ordered, and he went into Amanda's office and pulled the door shut.

He flopped into the ancient sofa and cast a critical eye around the office. "I know things are tight, but we could stretch to a tin of paint. Maybe even some office furniture?"

Amanda leant back in her ancient chair and it groaned back. "Yes, maybe when I get a minute, but I like it. Feels traditional."

Devoy shrugged. "Okay, what have you got?"

She handed him the report.

He glanced at it. "Can I have a cigarette?"

She handed him one. Devoy only smoked when things were bad. He returned to the short report and gave it a further review before throwing it aside and drawing deeply on the cigarette.

She waited, but she wasn't worried. The other good thing about Devoy was that he and Amanda thought much the same way.

He took another long drag on his cigarette and said, "Fuck," and leant back in the sofa. This was no laughing matter. Devoy began to laugh. "This ought to set the war on terror back about a decade." With which depressing but accurate forecast, he moved on to the present. "What now?"

Amanda told him about her progress and said, "I'm tailing Sebastian Mann and looking for Ray Common. But I'm minded to pull in Selena Thornton and the entire Canisp board."

"All of them?"

"Well, I fancy Katherine Carver and Jeremy Steel more than the others, but that's only a hunch. They are so disagreeable, but that's hardly evidence. Overall, I still feel several steps behind whatever's going on. So, if we pull them all in, it might give us little time, some breathing space."

"Surely this information gets us closer?"

"A bit, but I need more."

"Pull them all in if you want. Actually, it might be better. Jeez, I don't want this getting out." Without wasting energy on opening the office door, Devoy bellowed, "Bishop!"

A tall man arrived in the doorway. "Sir?"

"This is Gordon Bishop," Devoy said to Amanda. "Have you got a list of all these people?"

"Yes." She retrieved it from her desk and gave it to Bishop. "There's a couple of addresses missing. Can you find them?"

Bishop said, "Are they all board members at Canisp?"

"Yes, except Thornton. She's the acting chief executive."

Bishop nodded. "Where shall we put them up, sir?"

"Take them to North London. Let me know when you've got them." He added, "Oh, it is possible that one or more might claim diplomatic immunity or a CIA connection. You don't know anything about that."

"Understood, sir."

Devoy turned to Amanda. "How many guys do you want?"

"Two here, please."

Devoy did the maths. "Gordon, take three of the guys with you and leave two here with me."

Bishop nodded and left.

Amanda reached into a desk drawer. "You want a drink, Nick?"

He rose wearily and threw off his coat. "Yes, why not?"

She joined him with two glasses and they sat in silence for a few minutes.

"So, the money's gone," Devoy said. "We might be able to catch the people responsible, but so what? The damage is done."

Amanda said, "Not necessarily, there might be more operations planned – although not through Canisp, of course."

"Maybe, but surely we shouldn't give up on the money?"

"All gone, they tell me."

"Max is young. Let's get a second opinion."

It was Amanda's turn to bellow, and Max came into the office. "Boss?"

"I've been thinking, double-check with Cheltenham and make sure that the money's definitely beyond our reach."

Devoy chipped in. "Talk to Simon Gilchrist."

"Yes, sir."

"The analysts are sure getting younger." Devoy reflected.

"He's brilliant," Amanda said.

"Maybe he needs a bigger challenge."

"Ask him."

Devoy looked at her and smiled. He called Max back in. "Miss Barratt gives me glowing accounts of your progress, Max. What are your ambitions?"

"I'm happy here, sir."

"Of course, but going forward?"

"I'm very happy working with Miss Barratt, sir, I'm sure she'll let me tag along as she moves forward."

Devoy looked severe, then let out a laugh. "Thanks, Max." He looked at Amanda. "Very loyal staff, you have."

"Can be impertinent, I'm afraid."

"Seems he thinks that you're the star to hitch his wagon to. Maybe he's right, although clearing up this case might help your stately progress."

Business as Usual

Amanda said, "Assuming the money is gone, the Americans have got a great big hole somewhere. Maybe we can help?"

"What do you have in mind?"

"We've got the list. Couldn't we devise some sort of interdiction, financial or otherwise?"

"We could try but we need our overseas experts for that. Let's wait until we're clearer on what's going on. But you're quite right. Let's get on the front foot here and show these idiots how it's done."

With which Churchillian blast, they settled in for a long night.

Chapter 31

Battling through the crowds at an East End overground railway station was a pleasure Selena Thornton would have preferred to forego. It had only been a ten-minute tube journey, but that had been enough to convince her that the way the other 99% lived was not for her. Selena was a committed progressive and she gave to charity, but, when up too close, she didn't really care for ordinary people.

She emerged from a gated exit onto an inner-city street that, despite the number of people and the fact that it was five o'clock, felt unsafe.

According to reports, this area of the East End was undergoing impressive redevelopment, but it was far from complete. Modern offices and flats sat alongside derelict buildings with cleared land impatiently waiting for its turn.

At least the area hosted a vibrant artistic community with each gable end adorned with indecipherable but colourful graffiti. After taking, and then correcting, a wrong turn, Selena gained the optimum route: a minor road running alongside the motorway. After a long walk into a cold wind, she arrived at the metalled fencing boundary of the Low-Cost Car Rental Company. A leaf of the main gate stood open and a large part-tarmacked area was home to a couple of dozen mid-range vehicles. The main office was portable and its door refused to yield to her prompting, but, after ringing a buzzer, it was eventually opened by a tall, youngish man. His English was reasonable but she had to concentrate. He indicated a seat in front of his desk and, after an administrative effort, located her details.

"Miss Thompson?" he enquired.

"Yes."

He read aloud the relevant details of her booking and let her into his confidence about mileage charges. This done, he got to the key issue. Leaning forward, he said, "Now, I've ticked the boxes about ID etc., but, as I explained, if your driving licence is unavailable, I'll need a deposit."

She delved into her shoulder bag and produced a thick bundle of twenty-pound notes. "There's a thousand pounds there."

He started to flick through the notes and about halfway through the count declared himself satisfied and pushed a set of car keys towards her. He then insisted on accompanying her onto the lot, keeping up an unconvincing chatter on the merits of the car.

It had been a decent vehicle at one time, but that time was at least ten years ago, she reckoned. Nevertheless, it was clean, smelled moderately fresh and started first time.

With an effort, Selena shut down endless mansplaining on the vehicle's features and, a moment or two later, she drove out of the lot and started her weekend.

Leaving London in the Friday rush hour was slow and frustrating. Normally, this would have driven Selena crazy, but not today. Today was a good day; the first day of the rest of her life. Selena believed in predestination, especially for people like her: people who mattered.

The traffic lightened as she left the City and allowed her to drive fast, which she loved. An hour later it thinned to a trickle as she reached the county of Norfolk. She had gotten to know the Fen Country in the last year after a few passionate trysts. It was the perfect place to disappear for the weekend, or perhaps even longer.

After another hour, the car had taken her past the last major town in the county and she was only half an hour from the house. Like the car, it had been a cash transaction under a false name. She wasn't entirely sure whether such subterfuge was necessary, but she had decided to do what she had been told. She slowed the car as she neared the final junction, turned left and, a few hundred yards on, arrived.

The accommodation consisted of a large two-storey brick farmhouse with an attached smaller bungalow. Money was no object but discretion was, and she had rented both of the houses in order to be undisturbed.

The driveway entrance was tight, but once in there was plenty of space. In a small porch-cum-greenhouse she located the house keys. After a rapid tour, she decided that the smaller attached cottage would suit her better. It was spotlessly clean and looked comfortable, but the modern fittings in a house that might have been three hundred years old was an aesthetic disappointment.

Still, it felt better than the main house. The log burner worked and the sofa was big and soft. She reached into her bag and took out bottles of red and white wine. The glass which sat out on the dining table drained about half of the bottle and she sipped it continuously. Her body was relaxing. There were still minor pangs of anxiety, but she shrugged them off. What she was doing was the right thing to do and, she reasoned, might even change the world. That's what the Thorntons did.

She forced herself out of the sofa went upstairs and drew a bath. It was relaxing, but every few seconds she found herself glancing at her phone. At last, it rang, and when she heard the voice, her whole body felt lighter and tingled a little. The voice was strong, confident and soothing, and she closed her eyes and enjoyed it. It was talking business and she was listening to the details, but it was all about the tone. Unmistakeably, the voice was in love with her.

Business as Usual

Chapter 32

Amanda Barratt wasn't having a relaxing weekend, but she *was* making progress. Max and Ali had now accounted for all the money. Thirty-eight billion dollars was now reduced to a single sheet of A4 paper and a list of forty names, the ultimate beneficiaries of these transactions. Not that the money was in reach; it had long gone to God knows where, disbursed to smaller groups, all politically active and all violent. It was Christmas for the world's terrorists.

The good news was that it wasn't Amanda's fault and neither could the debacle be pinned on the British. That was about the only good news.

She lit a cigarette and discarded the previous one in a foil container swimming with cold, sweet and sour sauce. It wasn't a good look for her office and, crisis or not, she spent five minutes cleaning up.

Her mobile rang, giving her an excuse to cut short the tidy-up. The news was yet again negative. Neither Ray Common, Selena Thornton nor Katherine Carver could be located.

Devoy, who had left for a meal, returned and flopped onto a chair. Despite his experience and expertise, he had also struck out, having failed to contact Bob Frost, who he was naturally eager to chat to. He did, however, have an update on the Canisp board.

He laughed as he recounted some selected highlights from the uplifts of Leo King, George Black and, especially, Lord Jeremy Steel;

the latter having, predictably, tried a variation of "do you know who I am?"

"Did any of them try to play the diplomatic card?" Amanda asked.

"No, none of them." He added carelessly, "They're probably clear anyway, but we'll find out soon enough. What have you got for me?"

She handed him her list. "They've finished now. I've got them re-checking and monitoring, but this looks pretty complete."

Devoy glanced carelessly at the completed list and threw it down. "What a fucking mess."

It was tough to argue.

Her phone rang again. Surely, they had, at last, located one of her missing suspects? This hope again proved to be over-optimistic, although the news was interesting. "I have Sir Jasper Reed for you, ma'am."

"Put him through."

The voice couldn't do that. "Er, no, he is here, at the front door."

Amanda wondered what could possibly have derailed Sir Jasper, a man of unchangeable habits. "Bring Sir Jasper up."

Devoy looked across at her, sharing her surprise.

Sir Jasper didn't bother knocking and marched into Amanda's office. He nodded to Devoy and flopped down on a chair.

Amanda offered him a drink, which he declined. "No, I don't have time. I play bridge on Friday evenings, have done for thirty-five years."

He threw a buff A4 envelope at Amanda and said, "Just thought you would be interested."

"Have you identified our Russian friends?"

"Oh them? No, nothing further on them, I'm afraid. Doubt there will be. No, it's about that bomb of yours, the one in Surrey."

Amanda hadn't given that much thought. She opened the envelope and delved in.

The first item she extracted was a small, irregularly shaped piece of bone or something like that. She looked it over and, stumped, looked at him enquiringly.

"Oh, that's a bit of a tooth. It's not in good enough condition for identification, I'm afraid. I forgot I put that in."

Amanda put the tooth down gingerly and decided instead to turn out the envelope's remaining contents on to the table. The other items were a little more wholesome and a little easier to identify. Reed picked them up in turn.

"As you know," he said, "after the bomb explosion there was a catastrophic fire. In such a fire there are only a few things that stand any chance of surviving. Some metals, occasionally a piece of bone or, indeed, a tooth, as you have seen. The tooth is too damaged to do any dental or DNA matching, but at least it proves that there was someone in the place."

Reed racked his brains. "Ferguson, was that the name?"

"Yes."

Reed lifted up the other items. The first, he said, was a part of a finely-engineered watch movement. He left what turned out to be the best until last. He produced a handkerchief from his top pocket and applied it to something that looked like a small stone, which he carefully buffed on one side. Then he held it carefully between forefinger and thumb. "A diamond," he announced.

"Doesn't burn?" Amanda ventured

"Yes, but there's more." He turned the diamond round. "Have a look at this side."

"It looks pretty much like the other side."

"We don't use the phrase 'pretty much' in forensic science, Miss Barratt. Have another look."

Amanda looked again. "There's a little black imperfection near the centre, but other than that I can see nothing."

"Yes, you see it?" Reed didn't have time for a guessing game, so he told them. "Actually, that's part of a human ear. Hard to believe," he added wistfully.

"How do you know that?" Devoy asked.

"Well, there was a bit more of it than that; it had fused to the diamond. Must have been near to the seat of the fire." Reed let them into his conclusions. "There are two good things about this. Firstly, someone was wearing an earring – a diamond one. I don't think that there is any way that this reaction, chemically I mean, could have happened unless it was being worn. I'm doing some tests at the minute and tomorrow I'll be able to tell whether I've got enough to get a DNA reading, but probably not." Reed stopped and looked at them both in turn, as if waiting for praise.

Amanda asked a question instead. "Is there any suggestion that there was more than one person in the house?"

"I can't be certain. All I know is that I have only one trace." He continued probabilistically. "You see, as you add more people, then the chances of capturing traces increase. So, provisionally, one only." He looked at Amanda. "But I understood that the man lived alone?"

Amanda said, "Yes, he did, but who knows – he could have had guests."

"True enough," Sir Jasper agreed. "Time for me to go unless, of course, you have anything else."

Amanda was reflecting, deep in thought. Distractedly, she said, "No, no. Thank you for coming round."

"Does it help?"

Amanda sighed. "I don't know, but it might."

Sir Jasper got up and looked at her. "Cheer up, Amanda. It might never happen."

"It already has," she said wearily.

The pathologist slipped back into the chair and looked at her. "It's not about what's happened. It's about stopping what might come." Sir Jasper allowed himself a sigh of his own. "You know, last year, I handled my 2000th dead body. I actually counted them. Every one. Took me a whole weekend. Every name, well those that had a name, every one a human being. A lot of bad human beings, I would say, but human beings nonetheless. If I thought that my work didn't make any difference going forward, I couldn't do it."

"But you're always so enthusiastic."

"Yes, about the possibilities for the future."

Amanda smiled at him. "Thanks, don't you have bridge to go to?"
"Yes, I do, can't sit here moping all evening."
Amanda laughed. "I'll be in touch."
"I'm sure you will, and Amanda, leave these cigarettes alone. I've told you before about them."

Sir Jasper breezed out the door.

Devoy laughed. "I hope you were listening to these wise words?"
"Did I have a choice?"

Devoy didn't answer and got back to the future. "What now?"

Amanda called Max and Ali into the office and told them to sit down. She said to Ali, "I've a question about your colleagues. Did any of them wear diamond earrings?"

Ali considered. "Selena wears earrings."
"What about the men, David Ferguson, Ray Common?"
"Not that I know." She added, with a politically incorrect reference to the real world, "Men with earrings. I mean it's fine, but not really in the City. So many international clients have different values. Why do you ask?"

"I've been reviewing some forensic evidence."
"Why don't you ask Ray or Selena?"
"I'd like to, but I can't contact either of them. I don't know where they are. Have you got any ideas?"

"I don't know Ray all that well," Cairns said. "I mean outside work. I've heard that he's pretty ordinary, still lives with his mother, somewhere in South London, I think." She reflected further. "Over the last few years, he's only taken a few weeks off each year. I think he goes golfing with friends. I've heard him talking about it. Long accounts. Very boring."

Amanda said, "Yes, Jack Edwards plays golf and he goes on about it. But as for Common, has he a girlfriend?"

"Not that I know of."
"What about Selena?"

"I know her a bit better. She's quite inspirational, to be honest. She's American and she could be anywhere. I've known her to go to all sorts of places for the weekend."

"Does she have a partner?" asked Amanda.

Cairns considered. "She never talks about that sort of thing. Well, not to me, but I don't think so. I mean, she's just so busy. Not just with work."

"What else?"

"Oh, I mean she is terribly committed to her environmental beliefs. I think she's quite active in a few groups."

"Really? I thought that was just the sort of tick-box exercise that companies have to do." She added, "I mean, the hedge fund business is all about money, surely."

"Oh no, leaders like Selena are changing all that. Trying to make a difference." Cairns dropped her voice conspiratorially. "I think she has even gone on a few marches, although I don't think she likes people to know about that."

Amanda smiled. "Don't worry, I won't tell anyone. For the moment we'll concentrate on the fraud and the dead bodies."

Cairns looked upset and Amanda felt bad for her. "Sorry, we really need to catch up with them. Have you no ideas at all?"

Cairns said something more interesting. "Selena sometimes takes the company plane at the weekend."

Amanda swore loudly. Maybe she should have thought of this. Over-indulgent certainly, but it wasn't unusual for a major hedge fund to have an airplane. When there were millions, even billions, to be made from a single transaction, why not?

"Where is the plane?" she asked.

"Sorry. No idea."

Amanda looked at Max. "Planes need documents and things. Surely we can find it?"

Max was confident. "On it, boss," he said, and he and Cairns left the office.

Devoy asked, "What are you thinking?"

Business as Usual

"I'm thinking about earrings," she said, "Or rather a single earring."

Chapter 33

Bob Frost had turned off his mobile phone after receiving but not answering two calls from Nick Devoy.

He had a bad feeling. He had just learnt more details of the shooting incident the previous night in Buckinghamshire that Nick Devoy had mentioned earlier. A British agent had also been killed, and, although Frost knew nothing about it, it was getting harder to rule out that it was connected to Katherine Carver's racket.

He needed to get into the game now – partly to limit the damage, but mostly to keep himself in the clear.

His first problem, as ever, was Katherine Carver.

Frost had over-estimated her, which was quite an achievement, as he had absolutely no regard for her abilities. What he had failed to factor in was the exponential damage that someone could do – not when they knew nothing, but when they didn't *know* that they knew nothing.

He had told her repeatedly that this money plan should be avoided: plenty of challenges and not that much of an upside; but of course, she had explained to him why he was wrong.

He thought about Katherine reviewing her project. She would be certain she had everything in hand, blind to her personal failings. Failure would never occur to her. Why should it? If anything went wrong, she would deny, deny, deny. If that failed, and it usually didn't if you were favoured, then she would blame others, which was bound to include him.

He had warned others as well but no one was listening. Carver was connected, right up to the top of the firm, and so much money was invested in her that she was considered too big to fail. They had a plan for her and the sky was the limit.

As a further contingency, Frost had organised a tail on Amanda Barratt. She was way ahead of him and he needed to find out what she was doing. It wasn't normal practice to be following a senior director in British Intelligence, but under the circumstances this breach of protocol was the least of Frost's worries.

Sebastian Mann was a well-used contractor and Frost had contacted him following the meeting. Mann had not been as confident and sure of himself as usual. Maybe Amanda Barratt had got to him. Nevertheless, Frost had learnt something: namely that the manager at Canisp, Ray Common, had been the contact for the gunmen.

In the absence of anything better to do, trying to find Ray Common seemed like his best option.

Chapter 34

The clock had passed midnight when Devoy's phone rang. It was a short call. He got out of the armchair heavily. "Come on, Amanda, time to go. The car's outside."

In a fast car and at that time in the morning, it took only fifteen minutes to arrive at the Gothic mansion in north London that served as a multi-purpose facility. The outward appearance of the building, which stood in several wooded acres, had changed little in the last century. Inside was a different story. It was fitted with the most modern communications in London. The upper floors were home to offices and a variety of incident rooms, while the basement floors contained a number of holding cells.

The facility was designed exactly for the type of activity that Amanda and Devoy were embarked upon. The outer door was opened by a straight-backed man of about sixty, who nodded and, without a word, led them down two levels via a tight corridor with concrete steps.

The lower basement cells were unconventional. There were only four of them. They were large and comfortably appointed like superior suites in a superior hotel. There were no bars and no heavy metal doors. But comfort wasn't everything, and it usually took detainees only a short time to work out that facilities such as this were not an indication of the beneficence of the British State.

Business as Usual

In such well-appointed and self-contained subterranean units such as these, long stays, out of sight and out of mind, could be arranged with ease.

A man sat at a desk in a small alcove. Amanda said, "Have we got them all now?"

He shook his head. "Sorry, still only three, ma'am. Which one do you want first?"

"Let's start at the top. Sir George Black."

Their guide led them to the last door in the corridor and unlocked what looked like a standard meeting room door.

Whatever one did, the smell of detention could never be eliminated. Otherwise, the large, open-plan section was tastefully arranged with, at its centre, a three-quarter-sided arrangement of sofas. Sitting comfortably, and evidently anticipating a short stay, Sir George sat clad in a heavy overcoat and seemingly at ease.

At their entrance, his expression changed from surprise to what looked like relief. "Ah, Devoy, about time. What's this all about?"

Devoy said nothing and looked to Amanda. She said, "We are very sorry about this, Sir George. Things have moved forward a bit today, have got more serious, and it's possible that your life's in danger."

He took this reasonably well and leant back into the sofa. "Oh, I see. Can I go home now?"

Amanda ignored both this question and, instead, from a side cabinet, she poured whisky into a chunky tumbler and handed it to him.

This done, she and Devoy each helped themselves to a seat on the sofa. "Do you know Bob Frost?" she asked.

Sir George looked puzzled. "Yes, slightly, he's a member of a couple of clubs. He's been around for years." He added, "He's American, I think he works at the embassy. What's he got to do with this?"

She didn't answer this question either and continued with her update. "Sir George, as you know, I have been concerned about the possibility of a fraud at Canisp. More facts have come to light and it's now certain."

His features fell and his mouth opened a bit.

Amanda carelessly piled on the bad news. "Many billions of pounds, we think."

Sir George's face fell again, this time about as far as a face could fall. He squeaked a question. "Is it an inside job?"

"Yes, almost certainly, at least partially."

"What does that mean?"

"Can't you tell me, Sir George?"

His voice went up an octave. "It's nothing to do with me, Miss Barratt. I know nothing about it. Nothing. You can't think that, surely?"

There was an entire industry devoted to what was ambitiously dubbed the science of interrogation, but Amanda didn't need to bother with that. Sir George Black might once have been a feared corporate raider, but he didn't look fearsome these days. If Amanda had been running a fraud, she'd never have used Sir George. He hadn't the talent, the knowledge or the energy. She was sure that he wasn't her man. But why tell him that?

"Sir George, you are the chairman. You must know something?"

"Of course, but one doesn't expect these sorts of things."

This pathetic answer, Amanda ignored. "Not much of a defence."

"Why would I need a defence?"

"I'm no lawyer, but I think that anyone who knows anything about this affair could use a defence."

"Well, I don't know anything."

Amanda wasn't getting anywhere fast. "Alright, Sir George, I don't think that you had anything to do with this, but there's a lot at stake here, not just money. So, if there is anything at all that you can tell me, I need to know now. If you can't think of anything, I'll be happy to give you more time. These rooms will be free for a while."

Business as Usual

It didn't really matter who you were or what you had achieved in life when you were sitting in an airless basement with the door key under the control of the security services.

Sir George looked desperately at Devoy, but he slowly shook his head. This last hope dashed, he started talking. "Look, all I know is that Paul, Paul Riordan, was looking into something."

"He told you this?"

"Yes, he said that there were a couple of, well, dubious accounts."

"Did he mention the names?"

"No."

"No details at all?"

Black shook his head. "No, nothing at all, and then Paul died."

"Yes, he died."

"A tragic accident."

"Maybe. I am still making enquiries."

"What are you talking about?"

"As I say, our enquiries are not complete," Amanda said formally. "Do you know anything else that can help us?"

"Nothing, I've already told you that. Can I go home?"

"Do you want to go home?"

Sir George summoned up some defiance. "Of course I want to go home, what do you mean?"

Amanda said, "David Ferguson's dead, and if Paul Riordan was killed because he knew something and it is suspected that he has confided in you, I thought that might worry you."

"You mean I'm in danger?"

"Yes."

Sir George looked at Devoy. "Nick, can't you help?"

Devoy said, "We can't offer you 24/7 security, George, except, of course, in here." He added, "And we need you in one piece to handle Canisp going forward, or at least for the transition."

Black looked confused. "Surely it's finished?"

"Not necessarily. You see, it's not a traditional sort of fraud."

Sir George was curious, but Devoy added nothing.

Amanda was learning nothing now. "If you wish to leave, fine. I'll keep an eye on you, but check in every two hours for the moment."

Sir George seemed less sure now, but he said, "I'm too old to spend time here. I want to go home."

Amanda and Devoy left. She said, "I'm sure he knows nothing. What do you think?"

Devoy considered. "I've known him a long time. Not well, but I've never heard of him doing a dishonest thing. His ethics are the talk of the city."

"Maybe there's a first time."

"Maybe. Let's go and see Leo King."

***

The next-door cell was identical in every way, except for the man inside. Leo King was shorter and rounder than Sir George, and was rubbing his hands with obvious anxiety. His head was bowed and he didn't acknowledge their arrival.

Devoy said, "Evening, Leo. How are you?"

King looked up pleadingly. "What's this all about, Nick? What am I doing here?"

"There are problems at Canisp. You could be in danger."

"Danger, what do you mean?"

"Mr Riordan and Mr Ferguson are dead," Amanda said. "Who will be next?"

"I don't understand what's going on."

Amanda looked at Devoy. She produced her list of clients and handed it to King.

He reached for his spectacles and reviewed the list with shaking hands. "What is this, Miss Barratt?"

"I was hoping that you could tell me, Mr King."

King threw down the sheet. "It means nothing to me."

Devoy shrugged at Amanda. King was either a great actor or he was what he appeared to be: an old man utterly out of his depth.

Amanda decided to believe her own eyes. "Okay, Mr King, that's all at the moment. The issue is, do you want to stay here where we can guarantee your safety?"

"No, I want to go home."

Amanda got up. "I'll arrange that."

Outside the cell, Devoy said, "I think you are doing the right thing. He knows nothing."

"I agree, but it's worrying."

"How so?"

"Imagine him as the next Governor of the Bank of England."

Chapter 35

Amanda readied herself for what she imagined would be a more interesting, although possibly not a more enjoyable, experience.

Lord Jeremy Steel was a controversial figure and he represented a lot of things that Amanda didn't like. That really didn't matter to her. Steel would get a fair hearing whatever his politics. He was speaking on a mobile phone as they entered. That was annoying. So much for high security.

Devoy and Amanda sat down while Steel continued his conversation, walking towards the far wall in search of privacy.

He was in no hurry. Amanda checked her watch. Still Steel talked on. Amanda walked towards him, pulled his hand towards her and prised the phone from his hand. She ended the call by slamming the phone on top of a table at the far side of the room, then returned to her seat.

Steel opened and then shut his mouth. He glared at her and made to speak but he didn't. Then his features unfroze and he broke into a plastic smile. "Good evening, Miss Barratt." He nodded to Devoy, "Nick," and settled for a seat on a chair opposite them.

He was dressed casually in jeans that he was too old for and a garish shirt with one too many buttons undone. He hadn't shaved, either. He said with forced civility, "What can I do for you?"

Amanda looked hard at him and was already confident that she had his measure. She waited a few more powerful seconds, didn't bother apologising for damaging his phone, and then got straight to the point. "We have a major fraud at Canisp. There have also been deaths, and we are now fairly sure that there is a connection."

He took this news stoically.

"And there's a chance that this conspiracy goes right up to board level."

Steel flinched a bit, but still held his nerve.

Max and Ali had done some good work and had now undertaken some further, detailed research on Steel himself and the clients he had introduced.

Amanda produced a sheet of paper, which listed the most potentially controversial and egregious clients, a dozen in total. Sovereign wealth funds were Steel's favourite targets, and it had not been difficult to produce a range of countries with human rights issues or dubious political records. At the bottom of the list were the four clients directly concerned in her major enquiry.

Casually, she handed Steel the list. "Here are some of the client accounts that we are investigating."

He reviewed the list. Annoyingly, he came back with what seemed a truthful answer. "I am aware of the first eight clients, but the last four I have never heard of."

"Did you introduce these clients?"

"Yes, the first eight. I think so."

"And the last four?"

"No, I've told you. I've never heard of them."

She started with the undisputed clients and briefly focused upon the account of a Central American regime. "You do know that there are international sanctions against that country? Is that the kind of client that Canisp normally tries to attract?"

"As I understand it, these sanctions have only been recently introduced, and as you might be aware, a number of global interests are engaged in helping to rebuild the country. I believe that these efforts are helping."

Amanda doubted that this was true and was fairly certain that Steel couldn't care less. "The Progressive Global Alliance?"

"I believe that we have an interest. That's not a secret. None of these clients are connected to a fraud. Of course, I don't know about the bottom ones."

"We'll see about that."

He said testily, "So why am I here?"

"Our enquiries are at a crucial stage and there have been deaths. We were concerned about your safety, and I needed to have a chat with you. Find out if you can help me."

"I've already told you, Miss Barratt. There's nothing more I can tell you."

Amanda produced another sheet but didn't give it to Steel. "I'm advised that the Central American fund was initiated after the date sanctions were introduced. We think this is true of several other of the accounts, although I'm not quite there yet. It's not a tough job for account openings to be pre-dated. Simple errors in paperwork can easily happen."

"Obviously I don't ever get involved in paperwork."

"No, I'm sure you don't, but, well, a nod and a wink here and there. I've spoken to Mr Common about this list, and he was very helpful. His recollections are different to yours."

Steel said nothing.

"So," she added wistfully, "tomorrow morning my people will be all over the administrative department in Canisp. If there's a dot or a comma missing, even a spelling mistake, then we'll find it." She added, "And, of course, if your name comes up in any way then I'm going to have a lot more questions."

Steel shuffled on the sofa.

She wasn't certain, but she thought that, at last, she had him on the back foot. His face was steady, but she was down to his last layer of defence.

"Do you know Bob Frost, Lord Steel?"

Business as Usual

"Not well, but I know who he is. Longstanding CIA man in London. Everyone around British politics knows Bob."

Amanda returned to her original list. With a marker pen, she drew a crude square around the bottom four clients.

She raised her voice. "I ask again, what do you know about these accounts?"

Steel's voice held a trace of desperation masked as irritation. "Nothing. I have never heard of them. They are nothing to do with me."

Amanda lit a cigarette. She blew a cloud of smoke between them and gave him a few more seconds, but still he volunteered nothing.

"Okay, here's where I'm at. There are circumstances where I might overlook your sloppy paperwork, but only if I am sure that you are, as you say, ignorant of the last four client accounts."

Steel leant forward a bit. "How can I convince you of that?"

"I'm not sure, to be honest. I'll have a think about it. For now, I have to get on with my enquiries, and I think that for your own safety, it would be best if you stay here overnight, at least until I can confirm that your safety is not compromised. Do you have any objections?"

"Do I have a choice?"

"We prefer to work with your agreement."

Steel laughed. "Can I have my phone back?"

"Sorry, I'll need to keep that."

In the corridor, Devoy said, "I think you have him on those dodgy accounts, but what about the key four? Do you believe him?"

"I don't know."

"So, he's breaking some rules, got a few dodgy characters with accounts. Is that enough to account for this mess?"

"Probably not, in my opinion. Just a concurrent scam. If this is an American initiative, he wouldn't be my first choice. However, it does suggest that someone in the back office has got loose ethics."

"Ray Common?"

"Yes, he set up all these accounts."

"So, has Common bolted?"

Amanda looked grave. "Maybe, or maybe worse."

Devoy said, "Another death?"

"Why not? There's billions at stake."

They returned up the stairs whilst they talked. Amanda entered an anteroom and updated the guard on her decisions regarding his detainees. "Let King and Black go. Get their phone numbers, addresses and get someone to keep an eye on them. 24/7 until I call it off. Steel's staying." She reached into her pocket. "Here's his mobile phone. The one that should have been taken from him when he arrived."

"Sorry, ma'am."

"What about Katherine Carver and Selena Thornton?"

"No word, ma'am. I checked a few minutes ago."

"I need to know the minute you catch up with either of them."

Devoy and Amanda returned to their car.

"What now?" asked Devoy.

"Not sure. I need something to break or I need to find Ray Common, Selena Thornton or Katherine Carver. I'm going back to my office."

Devoy looked a little dismayed and she took pity on him. "I'll drop you off and update you tomorrow."

Having delivered her ageing boss to his London flat, she returned to her office.

Max and Cairns were still there, showing an admirable devotion to the cause. Max said, "How are you getting on, boss?"

"Slowly, but the work you guys did was great."

"What now?"

"Keep digging."

She headed to her office. Kicking off her boots, she reached for an overcoat from a stand and, a minute later, was lying on her sofa, half sleeping **again and** longing to be relaxing in Norfolk.

Chapter 36

Selena Thornton forced herself out of the bath and slipped on a robe. She was glowing and had never been happier. Time for another glass of wine. She flopped in an armchair and shut her eyes. Making plans for the future wasn't easy when there were so many exciting possibilities. It felt great.

A sound rose. A car a long way away. It passed, and again all was silent. She took a mouthful of wine and relaxed. And then she jumped, annoyingly spilling wine on her robe. Maybe she was hearing things? She wasn't. A knock on the door.

She put the wine glass on the table and stood stock still. Another knock, a bit louder. She wished she had put the car round the back. Too late. She could hardly cower behind the sofa, so she went to the door.

Katherine Carver was a tall woman, but looked huge framed in the low doorway. She flashed some large white teeth. "Hello, Selena."

"Katherine, what are you doing here?"

"Can I come in?"

"Yes, of course."

Katherine Carver swept past Selena. She cast an eye around the sitting room, and regally removed and held out her coat. Obediently Selena took it and laid it carefully over the back of a chair.

Katherine moved past her to the sofa and sat. "Sit down Selena."

Selena returned to her seat. She lifted her wine glass.

"Don't I get a glass of wine?"
"Yes, of course. White or red?"
"What type?"
"Sorry, just plonk from the local supermarket."
Katherine tutted. "I'll try some red, if it's bearable."
Selena went through to the kitchen. Her hands were shaking and she needed a couple of attempts to get the corkscrew into the cork.
She poured a glass and returned to the lounge. "Here you are."
Katherine looked at it, then sniffed it cautiously. "Here goes."
Selena waited on the verdict.
"Not too bad, actually."
"Good."
There didn't seem anything else to say. The silence went on and it wasn't comfortable. Why was Katherine here?
Katherine delved into her brown bag and produced a few sheets of paper, which she reviewed carefully. After another mouthful of the wine, she put down her glass and looked around the room. "This is a nice cottage. I didn't know you owned a property out here."
"I don't own it. It's just rented."
"For the weekend?"
"Yes."
"Strange place to come. So quiet. How long have you been coming here?"
"Oh, I just fancied a change. It's been so busy recently. I just wanted to get away from it all."
"We've all been busy," Katherine said.
Again, silence.
Selena tried again. "You look so different out of the office. I think it's the first time I've seen you in casual clothes. Where's the Dior and Gucci?"
Katherine laughed. "Just my office uniform. I can let you into a secret. I hate these clothes. I was brought up in New England with horses. You can't wear Gucci when mucking out stables."

Selena's main question couldn't wait any longer. "How did you know I was here, Katherine?"

"I asked your assistant.

"And when she couldn't help you?"

Katherine laughed. "Yes, that was a silly lie."

Selena persisted. "So how did you know?"

Katherine had lied and obfuscated to more important people than Selena Thornton so she moved on. "Selena, We need a quick word on an urgent matter. It can't wait."

"Ok, what's so urgent?"

Katherine walked across and handed the sheets of paper to Selena.

"These are the accounts we looked at earlier."

"Yes, what about them?"

"You can't see the problem?"

"No, the transactions seem to be through."

Katherine said. "Have a look at the last column. I don't recognise these names. Do you?"

"Yes, I think so. They seem to be the ones that were on the execution instructions."

"Not as far as I was concerned. Can you check?"

Selena said, "I can check on Monday."

Katherine's head shook slowly. "No. Now."

"I can't. I didn't bring my laptop with me. I was trying to get away from work for the weekend. I'll check on Monday. I'm sure everything's fine."

Katherine Carver shook her head. "I'm in a hurry and I want an answer now. That's a lot of money."

"Yes, I understand that. You still haven't told me how you knew I was here."

Katherine's voice was harsh and unforgiving. "Don't fuck me about, Selena, this is a matter of national security. I can find out anything. You're way over your head here."

Selena tensed. "I've no idea what you're talking about."

Katherine sighed. "Can these transfers be reversed?"

"I'm not sure. I've told you. I'll look first thing on Monday."

Katherine rose again, and walked over to Selena, towering over her and very close. "That's not good enough, Selena. Not even close. You need to come with me now."

Selena had seen Katherine in action many times, cheering her on when she was crushing and humiliating rivals, but it was different being the object of this force. This shouldn't be happening to her. A wave of anger overwhelmed her. "I'm the Managing Director Katherine. You can't order me about. Now sit down and get out of my space."

In the silence Katherine's breathing seemed urgent, and Selena could smell the cheap wine on her breath. As she turned her head, something cold and metallic brushed against her cheek.

She looked up. Katherine's eyes were dead and offered no hope. She looked older than her fifty years, and her muscles were only just holding up the skin on her neck. A well-formed neck, but badly defended.

The gun was steady, inches from her face. Death was close. There was no time to think. She fiddled in her robe pocket and grasped the corkscrew. She turned slowly not rushing. It went in deeply. Selena released her grip. The corkscrew stayed in Katherine's neck.

Katherine's eyes flicked towards the metal spike and her stare became fixed. The gun fell to the floor. She moved her hand towards the corkscrew but she never reached it. An eruption of thick red blood, jet after jet, burst from her neck. The torrent was strong and powerful, and as the pressure subsided, it decorated Selena's thick white robe.

Then a thud as Katherine Carver fell dead on the floor. She had issued her last directive. How would the world cope?

Chapter 37

Pam Riordan sat at the table, alone with her racing thoughts. Jack was still in bed, which was fair enough as it was barely 6 a.m. Despite the comforts of the house and of the master bedroom – one of about seven – she had slept poorly. Her head was full of scary thoughts. Things like people with guns who, without debate, would kill you for money and causes. She had learned some other things in the last few weeks. Specifically, that the forces of the British state were not the reactionary neo-fascistic force that many of her fellow university students believed. It was tough to hold that line when they had saved your life more than once. She liked Jack. And Amanda? Well, she liked her too.

Pam had grown up a lot in the last fortnight. Although her mother had died years ago, she had enjoyed a gilded life, or so others would say. There had been love and there was money, but now there was just money. She was nearly twenty but without a relation in the world, so on this criterion she was unfortunate. From time to time, the thought left her terrified.

They had arrived yesterday, and for a safe house, it was certainly well-chosen, with no neighbours in sight. Situated in the east of England, an empty region known as the Norfolk Broads, the house was old, at least in parts, and the blackened beams in some of the principal rooms went back to the 1600s. It was a good-sized, one-and-half-storeyed cottage with a thatched roof, and it sat in quite a few acres of mature gardens, set back from the road. All the rooms were comfortable and most were individual, some quirky. The kitchen was large and traditional with a large, recessed open fire with a massive and well-used oak table as its centrepiece. All this could be achieved in any house, but not love, and there had been love in this house.

The Broads was a popular tourist destination, but on the drive yesterday, she had only seen endless fields with a few scattered houses and no people. It looked a tough area to be poor in, but that was about the only problem that Pam didn't have.

She had expected a black reaction today, and it had arrived, but under the circumstances, she was coping well. On being exiled to this wilderness by Amanda she had again resisted, but now she admitted that Amanda was right.

Surprisingly, she found herself thinking about the face of one of the dead assailants. The last of the gunmen. He had been only a few feet from them when Jack had killed him. Two shots from a tiny little gun and he was dead. Jack had ripped the man's hood off, and she had looked at his face. A young man, only a bit older than her. Maybe he had a father or a mother.

The kitchen door opened and her godfather entered. He had also slept badly, if his crumpled morning face was to be believed. Like any man first thing, he managed only a grunt and stood staring vacantly ahead whilst the kettle boiled. He deposited two, or maybe three, spoonfuls of instant coffee in a small mug and joined her at the table. He lit a cigarette as a perfect accompaniment to the strong, black drink.

"Not much of a start to the day," she said.

Jack suppressed a cough.

"I suppose that it's not that important when set against fraud, spies and murder."

"Did you sleep well?" he asked.

"No."

Jack returned to his coffee and cigarette.

Pam said, "Do you ever get used to it? The dead bodies?"

"A simple 'good morning' would be better."

"Sorry, I've been up for ages. I've been thinking about things."

"It's okay," Jack said. "To answer your question, I don't, but I've found a way to live with it. Try not to think of it. Sorry, that doesn't really help."

"This is a nice house. Has Amanda had it long?"

"Yes, it was her parents' house."

"Are her parents alive?"

Jack shook his head.

"When did they die?"

"Her father only a few years ago, I'm not sure about her mother. I think it was a long time ago."

"Was she close to her father?"

"Yes, very."

"Amanda's nice."

Jack grunted in agreement.

Jack and Amanda both seemed ancient to Pam – around forty – but maybe just young enough to imagine them in a relationship. "How long have you known Amanda?"

"Ten years or so."

She looked at him and smiled, but he didn't respond to her silent prompt.

"And?"

"And what?"

"Well, you're both single."

Jack suppressed a yawn. "Yes, we're both single."

This was hard work, but she persisted. A thought flashed across her mind. "Does Amanda prefer girls?"

"I don't think so. She was married years ago."

She nudged him on the arm and laughed. "What about you, Uncle Jack? Are girls not your thing?"

"None of your business, and don't call me Uncle Jack."

"Okay, I won't call you that, but you must answer my question."

He sighed. "If you must know, Amanda and I are good friends – just friends. And before you start again, we do get on well, and there have been times when I thought we might be more than that."

"Oh, she turned you down?"

"Certainly not!" He pushed back his hair and stuck out his jaw. "How could you think that?"

Pam laughed.

Jack smiled at her.

"Why are you smiling?"

"It's nice to hear you laugh."

That was true enough, she hadn't laughed in a fortnight. Talking about other people was helping. "Never mind, Uncle Jack, perhaps Amanda will come round in time?"

Jack laughed again and was saved from further questions by his mobile ringing. He listened in silence for a while. "I need a pen and paper."

Pam looked around and handed him an envelope and pen.

Jack scribbled some information on the envelope and the conversation ended.

"Was that Amanda?"

"Yes."

"You look serious, is it bad news?"

"No, no, everything's fine."

"Can I see that note?"

He handed her the envelope.

"What is this? Secret service code?"

Jack laughed. "No, it's the registration of a private plane – one owned by your company."

"Hmm. Now you mention it I did know that Dad, well, the company, had a plane. Is that important?"

"No. Not really. Amanda says that it's sitting at an airfield quite near here. A private airstrip. She's trying to alert the aviation authorities and tell them to keep it grounded, but she's asking us to go and have a look. Just to check."

"That seems easy enough. Where is the plane?"

Jack screwed up his eyes in attempting to read his own writing. "South Deep International Airport."

"Never heard of it." Pam said.

"Me neither. See if you can find it."

A short online phone search was all it took. "Got it. About thirty miles from here."

Jack said, "Yeah, that's what she said. We are much nearer than she is, and it seems she's got no staff in this neck of the woods."

"When do we leave?"

"We?"

"I'm coming with you. I'm not sitting here alone. Besides, you said it was just routine."

"Fine. When is that airfield open?"

She returned to her phone. Nine to five only; not very impressive for an international airport.

Chapter 38

Amanda looked at her watch. 6.30 a.m. Yuck. She hauled herself off the sofa and, yawning and stretching, sat down behind her desk.

She had sent Max home a few hours ago and had let Ali Cairns go home too, but only after she had agreed to let one of Amanda's agents accompany her. She was pretty sure now that Cairns was sound, but Amanda was cautious. She had a decent record of judging people, but she hadn't always been right. In her business that could be fatal, and this was no time for unforced errors.

She took a mouthful of coffee from a mug. It was cold and bitter. Like the case. Surely something would break soon?

Hope was one thing, but otherwise there was no reason for this optimism. She had agents all over the place (God knows what she was doing to the budget) and yet Ray Common, Selena Thornton and Katherine Carver had still not been located. Maybe some were dead? She stretched and yawned again. Her mobile stayed silent.

At least others were also failing, most notably her boss, Nick Devoy, who, despite having access and control over almost all of the UK's surveillance assets, could not get in touch with Bob Frost.

Maybe she should go home? She could sleep for a week, but something told her to stay in the office. Still her mobile did not ring.

Jack had sounded relaxed and hadn't complained about his assignment. He was doing quite a good job. Maybe he was changing? In the last few days, he had seemed different – stronger – and he had killed two dangerous men. How would she get on with a new, self-confident Jack? She wasn't sure, but she reckoned that whenever she got this case closed, she might try to find out. She wished that she was with them in East Anglia, but wishing was no good. She got back to business and reflected on yesterday's events.

As she did, it wasn't the nauseating Sebastian Mann or the equally nauseating Lord Jeremy Steel that occupied her thoughts. She was thinking about Mrs Common sitting alone in her South Croydon villa. She would be smiling, but on the inside, with all her hopes invested in her son, Amanda dared not imagine how she would be feeling. Prospects for her son, previously poor, were now tending to non-existent, and there was nothing Amanda could do.

She pulled over the envelope that Sir Jasper Reed had delivered last evening and emptied the contents onto her desk. Once you were able to forget that some of the things represented all that remained of a human being, they were common enough items. She looked at the earring and shivered when recalling Sir Jasper's description of the fused human skin attached to the stone. She picked it up gingerly, looked at it closely and set it down again. Nothing.

She put the bits back in the envelope and pulled a file towards her. It contained only a couple of sheets: all that they seemed to know about Sebastian Mann. Being based in London and having worked with a number of foreign governments and intelligence agencies, he deserved a bigger file.

There were noises outside her office. It sounded like Max.

It was. "Don't you ever sleep?" Amanda asked.

"Sometimes, but remember, I'm young. I don't need much sleep."

"Well, I've been here all night."

Max looked at the sofa and her coat lying carelessly on it. "Working?"

"I might have had a short nap. Anyway, what are you doing back here?"

He poured himself a coffee and handed another to Amanda. "I thought you might need more help."

"Well, you're not wrong about that."

"What do you want me to do?"

She threw across the file on Sebastian Mann. "Have another look at this guy. I need to know much more about him."

Max scanned the file. "Not much here."

"No, and that's surprising given his connections."

"What do you want?"

Amanda yawned. "Everything."

Max smiled and turned to leave. "I'll see what I can find. Why don't you have another rest, boss?"

"Cheeky bugger."

Amanda yawned again when Max was safely out of the room. She was tired but he had given her new energy. She went back to Sir Jasper's envelope and delved inside. She pulled out the diamond earring again and examined it carefully. A thought danced across her mind. It seemed important but she couldn't capture it. Annoying. She stood up and walked around the office in a vain attempt to recover the thought. That didn't work either, then Max was back.

"This is interesting, boss."

She took a single sheet of paper from him and looked over it. "So what? I know Mann was a soldier. I want to know the real stuff – who really pays his bills."

"Yes, I'm getting to that, but I thought you might be interested in links between Sebastian Mann and Canisp."

"I am, but this doesn't tell me anything."

Max looked at her with a sadness reserved for a failing elderly relative. He moved alongside and placed another sheet in front of her. He pointed at similar entries on both sheets. "Look at these dates."

Amanda felt a frisson of excitement. It was interesting but not conclusive. And then the thought that she had lost came back into her head. She picked up the earring. Now she knew where she had seen it before. It burst into her head like a greyhound from a trap.

She was sure, certain now, and if she was right, this changed everything.

Chapter 39

The distance from the house to the aerodrome was re-estimated by the car's sat nav as just under twenty miles, but it turned out to be a slow drive, ambling through single-track roads which cut through endless, low-lying fields. That didn't matter much. It was a routine job, and they weren't in a hurry.

Despite this, Jack reasoned, it was one of Amanda's jobs, so he packed the Glock.

"Quite impressive having a company jet," he said.

Pam laughed. "Well, it would be if it was a jet. I think Dad told me that it was an old propeller plane with a couple of seats. It didn't cost much. A Piper or something, I can't remember."

"Not quite what I had in mind. I was thinking of a sleek luxury machine flying global elites across the world at a moment's notice."

"It might make France, if the wind's behind."

"So, what's the point of it?"

"I think it was just a modest management perk if you ask me. Dad and a couple of others were using it to get pilots' licences, I think."

"Others? Who else?"

Pam thought for a moment. "Don't know, but I think someone at Canisp is the real ace. A woman, I think, but I can't remember the name."

Jack had another look at the sat nav. It wasn't working. He tried his mobile but that was out of signal also.

"Great. How far have we come?"

"A couple of miles. Do you know the way?"

"No, not exactly, but we've got to get onto the main road for about, say, eighteen miles and then turn off. Keep going and we'll think of something. Jeez, I miss the old days. A big map book was all you needed, not all this modern guff."

"I'm sure we'll manage," Pam said.

And she was proved mostly right. After a few false turns, they gained the main road, and after a drive of about eighteen miles turned off in the general direction of the airfield. The road signs were no help now, but they at last got a break from a man working on a tractor at the side of the road. His accent was dense but intelligible, and his directions proved accurate. After what seemed like a long drive, Pam eventually spied a crudely worded metal sign, a growing season away from being covered in foliage, which indicated the way to South Deep International Airport.

The entrance was guarded by a filthy, unmanned portacabin with an extended front window covered in stickers.

No barrier blocked the narrow, grassy lane, and Jack drove on uneven ground for about a quarter of a mile before emerging onto a broad, defined, mown area with a collection of modest buildings on the near side and, in front, two or three carelessly parked and unprepossessing light aircraft.

There were a couple of cars parked alongside the chalet building, which looked like the administrative epicentre of the facility.

Jack pulled alongside the cars. From this point it was clear that the runway covered many acres and was laid to grass, not tarmac. It was marked by a series of unevenly placed traffic cones, which started quite near the buildings, but was mostly hidden as it curved behind a raised grassy bunded mound that might have been to deaden noise.

They passed by a couple of flimsy-looking polytunnel hangars and up a few steps into the wooden chalet.

The door was locked. Jack looked around and spied a round middle-aged man heading their way.

Business as Usual

He greeted Jack and Pam in booming tones. "Good morning. Welcome." He looked quizzically at them. "I haven't seen you two before. Are you new?"

He didn't wait for an answer and led them into the chalet building. It was basic but well-kept with a sitting area served by a coin-operated coffee machine. On the other side, a selection of wares for the discerning flyer was tidily presented in a way that suggested a low volume of sales.

Dominating the scene was a large central desk, behind which the middle-aged enthusiast now sat, battling with a large collection of paperwork.

There were a couple of shaky-looking plastic seats beside the desk, and Jack and Pam sat down.

"I'm Jack Edwards, and this is Pamela."

"How can I help you?"

"Have you received a call from a Miss Barratt?"

"No, not this morning, but I've been out on the strip most of the morning. It's just me today."

So much for that. From his pocket, Jack produced the envelope with the registration number written on it and passed it across. "I'm looking for this plane."

When you knew every member, it was a fair bet that the man would have just as good a recall on the airplanes. He did. Checking his memory a second time, he then leafed through the pile of papers and produced a single sheet. "Yes, I think I know this plane. It belongs to one of our members. However, this information is confidential. What's your interest in this?"

Jack was usually tolerant with these objections, maybe because he never felt that he had any official status. But today he felt differently and reached into his pocket for the warrant card that Amanda insisted he carry. He slapped it on the table. It was the first time he had ever deployed it, and it felt powerful.

The man sat up a bit, decided that he was in favour of law and order and the debate was over. "Yes, this airplane is owned by Canisp – a

City finance company. The authorised users are listed as Mr Riordan, Miss Thornton, Miss Carver and Mr Common."

Jack nodded. "Where is the plane?"

"On the runway, of course. That's where I've been, preparing it for take-off."

"Take-off? Who's using it?"

"I don't know, I got a call yesterday. But no one's arrived yet."

Jack got up. "Show me exactly where the plane is. Quickly."

The man led him to the front door and pointed across the grounds.

"Behind the bunding, left hand side of the strip, there is a small holding area there."

"Are any other take-offs or landings scheduled today?"

"None today."

"Keep it that way." He reached for his mobile. No signal. "Have you got a real phone here?"

"Yes, over here."

He scribbled down a phone number and said to Pam, "Call Amanda, then wait here. I'm going to have a look."

Jack headed onto the airstrip. Even the most modest airport covered a lot of ground, and the raised bunds that masked the holding area and runway were about half a mile distant. It was dry, the ground was firm and Jack made quick time. The bunding was broken to admit taxiing planes, but Jack decided on a more covert approach.

The grassy bund was at least twenty-foot high and was steeper than it looked from a distance. The wind was light. His feet crunched on the gravelly soil as he climbed. But that didn't really matter; the deafening burr from an airplane propeller was all he could hear.

He slowed just before the ridge and sank to his knees, completing the last few feet on his belly.

A figure at the far side of the aircraft was poking around. Pre-flight checks perhaps? Jack knew next to nothing about airplanes – he hated flying – so he waited. It seemed a long time, but probably only a minute or two before the figure came nearside. Annoyingly, he couldn't see her face, but now he was sure it was a woman. It was. And then she turned and looked straight at him. He pulled his head back just in time, he thought.

Selena Thornton hadn't seen him, although that didn't really matter. Detaining her wasn't going to be tough for a big strong man like Jack. He wouldn't even need a gun. Amanda would be pleased.

He inched forward again. Thornton had her back to him engaged in a close examination of a side panel of the plane.

Jack started to lift himself to his feet and reintroduce himself, but that never happened. There was a complication. He slid back to the ground.

From the far side of the field, Jack saw a dead man approaching.

Chapter 40

Selena Thornton's boots were muddy and her hair was in disarray, but none of that came close to upsetting her day. The checks on the plane were nearing completion and she was beginning to experience the thrill that she always felt before a flight.

But today was like no other. She pushed back those thoughts and ticked off the landing lights and the air inlets. She turned off the propellor, then pulled over a short set of metal steps which allowed her to check the fuel tank from the top of the wing. This was also fine. It was a great day to fly. She was nearly finished, but she lingered on top of the steps and took in the vista that the height afforded. She stared across at a dense copse sitting just outside the airfield boundary.

From the dark interior, two figures emerged. Her excitement mounted and her heart thumped as she strained to make out their features. On they came, heading her way. Slowly, she descended the steps and moved towards them.

David Ferguson was a beautiful man. Tall with cropped black hair and a rugged jawline with a hint of stubble, his dark eyes regarded her. She rushed towards him and held him tight. He responded and she melted into his body. His fingers combed through her hair, and his lips danced over her face and ears. Selena, for a moment, remembered what bliss was. She held him even tighter, but this time his response seemed weaker. She tried again. Just one more kiss. Not so good this time. His body moved from neutral to reverse. She disengaged and smiled at him. His smile first weakened and then, in imperceptible decrements, disappeared.

"Is everything okay, David?"

A smile returned and flickered across his face. "Yes, everything's fine. Did you do what we discussed?"

"Yes, exactly as you told me."

"You're sure no one knows you are here?"

She hesitated. Today of all days he would pick up on this. "Is there a problem?"

Her mind raced. It was a long story; a complicated story. There was no time. She gave him some of the truth. The rest could wait, maybe forever.

"Katherine came round last night."

His eyes widened in alarm. "Came where?"

"Round to the house."

Ferguson looked concerned. "And?"

"She was talking about the money."

"What did you tell her?"

"That everything was going smoothly."

"And she just went away?"

"Yes, I said we'd catch up on Monday. She seemed satisfied with that. Why not? She doesn't have a clue how things work."

Ferguson persisted. "And you said nothing about coming here today?"

"No, of course not. Anyway, we can talk about it later. I need to do a few last-minute checks. The air inlets, that sort of thing."

Loud banging sounds came from the plane. *Damn, concentrate, Selena.* She turned to Ferguson. "What's going on there? Who's that guy?"

David said casually, "Oh, that's the pilot."

And here it was, the betrayal. *Keep calm, Selena.* "Why do we need a pilot. I can fly. Why involve someone else? Three's a crowd."

Ferguson said, "Yes, three is a crowd."

The penny dropped. "But there won't be three of us, will there, David?"

Ferguson shrugged. "No, I'm afraid not."

Selena said bitterly, "You needed my expertise and that was it?"

"Sorry."

"And our environmental causes?"

"Your cause, Selena. I've got another cause."

"And nothing can get in the way of what you want. Is that how it is, David?"

"If you like."

Ferguson's face didn't look as if he would ever smile at her again. A face of granite. Hate, all now directed at her.

She backed away from him a few paces. "You won't get away with this, David."

At last, she got a laugh. "Just shut up, Selena. Time to say goodbye."

From a pocket in his leather jacket, Ferguson produced a gun.

Selena backed off a further few paces.

His hand was steady. He was going to have the courage to kill her. She hadn't thought he could do that.

The gun levelled out, pointing at her now. He started walking towards her. This would be no protracted break-up.

Chapter 41

Jack had been disorientated by the appearance of David Ferguson, but as he had never been in love with him, his thinking was less clouded by emotion. A few of the words between the former lovers had floated through the air clearly and, although most had drifted off in the wind or been drowned out by the aircraft engine, Jack felt he was now as well briefed as the unfortunate Selena Thornton. He felt a pang of pity for her. As for Ferguson, Jack had less ambiguous feeling, and now Ferguson had a gun blended naturally in his hand. His face was hard and fixed in a dangerous thin smile. He was going to kill her.

So, what are you going to do, Jack?

Nothing was probably the right answer. What did it matter if Ferguson killed Thornton?

Jack felt in his pocket. The Glock slipped into his hand easily. Annoying. His bones were heavy and muscles uncooperative, not buying into this plan. Something touched his shoulder. God knows why he didn't shout out loud. Pam was lying beside him. Her mouth opened to speak. Frantically, he put his hand roughly over her mouth, only releasing it when she had nodded to indicate her understanding of the situation.

This was an unwelcome complication, but Jack had made up his mind and was fully invested in his next move. The time that her arrival had wasted, luckily, proved immaterial as Ferguson, cruelly, had allowed Thornton a few more seconds, apparently in making further ineffectual pleadings.

Jack had a last review of his options. The pair of former lovers weren't far away – probably no more than twenty yards as a bullet flew – but twenty yards was a long range for an accurate handgun shot. In reality, the shot wasn't that difficult if you were a professional like Amanda, but Jack was an amateur.

A rapid descent and urgent assault would close the distance, but that also had risks, especially as the other man had just left the cockpit to join Ferguson. He wasn't holding a gun, but he was tall and powerful and looked like he might have one.

Logic screamed "Leave things alone": getting himself killed and leaving Pam alone wasn't a risk he was happy to take. And for what? But something was compelling him. A sense of justice, maybe. He didn't know.

Jack stood up, stumbled a few steps down the grassy mound and shouted something. Whatever it was, it got their attention. Ferguson, Thornton and the other man looked round. Jack risked another step forward.

A reasonable discussion proved out of the question with Ferguson's gun now pointing at him. Who fired first wasn't certain, but after the explosion, Jack was still alive. So was Ferguson but he was hit – somewhere in the shoulder area. He didn't fall but staggered backwards, and, as he processed what had happened, he looked at Jack. So did the other man, who was reaching into his jacket now.

Again, Ferguson raised his gun.

Jack's second shot did knock Ferguson down. Thornton fell to her knees screaming. Jack rushed for Ferguson's fallen gun.

Too late. The other man was now in the game and he was way ahead of Jack. Out came his gun. He looked as if he knew what he was doing. Jack fell to the ground. He felt strange. Strange but, not dead. He looked across at the other man. *He* looked dead. A good-looking powerful man of about forty. Or at least he had been before a single bullet exploded into his temple and then four, maybe five, more shots had thundered into his chest wall.

Not for the first time in his life, Jack had been lucky. A real professional had arrived.

Chapter 42

Amanda leant over the dead man, put her hand on his neck and then poked her nose into the aircraft. She moved across to Ferguson and then to Selena Thornton. After a short assessment, she barked out a series of instructions and soon had total control of the scene, supported by about a dozen additional professionals – large men with guns. One came across to Amanda. "What about these two, ma'am?"

"Take the woman to the terminal building, find somewhere quiet. Leave the man here. I'll wait with him until the medics arrive. Have you searched the plane?"

"On it."

The man left and Amanda turned to Jack. "Are you alright?"

"I think so."

"Out of breath?"

"A little, but not permanently."

Amanda dipped her head. "Sorry."

"Sorry for what?"

"I sent you here. That was stupid of me."

"You don't think I can handle these things?"

Amanda laughed.

Fair comment, Jack thought.

They turned in response to a hail from the direction of the grass mound. A moment later, a burly agent arrived with Pam at his side. "She's clean, ma'am."

Business as Usual

Amanda looked at Pam, who looked close to tears. And then they came. Amanda took a step forward and hugged her for quite a long time. Jack felt he should do something, but he couldn't think of anything, so he and the agent looked on.

Eventually they broke free of each other. Amanda withdrew a few paces to confer with another colleague whilst Pam moved alongside Jack.

And then Jack realised he had made another mistake. Ferguson's gun was lying on the ground, out of his reach – which was fine – but Pam had spotted it, an instant before him, and it was now in her hand. She was glaring down at Ferguson.

Whether she knew how to use the gun, Jack didn't know, but as he knew, firing a gun was not a difficult task.

Pam continued staring at Ferguson with a face of granite. She raised the gun, but to Jack's relief, she didn't fire. "Did you kill my father?"

Ferguson tried to get up but he couldn't. A torrent of blood streamed from his mouth.

"I asked you a question. Did you kill my father?"

Ferguson grimaced, probably with pain, but it looked like a smile. It didn't work well.

Jack tried to speak but he couldn't get any words out.

The gun in Pam's hand was steady now, and her finger was moving towards the trigger.

Jack moved forward gingerly, but Amanda held him back, moved alongside Pam, and in a single efficient movement slipped the gun out of her hand. "That's not the way. You need to leave this to me."

Pam uttered a minor protest but her energy was spent, and she gave up without a struggle and joined one of Amanda's men in a slow trudge back to the terminal.

Amanda wrapped a handkerchief around her hand and started looking intently at the handgun. "Glock 17, just like yours." She removed the magazine and flicked out a few rounds, which she looked at closely. She then beckoned an agent across and handed him the gun with a few instructions that Jack couldn't hear.

She turned to Jack. "You're not much of a godfather, Jack. You just can't seem to keep this girl safe."

Another fair comment he thought. "Thank God you got that gun from her."

"I don't think she would have fired."

"I'm not so sure, she's pretty headstrong, but I hate the thought of her spending a lifetime wondering whether she had been justified in killing a man."

Amanda said, "Hmm."

Jack knew what she meant and spent an unpleasant few seconds thinking about the people he had killed. He wondered whether Amanda was doing the same.

"So, can you tell me what's going on?" he asked.

"Not completely."

"And how come you're here? I thought you were in London?"

"Well, I was, but let's see what we can find out."

Ferguson decided *he* should ask the first question. He looked at Amanda. "Who the fuck are you?"

Amanda smiled sweetly. "I am Amanda Barratt, Mr Ferguson. I've got some questions for you."

Ferguson spat out more blood. Jack wondered if he was about to die.

Amanda was also professionally concerned. "There'll be an ambulance here very soon, Mr Ferguson. You dying's not going to help me much."

Ferguson managed a weak smile. "It was your man who shot me. Fast gun-play for a financial inspector."

"Paul Riordan was a friend of mine," Jack said.

A trickle of blood again burst out from the corner of Ferguson's mouth. He said reflectively, "A friend of mine also."

Jack felt a flash of fury, but Amanda shook her head, which he took to be an order to avoid further conversation. He shut up, and it wasn't long before the ambulance arrived.

Business as Usual

Amanda led Jack a little way back and they let the medics get on with it. It wasn't a long wait. A few minutes later, a smartly dressed woman in tweeds and wellingtons, aged about fifty, strode over. "Hello, Amanda. What's a nice girl like you doing in a place like this?"

Amanda laughed. "Just a quiet weekend in the country, Angela."

"Quiet by your standards, Amanda. At least there's a couple left alive today. The man died instantly, bullet in the head. The other shots would also have killed him. The woman's uninjured and the guy on the ground …"

"Mr Ferguson."

"Ferguson. He'll live. A bullet in his shoulder, still there, and another which went through him. As far as I can see it missed the vital organs, but I need him in hospital to be sure."

"When does he need to go to hospital?"

"Immediately, obviously."

"Can I question him first?"

"Sixty minutes tops."

"What about making him comfortable in the terminal building, just for a short time?"

"If you must."

Jack said, "What about that blood coming out of his mouth?"

Angela looked at him hard and said to Amanda, "Who's this?"

"Jack Edwards, he works for me."

Angela studied Jack carefully. "Looks a bit out of shape to me. And a bit old."

Amanda said, "True enough. He's part-time."

Angela looked at Jack again. "A medical man?"

"Er, no."

"Well, Mr Edwards, don't worry about the blood. He bit his tongue. It's quite common in shock cases. Anything else?"

"No, thank you."

"Good. I'll set up Mr Ferguson in the terminal building. Get over as soon as you can. One hour, remember."

"Thanks, Angela."

"Who was that?" Jack asked.

"Oh, Angela Power. Home office pathologist."

"Well named," Jack observed.

"Yes, she's really good. You can have as much attitude as you like when you're always right."

"How true."

The ambulance moved off and Jack and Amanda followed it back to the terminal. She said, "Seems that it takes more than a couple of shots from you to kill someone. I'm going to have to get you some shooting lessons. This has happened before."

"True enough, but luckily you're usually around."

"One day I'll be late."

As Jack considered his bad marksmanship, they had passed through the gap in the grass bunding. The administrative block and the car park were packed with vehicles and people.

"They all yours?" he asked.

"Mostly, plus a few local police and ambulance. Let's say they're all under my control at the moment."

"Impressive. But why so many?"

"I don't want anyone to know about this, not just yet."

"The public?"

"Don't be silly. The CIA, MI6 … I don't want them poking their noses in."

They entered the administration building and, like outside, it was clear that Amanda was taking no chances.

The manager seemed to be enjoying the activity. A couple of enthusiasts were less happy and loudly demanding to know when they could leave the airfield.

Amanda and Jack swept past these anguished conferences and into a back office where they found Pam, sitting alone but calm.

Jack asked, "You alright?"

"Yes, I'm fine. Sorry about that gun thing. I don't know what happened. I just lost my mind."

Business as Usual

He lit a cigarette and handed one to Amanda, who shook her head but took it, and all three sat in silence alone with their own thoughts.

Chapter 43

After two or three watery black coffees and as many cigarettes, Amanda received word that they were ready for her. She said firmly to Pam, "This time I need you to stay here. Okay?"

Having extracted a promise, she grabbed Jack by the arm. "I need you to come with me." He followed. The immediate area outside was now free of people who had, presumably, repaired to the hangars. Without warning, she turned towards him and kissed him hard on the lips. It was as pleasant as it was unexpected.

"What's that for?" he asked.

"Just saying sorry again."

"I still don't see what you could have done."

"I don't know either, but I am meant to be in charge."

"True enough. I enjoyed that kiss. What about another?"

She puckered her lips but didn't come nearer. "Maybe later. We've work to do."

Jack decided he was through being bossed around. He pulled her towards him and kissed her again.

"You're right, that is nice, but we've got to get on. I haven't got time to hang around kissing the help when there's an international crisis to manage."

"That's fair enough, I suppose. What about later?"

"I'll think about it. Come on."

Business as Usual

The first of the flimsy hangars was clear of aircraft but was home to about a dozen people who stood around in groups doing nothing in particular. They straightened their backs a little as she passed by. In the far corner in a separate section, a table and some chairs had been requisitioned and a rude interview area created.

Amanda dismissed all but one of her agents and took a seat, offering Jack a chair alongside her. Selena Thornton was seated opposite. Out of her natural habitat, she didn't look very formidable. Her clothes were all wrong for a cold aircraft hangar in the remote east of England. Jack could see only a middle-aged woman, desperately unhappy and with a lot of problems.

Amanda lit a cigarette and gave one to Jack.

"Hello, Miss Thornton. I'm Amanda Barratt and I'm a director in British military intelligence. I'm investigating fraud and conspiracy at the Canisp Hedge Fund and offences under numerous terrorism Acts." She added menacingly, "Just in case you are wondering about your legal position, it is as follows: I have probable cause to detain you under emergency terrorist powers … indefinitely."

Thornton's head was bowed and her eyes were wide open and faraway. She didn't move or say anything, so Amanda tried again. "Miss Thornton. Do you understand what I am saying?"

Her head must have been very heavy because it took her a long time to lift it and look at Amanda. "You think I'm a terrorist."

"Why not?"

Thornton's voice was desperate. "I'm American."

Amanda lit another cigarette, maybe because she suspected it would annoy Thornton. "I already know that, Miss Thornton. I'm afraid that your nationality is not going to be enough to convince me."

Thornton jerked her head away from a long plume of cigarette smoke. "What do you want to know?"

Amanda said, "Let's start with where you've been in the last thirty-six hours?"

"In the country."

"At a hotel?"

"Yes."

"What's the name of the hotel?"

Selena shook her head wearily and shrugged.

"How did you pay?"

Selena stared at Amanda. "What does that matter?"

"Just answer the question."

"Oh, cash, I think. I really can't remember."

Amanda moved on. "Let's talk fraud. Let me tell you where I'm at. I'm not yet convinced that you are the driver behind it. If so, then there will be other people I am more interested in than you. If you tell me everything you know, then I promise you I will get you the best deal I can. It might not be great, but it'll be the best you can get."

Thornton wiped her nose with the back of her hand, and they waited. Then she laughed and said, "I can't tell you anything."

"Oh, I'm sure you can, Miss Thornton. As I said, it will be better for you if you can save me time."

"No, I want to see a lawyer."

Amanda laughed too. "I can quote you a number of anti-terrorist Acts but I don't have time. Let's just say this is not a Hollywood movie and you can forget lawyers, and – before you ask – a telephone call."

Selena folded her arms in an act of defiance, but it wasn't really credible. Even Jack could see that.

Amanda said, "I'll give you a minute, Miss Thornton. If you don't start talking, I'll detain you somewhere else until you do. It's your call."

"Where will I be taken?"

"None of your fucking business. You've got about forty seconds now."

Jack was sure that she would talk. He was right, but never in a million years could he guess the words.

In a thin, apologetic voice, she said, "I've killed someone."

Amanda's face didn't change. Well, she had heard everything. "Who have you killed?"

"I didn't mean to. It was self-defence, but why would you believe me?"

"You'd be surprised what I believe, Miss Thornton. Who did you kill?"

"Katherine, Katherine Carver."

Amanda took this in her stride again. "Where?"

"At the cottage, last night. She came. Came to kill me. She pulled a gun, what else could I do?"

"I haven't heard what exactly you *did* do."

"She was going to shoot me. I just lashed out. I had a corkscrew in my hand. It hit her in her neck and she just died."

"A cottage or a hotel?"

Selena said, "I wasn't in a hotel, I rented a cottage."

Amanda sighed and pushed across a pen and a sheet of paper. "The address, please?" She reviewed the paper after Selena had written it down. "This better be right. I haven't got time or patience for any more pathetic lies."

"It's right."

"Is Ms Carver still there?"

"Yes. It's horrible."

"Why would Katherine Carver want to kill you, Miss Thornton?"

"I have no idea. Maybe she wanted the money."

"For herself?"

"Who else?"

"That's for you to tell me, Miss Thornton."

"I have no idea."

"Didn't she say anything?" Amanda said impatiently.

Selena sighed. "She said something about national security, and that I was involved in something that was way over my head."

"She was right about that much. Go on."

Selena overcame a tremor in her voice and said, "I've made a real fool of myself." She clasped her hands tightly. "David Ferguson and I have been lovers for about a year." She worked hard to stop her voice cracking. "I love him."

Jack watched Amanda. Her eyes blinked shut, and her head perceptively shook. This was an old, old story.

Selena ignored this silent rebuke, composed herself and resumed. "About two or three months ago, he said to me that he had been approached, through intermediaries, by an organisation that had accumulated a lot of cash and needed to move it quickly. I asked him more about the source, but he said he couldn't give me any more details.

"He said that, if we arranged to move the money, we could charge huge commissions – maybe up to 50%." She added an ethical consideration. "It all sounded a bit iffy, really – obviously. Nothing more happened for a few weeks and then David came back to me. He said that he had sorted everything out, checked everything out and it was all legal. I wasn't sure, but then he said that the commissions could go to environmental groups. That's a cause I strongly believe in."

Amanda didn't look as though she was awarding any prizes for loving good causes. "Go on."

"Well, I can't say that I was completely satisfied about the source of the money but …" She reflected and seemed to plead to Amanda as a woman. "I loved him and I trusted him."

It was a waste of a plea. "Why did he need to involve you?"

"I know my way around international banking better than David. He needed a route that was obscure."

"Surely that was suspicious?"

Thornton shrugged.

Jack was keen to intervene here but left it to the boss. Amanda changed her focus of attack. "And what about Paul Riordan? Were you involved in killing him?"

Thornton's voice rose several octaves. "Paul? What are you talking about? That was a road accident. What do you mean?"

Having dropped her bombshell, Amanda moved on to what seemed a key question. "There have been other killings as well and I'll come back to them, but tell me this, Miss Thornton – if this was to be a legitimate transaction as you described, why would you and Mr Ferguson be planning to leave the country?"

Business as Usual

It was a tough question, but against the odds, Selena had quite a good answer. "Things changed after the bomb at David's house. He came to me that night and said there was trouble. The transactions were in progress at the time. He said that he was being pressed to return the money and pay a huge penalty. He had refused, but said that the group who controlled the money were trying to kill him and it was them who had bombed his house."

Amanda said, "And you believed all this?"

"I suppose I did. He said he had to disappear. One thing led to another and I decided that I would leave with him." She added unnecessarily, "I love him, you see." She rocked her head back and laughed wildly. "What a fucking fool."

Amanda's face was granite. At last Selena Thornton had said something she agreed with.

Chapter 44

Selena Thornton's accurate self-assessment served as a suitable time-out for Amanda, who got up and led Jack into the body of the hangar. "What do you think?"

"Possible. Naïve, but possible."

"For love of a man and the environment. She's right. She is a fucking fool."

She dispatched a man to next door's hangar. He returned with news that Ferguson was fit to receive them.

"Right. Let's go and hear what this bastard's got to say."

Ferguson was in control of his emotions but physically was in worse shape than his ex-girlfriend. Despite medical bulletins to the contrary, it seemed to Jack that Ferguson was seriously injured. Propped up on a part-raised portable stretcher, his face was grey and his chin sat heavily on his chest.

Amanda said, "How are you feeling, Mr Ferguson?"

"They say I'll live, unfortunately."

He looked across at Jack and said, without animosity, "Here's the man who shot me. I can't believe that I missed you. I'm a terrible shot. Guns are not usually my thing."

Amanda wasn't in the mood for small talk. "I'm in a hurry, Mr Ferguson. The doctor says if I question you for more than" – she looked at her watch – "twenty minutes you might die."

"Well, you'd better get on with it then."

Business as Usual

Amanda said, "Okay, Mr Ferguson, I'm detaining you under the provisions of so many terrorist Acts that I can't be bothered reciting them all."

Ferguson shared her disdain for bureaucracy. "Yes, I know all that, and I don't give a fuck. What do you want to know?"

Amanda looked concerned. Jack wondered why. Surely this was an interrogator's dream?

Amanda said slowly, "Should I be congratulating you, Mr Ferguson?"

He laughed, "In a way. Nothing matters now. It's done."

For a man with a bullet in him and prospects no better than life in prison, he looked serene, almost happy.

"Let's have it."

Ferguson grimaced with pain as he shuffled himself up in the stretcher, and got himself comfortable. "This is a long story, but I think we have time.

"Twenty years ago, I was a young man working in the Middle East. I had a wife and a daughter." He paused for a moment, his face twitching, evidently trying to control a powerful emotion. He restored control and continued. "All went well. I liked it there but I missed my family. So, I arranged for them to come out and live with me. Why not?

"The country was pretty stable politically except for a few peasant revolutionaries. They were very little trouble: small in number, poorly organised and lightly armed, and they had no real support in the country. Their insurrectionist activities consisted of a few stabbings a year, some graffiti, and, once, a letter bomb. Nothing really."

He went on, "Well, that was before. And then someone decided that this little country should become part of a great game. And overnight these people had machine guns, rocket launchers, grenades, explosives, everything. Like giving these things to children."

Ferguson stopped for a moment and got to the heart of the matter. "Maybe you have guessed the rest. A rocket launcher, a plane hit and suddenly I don't have a family." He looked at both Amanda then Jack.

"My daughter, my wife, and the child she was carrying. The future. Gone. That changes you."

Jack had to admit, Ferguson could tell a compelling story, albeit with a few gaps. They were soon closed.

"After the initial grief passed, I started to get angry ... angrier than I knew I could. Surprisingly, I wasn't really angry with the ones who fired the rocket – more with the individuals who supplied the weapons. What did they expect would happen? Whatever, they were quick to deny involvement. Irresponsible? Yes. Cynical? Yes and, of course, ultimately responsible?"

Fire burst from Ferguson's eyes. "Like any human I was burning for revenge, but how? I mean, how does one get revenge on the CIA?"

Amanda could only lean forward in anticipation.

"Anyway, years passed. I did well. I never re-married. Thoughts of revenge were always there, but to be honest, what could I do? A futile gesture? What would be the point? And then, years later, the means fell into my lap."

Jack leant forward in his seat too.

"Katherine Carver came into my office one day. For some reason, she thought I would be more sympathetic than Paul. What a fool. Anyway, she described to me an operation that she was arranging for, what she called, the American government. With typical complacency and arrogance, she asked me to help."

"Have you seen Miss Carver recently?"

"No, why would I want to see her?"

"You say she was the instigator of this project."

Ferguson shrugged. "True, but once I had the details, I didn't need her any more. She's an idiot anyway. When you go to hire people, Miss Barratt, try to do some basic due diligence. Establish whether they hate you and your organisation before you employ them."

He continued, "Anyway, there it was – would I help the CIA move about forty billion of their dirty money from the Gulf to some of their secret accounts? Katherine didn't say – well, she didn't need to – it was the sort of money, unofficial money, off the books. The money that funds covert, illegal operations, just like the one all **those** years ago that killed my family."

Ferguson took a deep breath. "What an opportunity. Almost providential. Revenge on the CIA. Something that would really hurt them."

It was hard to argue, almost impossible not to sympathise. And then one thought of the horrors to come.

Ferguson continued, "Well, you probably know the rest. I programmed the execution of the trades, but also created a back door in the program. It was a nice piece of work, quite elegant. Anyway, the net result is that I arranged for the CIA to fund their deadliest enemies to the tune of about forty billion dollars."

He added, with cold satisfaction, "They'll be killing Americans for years."

Chapter 45

There followed a short period of silence and reflection, which this story certainly deserved, and then Amanda said, "And who did you kill, Mr Ferguson?"

"No one."

"Paul Riordan?"

Ferguson contrived a look of genuine shock. "No. Paul died in a car crash."

"Did Paul suspect that you were moving this money?"

"No, why would he?"

"I understood he had suspicions."

"Not as far as I know."

Amanda looked at her watch again. "What about the bomb explosion?"

"What about it?"

"Are you a skilled bomb-maker, Mr Ferguson?"

"No."

"So, who helped you?"

"Sorry, this is down to me."

Amanda tried again. "Did the Americans help?"

Ferguson replied, "I have global contacts. Let's just say that."

"What about Sebastian Mann?"

"Never heard of him."

Amanda said, "Hard to believe. Especially as he's lying dead on the airfield. I know that because I killed him."

"So you did, Miss Barratt. You're a better shot than me or your man here."

Amanda waited.

"Sebastian was a friend."

"You worked together in the Middle East?"

"Seems you've done a little research, Miss Barratt."

"Did he get the explosives?"

"I've no idea."

"Through British Army friends?"

Ferguson shook his head. "Please, don't ask me again. Even if I did know, I wouldn't tell you."

"What about Ray Common?"

"Poor Ray. I needed him to sign off some paperwork. I gave him fifty thousand pounds, but when your inspectors arrived, he got nervous and asked for more money or he would expose the transactions. A weak link. I couldn't allow that."

"Did Common do anything else for you?"

"No."

"So Common was in your house when the bomb went off?"

"Yes, I killed two birds with one stone –got rid of a blackmailer and allowed me to disappear."

"It all sounds so easy, Mr Ferguson."

"It was, I'm sorry to say."

Amanda said, "And then these gunmen. Did Mr Mann arrange those too?"

Ferguson shrugged. "It hardly matters now. Let's just say putting Ali Cairns out of the way would have helped. She's about the only person who really knows how we work. Also, I just needed to slow you down until the transactions had gone through, but you killed them as well, Miss Barratt. You're a very dangerous woman."

Amanda was nearly at the end of her charge sheet. "And what about Miss Thornton? Would you have killed her?"

Ferguson was nothing if not honest. "I didn't intend to. Not at first. I probably should have because I didn't need her any more, and she was the only one who knew I was still alive, but I changed my mind."

"And with Selena dead you needed a pilot, hence Sebastian Mann."

"Something like that."

"How much does Miss Thornton know about all this?"

Ferguson laughed. "Not much. She gave me a bit of advice about which banks to go through and ensured the trades went through smoothly. She knows a lot about banking so that was quite useful." He laughed maliciously again. "I told her that some of the money was going to help environmental campaigns."

Amanda said, "Did she know anything about the killings?"

"No, nothing."

"And what about the ultimate bank accounts? The terrorist accounts. How much does she know about them?"

"Nothing, so there's no point in trying to torture it out of her."

"Where did you get these details."

"I told you, I've got global connections."

"That's a lot of connections to a lot of bad people."

Ferguson nodded. "Yes, quite a good job I would say."

"Very good job, Mr Ferguson."

"Praise indeed."

Amanda said, "How did you select the beneficiaries?"

"All my own work. I read the papers."

"No help at all?"

Ferguson shook his head.

What about the board of directors?

Ferguson laughed loudly this time. "Come on, Miss Barratt. Would you use these fools?"

Chapter 46

With Ferguson off to hospital, Amanda and Jack sat on a two-seated bench in front of the aerodrome buildings. Amanda said, "What do you think?"

"I think you need to ask more questions."

"Of course, but do you believe Ferguson?"

Jack lit a cigarette. "Yes, I do."

"Would you do that for your family?"

"Maybe, although I'm not sure I could organise something like this."

"I know that," Amanda said harshly but fairly, "but you know what I mean. Could you do it?"

Jack shook his head. "No, I don't think that I could keep the fires of revenge burning for so many years. But it'll never arise. Everyone that killed Marion's dead."

Amanda looked at him. "Sorry, clumsy of me." She put her hand on his arm, and they sat in silence for a moment.

Jack said, "Ferguson has certainly outsmarted the Americans, really stuck it to them."

Amanda wasn't ready to award prizes just yet. "Not just the Americans, I'm afraid. Some of the bullets and the bombs will find our guys." She repeated Ferguson's words. "For years."

"Well, what happens now?"

"If you were the Americans, what would you do now?"

"The money's gone, they will check that of course. Maybe try to get it back somehow. But, assuming they can't, then I doubt I'd want such a cock-up publicised. They'll try to keep it quiet. I would. I mean, it's hardly their finest hour. Carver's dead and they've indirectly funded international terrorism."

"Yes, and the London end telling lies to their closest allies. Such a pity. I always liked Bob Frost."

She gestured to a man in a suit. "Peter, I think we can give Mr Appleton his aerodrome back now."

"Yes, ma'am."

"Have we got a twenty-four-hour guard on Ferguson?"

"All arranged."

"Good, and remember, no lawyers, no phone calls, and no suicides. I have a lot more questions."

"What about other agencies?"

"No, let's keep this to ourselves for the minute."

"Understood, ma'am."

Jack and Amanda returned to the office. Pam was quiet and pale, and her eyes were heavy. This time, for sure, there would be no escaping a black reaction.

She looked up. Her voice was weak. "Is it over now?"

Amanda put her arm round her shoulders and pulled her close. "Yes, I think so." Pam leant her head on Amanda's shoulder and closed her eyes. "I'm very tired."

Pam slept in the back of the car, which Amanda drove back to her Norfolk home. Jack carried her up the narrow stairs over his shoulder and, after depositing her on the bed, joined Amanda in the kitchen.

She poured him a strong, black coffee and passed him a cigarette. It was comfortable being around her.

"Nice kid. Wonder what she'll do now?"

"I've been thinking about that," he said.

"Have you something in mind?"

"Not really. Just an overwhelming feeling I should help. Do something?"

"What can you do?"

"I don't know, but I've been doing nothing but thinking about myself for the last few years."

Amanda touched his hand. "It's understandable."

"Oh yes, I've got an excuse. I've got lots of excuses and, in a way, hiding out in the north of Scotland's fine, but …"

"It's not enough?"

"I don't think that it will be."

Amanda said, "You have choices. Lots of them."

"Yes, yes," Jack said impatiently, "I'm not complaining. How can I?"

"Well, what do you want to do?"

Jack dragged on a cigarette. "Fuck, I've no idea."

Amanda smiled. "Maybe you need a girlfriend or something?"

"I'm very fussy."

"Me too."

With this, she got up and returned with a photograph from the drawer of a Welsh dresser. It was an old photograph, taken about thirty years ago, Jack reckoned. A simple beach scene: a mother, a father and two children of about five or six years old. Everyone looked happy. She said, "Which one's me?"

He pointed at one of the children.

"No," she said, "That's my little sister." She gazed into the distance. "That was at Ballycastle Beach."

"Where's that?"

"Northern Ireland. County Antrim. It was a long time ago. I think I was seven, but I remember it. Just running about and kicking a ball. Paddling in the sea. It was cold."

"Never heard of Ballycastle Beach. Did you often go there on holiday?"

"Not a holiday. Just a day trip."

"Long way for a day trip."

"No. We lived in Northern Ireland then. In fact, I was born there. Left when I was eighteen, for university."

Jack looked at her. "Why didn't I know that?"

"You never asked." Amanda picked up the photograph again. "My mother was born there. And my sister, of course."

He was getting deep now. Jack had never known Amanda's sister but she had been in the family business and had ended up dead. He didn't need to say anything.

"And now there's just me."

"And you're doing okay," Jack said awkwardly.

"Most of the time."

Jack touched her arm. "How about we stay here a day or so?"

Amanda exhaled a lungful of smoke and rocked her head back. "Oh, that would be nice, but I'm afraid duty calls." She squeezed his hand. "Maybe when I'm cleared up in London."

"When do you need to go?"

She stubbed out her cigarette and disappointed him again. "Right now."

Chapter 47

Just in time for a late lunch, Amanda walked into the library at the Colonial Club. Nick Devoy already had a visitor.

Bob Frost greeted Amanda with the exaggerated courtesy of the old-fashioned American gentleman that he was.

She smiled back. Frost had told her quite a few lies, but one advantage of being in the intelligence community was that it was always business and rarely personal. Normally the issues involved were so big and so remote from the day-to-day lives of even those most closely involved that it could only be treated as a never-ending abstract game.

Nick Devoy opened the conversation in that spirit. "Well, Bob, from what I understand, you've made a massive fuck-up."

Frost sipped his brandy and considered. "As I mentioned yesterday, our official position is that we have no knowledge of, or interest in, whatever has been going on at the Canisp Hedge Fund. Although I understand that we've lost quite a bit of money in a failed investment."

"No chance of recovery?"

"The accountants say not."

"Bad luck," Devoy said blandly. "Plenty more where that came from?"

"We can afford it." Frost said complacently, still focused on the brandy.

"I have news about Katherine Carver."

"I was minded to ask for your help. Officially," Frost replied.

Devoy shook his head. "Bad idea, Bob."

Frost mouth fell. "Has she met with an accident?"

"Yes, Bob. And that's officially and unofficially true."

"A bad accident?"

"As bad as accidents can be."

"Poor Katherine. She was destined for the top."

"Not now, Bob. Sorry, there was nothing we could do. We didn't kill her. We think she was trying to kill someone but ended up dead herself."

Frost was philosophical. "Always a risk to send these academic types out into the field."

"She was highly regarded, I understand."

"She was."

"Won't she be missed?"

"She already is being missed. Langley and Washington are going fucking crazy at the moment."

"Don't make it official, Bob. She's broken about every protocol I know. We need some time. We'll talk to you when we have something."

"Can I have the body?"

Devoy looked at Amanda. She said, "Yes, in a few days."

"That will do for now. Can I call it an accident?"

Amanda said, "I'll see how far our pathologist can stretch things."

"Fine, I'm sure we'll get over it. You know, they'll find someone else with that particular skill set. We've got thousands like her, I'm afraid."

Devoy said, "And what about you, Bob?"

"Seems like old-fashioned is back in fashion. They've asked me to do another two years."

"Impressive, especially in this political climate."

Amanda said, "Good news. I'll look forward to seeing you around, Bob. Maybe you can help me with a few things. Give me the benefit of your experience?"

Bob said agreeably, "Of course, if I can."

"Let's start now. I've got a couple of questions"

"Shoot."

She said, "If you were running an operation like this, would you have sanctioned the killing of Paul Riordan?"

"No."

"Why not?"

"Obviously I have no official knowledge of this operation. However, when Mr Riordan was killed, as I understand you, the transactions had not begun, so why not just make alternative arrangements? No need for violence. Of course, given what we know now, that would not have suited Mr Ferguson. He had, what is now clear, the strongest interest in things proceeding as planned."

Amanda said, "Hypothetically, of course, would you have involved more than a single board member in such an enterprise?"

"My practice is always to have a single manager on every project."

"And that would have been Katherine Carver?"

"Why not?"

"What about Lord Steel?"

"I wouldn't touch him with a barge-pole."

"Not much of a testimonial."

"Not much of a man," Frost retorted. He downed his brandy and looked at them. "Well, I'll let you get on with things. If you get any more specific details of the unexpected beneficiaries of Mr Ferguson's largesse, let me know. Maybe we can sort this out with some good old-fashioned intelligence work."

Amanda smiled. "Of course, Bob."

Frost laughed. "I'll look forward to working with you, Amanda." He waddled out of the club.

Devoy said, "I'm going to have a sandwich and another drink. You want something?"

"Yes, the same."

Devoy stuffed a sandwich in his mouth and took his time eating it. "What now, Amanda?"

"I'm not completely sure. Talk to Ferguson. See what we can get out of him."

Devoy looked at her. "Nothing else?"

"I'm not sure, Nick."

"You want to talk about it?"

"No, I'm waiting on a few calls, some analysis. Just testing a few ideas."

Devoy picked up another sandwich. "Do you need anything?"

"Just a good break."

Chapter 48

A long black Jaguar pulled up outside the club, and Amanda got in the back. "Where to, ma'am?"

She told him, switched off her phone and, for the next hour, let her eyes close and her aching body rest.

All too soon she was woken. "Here we are, ma'am – 45 Park Road."

Mrs Common responded to the doorbell with a typical lack of urgency. She smiled at Amanda. "Hello, Miss Barratt. Have you got news for me?"

In the same bay-windowed sitting room that she had sat in one – or had it been two? – days ago, Amanda again waited as Mrs Common prepared tea. She retrieved the photo from the mantelpiece and looked at Ray Common and his friends en-route to the football match. When you were looking for something, suddenly it was quite obvious. The diamond earring was his pride and joy and it shone out of the picture.

This time, as if in preparation for a long and difficult conversation, Mrs Common emerged rolling an antique two-level trolley laden with tea, cakes and also sandwiches.

Amanda was one of the busiest people in London today, but she was determined to give Mrs Common all the time that they both needed.

Mrs Common carefully poured out two cups of tea. And it was she who opened the conversation with a realisation that stunned Amanda.

"It is very nice to see you again, Amanda, but" – she was still composed – "I imagine you have bad news for me."

This stoic acceptance of misfortune should have made things easier for Amanda, but somehow it didn't. Somehow it transferred the mourning duties partly on to her, and although she had never met Ray Common and knew him only by his criminal deeds, she already regretted his death.

Mrs Common was waiting for an answer and it couldn't be avoided.

"I'm so very sorry, Mrs Common, but we believe that your son is dead."

Mrs Common didn't flinch. She said ruefully, "I feared as much. I knew he wouldn't miss the match. Besides, he would always have contacted me."

There was a cold logic in this, maybe the type of logic that only a loving mother could believe in.

Without flinching, she said, "What happened to him?"

Amanda lied. "It was a gas explosion, I'm afraid."

Mrs Common took this in her stride. "Yes, there was a lot of that in the war. I was very young, but I remember. One day the houses and the people were there, and the next day, …" She let the sentence fall away and then, for the first time, asked Amanda for something. With a gaze full of hope, she asked, "Last time you said he was helping you; did he help?"

Amanda's business was built on lies, but she almost believed it when she heard herself saying, "Yes. He was very helpful, very helpful indeed."

Mrs Common had needed to hear this, and Amanda was just happy that she could give her something. Of all the actors in the case, Ray Common's part was the easiest to ignore. Amanda wondered how she would navigate the fact that only the diamond earring remained of her son, but Mrs Common was a remarkable lady and had also anticipated this.

Without emotion she said, "I suppose that, with a gas explosion, there isn't much left for me to bury."

Amanda was holding back her own tears now and could manage only a nod in response.

"Well, it won't make any difference to God. Would you like some cake, Amanda?"

Amanda was struggling badly now, but, mercifully, Mrs Common moved on to more prosaic matters., "Oh, I have something for you. Let me go and get it." She shuffled out of the room and eventually returned with a small attaché case, which she set before Amanda.

"There is fifty thousand pounds here. Is that part of your enquiries?"

Payments that Ferguson had made to Common for services rendered were of no interest to her. She knew that the money wouldn't matter to Mrs Common either, but it was tough to know what else she could do for her. Amanda said, "No, nothing at all. I'd get that into the bank as soon as you can."

Mrs Common smiled indulgently. "Oh, you can't always trust banks, Amanda."

"Very true, Mrs Common, very true. Now is there anything that you would like me to do for you?"

"No, Amanda, I expect that I will get some kind of official notification, and I can take it from there."

Amanda asked respectfully, "May I know your first name?"

"Sorry, I should have said. It's Margaret."

"Well, Margaret, if there is ever anything that I can do for you, I need you to promise that you will call me."

"Thank you, Amanda. I will." She looked as if she meant this, and it made Amanda feel better.

Margaret escorted Amanda to the door and hugged her. "Thanks for coming to see me. I'm glad it was you that told me. Good luck with your work. I expect you still have a lot to do."

Amanda headed back to the car and wiped wet tears from her cheeks as the car pulled out, with her wondering if she would ever be as strong as an old lady from Croydon.

Chapter 49

The drive back to London gave Amanda another chance to rest, but now she didn't feel like resting. Sadness had morphed into anger and a firm conviction that this case wasn't quite over. Maybe she didn't want it to be. Her mobile rang. At last, interesting news.

She called Jack. He took a while to answer and managed a couple of grunts.

Amanda said, "Morning."

Another grunt.

"I'll be passing your flat in about thirty minutes. Can you be ready?"

"Must I?" Another yawn.

"Late night?"

"Yes, we got back about two in the morning."

"I'll forgive you. Can you meet us on the street?"

"See you in half an hour."

Despite her worst fears, Jack was on time, well-scrubbed and quite sharply dressed. He shuffled into the back of the car alongside her and smiled. "Hello. What's up? I thought we were finished?"

"Hardly."

"Have Ferguson or Thornton told you more?"

"No, not yet."

"Well, what then?"

"I'll fill you in later."

Business as Usual

The black Jaguar drove onto the pavement outside a modern glass-fronted office building in the City of London.

Amanda said, "This is Sebastian Mann's office."

"That's the guy you shot at the airfield?"

"Yes, the one who was about to shoot you."

Amanda walked past two suited men and through the front door into a small unstaffed reception.

"Quiet," Jack said.

"Yes, there are no staff here, except mine of course."

A door opened and they went through and waited as a lift door opened, shut and opened again to admit them to another empty area, off which led a narrow corridor. Jack followed until Amanda stopped at the last of the doors.

It was protected by a keypad. Amanda entered five or six numbers and the door lock yielded. Another bland waiting-room. One further door – surely the last. Again, Amanda entered a code and they went in.

This time, Jack didn't ask for an explanation. It was all too clear, and it nearly made him sick. Ahead, six curved screens each flashing views of a road, and before them a low seat with a steering wheel and pedals. The view from the screens changed in real time. The configuration was not unlike some kind of driving amusement game, but there was nothing funny about this.

The door opened behind them and Max Harris came in. "Hi, boss."

"Hello, Max, are we done here?"

"Yes."

"Any physical evidence?"

"None at all. A few smudges. Gloves, I think. Otherwise, everything's clean."

Amanda's face fell.

Harris wasn't finished. "Never mind that, boss. I've got something much better; I think. I'm waiting on a phone call. It's due any time."

Jack took a pace or two forward and sat down on the seat. His knees were at his chin. Far too near the pedals. He looked around and spotted a lever. Amanda grabbed his hand. "Leave that."

He looked at her quizzically.

"Let me sit down."

She replaced him in the seat. "See, fits me perfectly."

"Well, obviously, you're about six inches shorter than me."

"Quite."

Jack looked at her. "You think that's important?"

"Suggestive."

"Okay, but surely your guys have been moving it?"

"No, nothing has been moved here."

"Were you here earlier?"

"No, I just arrived with you."

Jack looked at her and asked a surprisingly intelligent question. "If this is your first visit, how did you know the code numbers for these offices?"

Amanda smiled. "I'm impressed, Mr Edwards. To answer your question, the reason I knew the passcode numbers is because we found them recorded on a mobile. You know how people record these things on their phones."

"Yes, I do it myself for my credit cards."

"Not a very secure thing to do. You could lose the phone or it could easily be hacked."

"Yes, by departments like yours."

"One of our specialities." Amanda admitted.

"Did you hack a phone to get this number?"

"No, we got it from one of the phones we picked up at the airfield."

"Sebastian Mann's."

"No."

Jack hadn't been out of bed long, but this also was interesting. Before he had time for his next question, the door opened again.

This time, there could be no doubt that further progress had been made. Harris was beaming. A kid with a new toy.

He sidled up beside Amanda and opened a folder, which she and he studied carefully.

Amanda said, "How sure are we?"

Business as Usual

"According to our experts, 99% confidence."

Chapter 50

As the Jaguar sped out of the City. Jack said, "Are you going to let me in on the secret?"

"Soon, I'm thinking."

"Where are we going?"

"North London. I need to speak to Ferguson and Thornton again."

"Can't you tell me anything?"

"In a minute. I'm still thinking."

"Do you know who killed Paul?"

"I think so."

"And that set-up was where it happened."

"Yes."

"How do you know that?"

"Max got into the software. The record was deleted, but he knows how to retrieve these things."

Jack sighed. "Are we really any further forward? We know that Sebastian Mann was working with Ferguson, he told us. The equipment's in Mann's office. Mann or one of his agents drove the car. That's it, surely."

Amanda didn't reply.

Jack tried again. "I can't see why Ferguson would lie. I thought you said that you believed him?"

"Yes, I do believe him, but I need to confirm a few things. We're here now."

Business as Usual

The Jaguar crunched its way up the serpentine driveway and stopped.

"Scary place. What happens here?"

"Multi-purpose. We use it for a few things, including holding people. Ferguson and Thornton are here."

The front door was heavy and ornate, but, when opened, thoughts of a luxury stately pile were dispersed almost immediately. The reception was ultra-modern and home to a buzzing swarm of agents and administrative staff. Amanda got a few acknowledgements as she swept in. Behind them, the door slammed shut.

Jack was glad he was with Amanda. There was nothing that he could put his finger on or later describe, but whoever the interior designers had been, they had done a great job. The reception was huge but it felt claustrophobic, comfortable but felt spartan and, worst of all, welcoming but oppressive. This was one of the places where plots were ravelled and unravelled and people, unaware, were monitored and talked about as they teetered towards personal disaster. Power lived here.

He stood aside while power was talking to a couple of men at a reception area. This finished, Amanda returned. "We're going to have a chat with Ferguson. Don't say a word, not one word. Just sit beside me and look professional."

"And Thornton?"

"She's ready to be released, but let's talk to Ferguson first."

"Yes ma'am," Jack said, getting into the spirit of things.

It was a long walk through well-appointed but dismal narrow corridors before Amanda stopped. She pressed a button; the lock unfroze and Jack followed her into a large bedsit room.

Ferguson was in the bed with a couple of tubes in his arms. His pallor was greying and his designer stubble was already breaking out of its former well-defined boundaries. He was watching a television screen on the wall, blaring out some fake news from one of those fake news channels that used to be trusted. He turned a heavy head towards them, an effort that cost him a lot of energy. "Hello, Miss Barratt, no flowers, chocolates?"

Amanda pulled a couple of chairs and placed them bedside. "No sorry, I forgot about that, but of course you can have all the chocolates you want if you give me a more detailed statement."

Ferguson smiled. "I'll keep that in mind, but I've nothing else to say. What happens now?"

Amanda smiled back. "I haven't decided. It looks like I'm going to have to waste quite a lot of taxpayers' money on you."

"Sorry."

Amanda flicked off the television. A cheap clock ticked. A twenty-four-hour clock. For Ferguson it might have been a yearly clock. It was a dismal thought, but he seemed in remarkable spirits for a man who had gone from multi-millionaire to convict in a week.

Still Amanda said nothing.

"So, why are you here, Miss Barratt?"

"Oh, just routine. I wanted to confirm some details of our chat."

"If you must."

"If you won't tell me about the terrorist connections, what about the killing of Paul Riordan?"

"Why do you say killing?"

"Because I'm not satisfied it was an accident."

"Strange that you focus on this. You're MI5, aren't you?"

"Yes."

"Surely the terrorist stuff is your priority?"

"It is, but I don't like loose ends."

"Strikes me there aren't any. Paul crashed his car. These supercars are dangerous."

"Did you ever drive it?"

Ferguson laughed. "No, never."

"You sure?"

Ferguson said. "Quite sure. You see, I don't have a driving licence, Miss Barratt. I haven't driven a car for years. I have epilepsy, mild really. I haven't had an attack for ages but I gave up my licence, oh twenty years ago. Maybe I could have got it back, but I didn't really need it. I could afford to be driven, although I like the train."

Jack noted this disclosure as interesting, although Amanda moved on. She said, "Do you have anyone that you wish me to inform of your detention?"

"Decent of you, Miss Barratt, but there's no one."

"No girlfriend? **Friend?** No one?"

"No one?"

"Tough to believe, Mr Ferguson. You, living like a monk?"

"Mostly, to be honest. I died a bit that day."

"You must have been close to Selena. She was in love with you."

Ferguson smiled. "Was she?"

"So she says."

"I'm sorry about that. I led her on a bit. I needed help, you see."

"You told me."

"She'll get over it. Look, I don't want her to get into trouble. This is down to me, and me alone."

Amanda got out of her seat and Jack followed. "Do you need anything, Mr Ferguson?"

"That's good of you. Yes, there is something. It's a bit of a cliché but I seem to have a strange craving for fruit. Oranges mostly."

Amanda nodded, returned the TV remote control to Ferguson and they left.

Alone in the corridor, Jack said, "That was a real tough interrogation. You learned nothing and now you're sending fruit."

She laughed. "You're right, I'm such a softy. Do you believe Ferguson?"

"Does it matter? It seems clear that you do."

"Yes, I do. Let's go and arrange that fruit."

Chapter 51

Oranges and a few apples were ordered via a suited, hard-faced man, about a foot taller than Jack, who looked as if he would be more comfortable in a gun fight, then Amanda returned to the dismal corridors and entered another room.

This room was similar but more welcoming. Not having a sickbed with a grey faced man on a drip helped.

Selena Thornton had also been well looked after, and a couple of open suitcases full of what were presumably her own clothes had been delivered. There was a bottle of whisky and one of vodka with a few mixers sitting on a side table and the television was sitting in front of an L-shaped sofa.

Thornton looked up as they arrived. Her hair looked in good shape and her face bore a trace of make-up. Maybe more than a trace. Either way, she had restored a sense of the powerful business woman.

Amanda slid casually onto the sofa quite near Thornton and Jack sat opposite.

Thornton tensed a little. Amanda smiled. "I've read your statement about Katherine Carver."

Thornton's lips tightened.

Amanda threw down a couple of loose sheets of paper. "I'll need to have a signature. Read it first."

Selena read it carefully, then picked up the pen that Amanda had placed on the table. She hesitated. "That seems in order. I mean, it's what happened."

"Fine, so just sign it."

Again, Selena hesitated. "But Miss Barratt, are you satisfied?"

"I'm neither satisfied or otherwise. I just need the truth."

Selena signed. "Here it is." Again, she made to speak but didn't. Jack thought he knew what she wanted. What anyone would want. Was she free?

She looked expectantly at Amanda, who was re-reading the statement deliberately.

She put the two sheets together and placed them on top of a small briefcase now on her knees. Jack's heart was racing. *Christ, get on with it.* Amanda still looked pleasant enough, but now her silence was scaring Jack. God knows what it was doing to Selena Thornton.

The room was huge, there were no bars on the windows and it smelt fine, but it seemed the most claustrophobic place in the world. Selena's hands were shaking. She trapped them under her legs. Still, they waited.

Amanda's phone rang.

She listened, rang off and then, looking at Selena, said, "You ready?"

Selena went to her suitcases.

"No, leave those, Miss Thornton. I'll have someone bring your things."

They walked in silence out of the room and upstairs, through the reception area, and out of the main door. In the broad gravel reception sat a sleek, black saloon car. An agent opened the passenger and rear doors.

"Take the front seat, Jack," Amanda said.

He did as he was told. Amanda ushered Selena into the spacious rear and sat alongside her.

The agent moved into the driving seat and started the car, then conducted a short series of what looked like checks. Jack had no idea what he was checking, but it didn't matter, for he was finished quickly.

Jack turned for the seat belt. He clicked it into place. The driver was gone. The ignition still on. The central locking clicked, and the car started to move, slowly at first as it followed the gravel track past the gable end of the building, heading away from the main entrance.

Selena let out a low noise.

"Our latest technology, Miss Thornton. Remote driving."

The gravel crunched as the car continued along the long straight track, heading into what seemed acres of grounds. A minor twist on the track was ahead. Powerfully, the car accelerated. Close to sixty miles an hour. Not fast for this car, but under the circumstances it felt like a rocket. A frothing steering wheel, late braking, then a smooth taking of the corner with a tiny bit of oversteer easily corrected.

Jack was going to have to spend a lot of time getting used to this, but Amanda seemed relaxed enough. "Well, Miss Thornton, what do you think of remote driving?"

Jack looked in the mirror at Selena's face, strained now. She said in a low, faltering voice, "What is the point of this demonstration, Miss Barratt?"

Amanda looked at her. "I would have thought that it was obvious. I thought you would like this. I understand you're an excellent driver."

Selena said nothing.

Amanda clicked open her briefcase and pulled out a couple of sheets of paper, which she handed to Selena. "These are quite impressive, Miss Thornton. I'm told that your best lap is still on the all-timers board. You never mentioned that you often accompanied Paul Riordan on his track days."

"Yes, once or twice. You didn't ask. Is it important?"

The car continued on from time to time, negotiating corners at an alarming speed. Jack had come to terms with things now. Ahead, he had no control, so he turned and looked at Amanda and Selena.

Amanda said, "You're quite right. I didn't ask. It took a while for me to see why it might be important."

"And why is it important?"

Amanda retrieved the papers from Selena and put her face nearer hers. "Because whoever killed Mr Riordan had to be a great driver. Like you."

"This is confusing. I have no idea what you mean."

"I agree things are confusing. All this technology. My staff have explained it all to me dozens of times, but I'm still not clear, so maybe you can bear with me."

Amanda looked at Selena, but she didn't say anything.

"Remote driving is an emerging technology. Modern cars have a CAN bus. It's a computer network, they tell me. To keep the story short and simple, computers can be hacked. So, cars can be hacked. We believe that's what happened to Paul Riordan's car."

"You're saying that someone took control of the car and ran it off the road?"

"Yes, exactly that. I did explain it properly."

"I thought it was an accident."

"Come on, Miss Thornton. The quicker we get this cleared up the better."

"I really can't help you. I understood that I was free to leave."

The car straightened after some more sharp cornering.

Amanda sat back in her seat. "I don't remember saying that, Miss Thornton."

Jack flicked his gaze to Selena. She tensed but took this blow well. She said, "What now? You tell me this wild theory that because I'm a good driver, I must have killed Paul. Remember I'm a lawyer, Miss Barratt, you're going to need a lot more than that."

Amanda said, "Quite right. It certainly sounds thin."

Jack thought so too.

Amanda went into her briefcase. "Sorry, I didn't explain this as well as I should have. I'm hopeless with technology. I should have explained how this works. After the vehicle's hacked, well, you need physical equipment to drive the car. A layout like a car. A seat, brake, accelerator, gears, and, of course, a steering wheel. Apparently, the set-up's got to be quite precise. Very like the car in question. Especially with these supercars. What I forgot to say is that we found the place where this was set up. An office in London."

Selena said, "Are you saying that David had Paul killed?"

"No, I'm saying *you* killed Paul Riordan."

Chapter 52

Selena's eyes flashed anger and shook her head violently. "You're mad, mad."

"No, I'm not mad."

"It was David's scheme," Selena said.

"Yes, but he didn't kill Riordan. He told me that."

"And you believed him?"

"Not really, but when I learned that he couldn't drive this supercar, he fell a little down my suspect list. Why would he kill Paul Riordan?"

"You said Paul was suspicious."

"Yes, he was. We think that he shared his suspicions with someone. I think it was you. When you heard that, you had to do something. A postponement wouldn't have suited you, Miss Thornton. You needed Ferguson to go ahead."

"Why?"

"The oldest reason in the world. Money."

"I've got plenty of money."

"Hmm, not real money. Not like your family used to have. Not enough to do some of the things you want. I need to tell you, Miss Thornton, I've got financial experts all over this, and I think two of the accounts are yours, maybe more. I will be able to prove it. If Riordan had lived, the scheme was over. A once in a lifetime chance for billions of dollars. Tough to resist and you didn't. It was easy for you – after all, you're the banking expert."

Amanda paused, but Selena went for a tactical silence.

"I've got some more stuff here in my briefcase." Amanda affected to be conducting a search. "Here we are, more analysis."

Selena grabbed the paper from Amanda. "What's this?"

"Analysis of the driving pattern from the time when Mr Riordan's car was being remotely controlled."

Selena smiled and seemed to relax.

"I know you wiped the record, Miss Thornton, but you know, I work for MI5. Getting into computers is what we do."

Selena said, "Here's your paperwork, Miss Barratt. I don't understand all these statistics."

"I know that you do, but I'll go on if necessary." She looked up. "Jack, stop the car, there's a button just under the steering wheel. Press it twice."

After a short fumble he found it, and, almost immediately, the car came smoothly to a halt beside a large oak tree in the meadow. It was a nice spot.

Amanda said, "Our experts did another analysis. This time comparing your driving records at the track with the analysis from the simulator. They tell me they're 99% certain it's the same driver."

"I don't understand any of that. You're reaching here, Miss Barratt. I've told you what happened. And he …" She pointed at Jack. "He saw everything at the airfield. David was going to kill me."

"Yes, I think that he intended to. But you knew he couldn't. Not with a gun loaded with blanks."

"Blanks?"

"Come on, Miss Thornton. Sebastian gave Ferguson the gun, just like you arranged."

"Sebastian?"

"You know Sebastian. Sebastian Mann. Private military contractor in the City. The dead man at the airfield. Your lover, Miss Thornton."

"No."

Amanda delved into the briefcase. Jack couldn't make them all out, but she produced and laid down photograph after photograph.

Selena picked up and looked at a few only. This time her expression did change.

Amanda was relentless. "I've more here. Here's a nice one in Highgate Cemetery. You see, I've been following Sebastian Mann for a week. You really shouldn't have met, but" – she pointed at another – "I guess it was just true love. That was a terrific performance at the airfield. The things you told me, some of them were true, most of them, in fact. That's what makes a convincing story. You just left out a couple of things. The bit about you and Mann being lovers, and the bit about you and he conspiring to kill Ferguson."

Amanda added, "Actually, despite myself, it's David Ferguson I feel sorry for. Betrayed by his lover and best friend. Piggybacking on his misery."

"Well, that's your theory."

"Yes, and quite a neat theory, I would say. Anyway, here's your phone. I forgot to return it to you. It is yours?"

"It looks like it."

"That's another thing, it's a bad habit to record things on your phone. Bank details, credit card numbers, or perhaps the keypad code for Sebastian Mann's remote-driving facility. That was another mistake."

Selena sighed deeply. She was done. "What now?"

"I'll take that as an informal confession and tell you what happens next. You're the banking expert. I want every detail of every movement of this money, everything. And, of course, we can start with the eight billion or so that you've got."

"And if I don't?"

"You will."

"I know some of the best lawyers in the world."

Amanda looked at yet another sheet of paper. "There are fifteen terrorist groups on this list. How long are you going to last when I tell them you're helping us to investigate them?"

Selena stuttered, "B-but I wouldn't be."

"Sorry, Miss Thornton. You don't get the protection of the truth now."

Chapter 53

Before eight on Monday morning in a city centre coffee bar, Jack, unhappy at being roused at this time, was again suited and booted and purchasing over-priced coffees.

Amanda, Pam and Ali Cairns accepted the cups without comment, and they all stood around a shaky, tall table.

Jack had all the money he would ever need and had confidently expected never to have to re-enter the world of work. But today he was going to have to. It was the least he could do for his goddaughter.

Admittedly this decision had been forced by a supplementary lecture from Amanda, but Jack had already forgotten about that and rationalised this as his own idea.

Pam and Ali Cairns were enthusiastically engaged in reviewing a small, bound report and looked like they knew what they were doing, and his black coffee had barely cooled when Pam announced that they were ready to leave.

Pam and Ali Cairns led and Jack and Amanda followed them as they entered into the reception area of the Canisp Hedge Fund. The receptionist, so indifferent when Jack had visited last week, seemed to have rediscovered enthusiasm and buzzed around Ali and Pam, while Jack and Amanda sat wearily on the reception sofas.

All too quickly, Ali came across with a couple of security badges and led them up the broad staircase. One thing that Canisp wasn't short of now was vacant executive offices. Like a couple of elderly relatives who were in the way, Jack and Amanda were dispatched to the boardroom and served some decent coffee while Ali and Pam did what they needed to do.

Amanda looked him up and down with a smile and conducted a critical appraisal. "Not bad," she provisionally concluded. "I think I could get used to seeing you in a suit."

"Sorry, but this is the last time for a while. At least I don't have to wear a tie today. I think that would have been too much."

"Hmm, maybe I can get you a tie."

"No thanks. When does this meeting start?"

"At nine. Not long now."

The new management were certainly efficient and at 8:55, Pam and Cairns arrived in the boardroom. Cairns said to Amanda, "Everything's boxed and being dispatched, although I doubt there'll be much."

Jack enquired as to what they were talking about.

Pam said, "Oh just papers from Thornton's and Ferguson's offices."

There were five minutes before the meeting and the new management did not believe in wasting time. Ali exhausted Jack with further updates about staff meetings, presentations and a few key appointments pending.

Jack poured himself another coffee. He didn't ask, but Pam had already anticipated his concerns. "Oh, and Jack, don't worry about the board meeting. Ali and I will do the talking." Having received these welcome assurances, Jack concentrated on his coffee.

Right on nine, they were joined by Sir George Black and Leo King. Despite their recent experiences, both were composed and looked happy to be back in their natural habitats.

They poured coffees and sat down.

Pam led for the new regime. In crisp, business-like tones and with an assurance Jack found impressive, she put them in the picture. "I am Pam Riordan. Paul's daughter." She didn't stop for sympathy. "I now control his shareholding and, also" – she nodded at Amanda – "the shares of Mr David Ferguson."

She did the maths for them. "This makes me the controlling shareholder." She gave them a second for this news to sink in, but neither Sir George nor King had anything to say.

Pam carried on. "At board level we now have two vacant positions. Katherine Carver and Lord Steel have both resigned." She produced a couple of single sheets and laid them in front of her. She said, "I am hoping that both of you, Sir George and Mr King, will agree to stay. Despite our recent challenges, we believe that the underlying business is strong and any reputational damage is contained."

Whatever doubts Jack had had about Pam's readiness to run a business such as this had now largely evaporated. King and Black both managed mumbles of assent and she went on. "Thank you. Now, Mr Edwards will join our board. He has an academic background in finance and economics and a wide range of experience."

Jack nodded meekly in response to their glances and said nothing.

Pam continued, "I will join the board and also take up a junior executive role." She looked at Sir George. "I hope that you will agree to continue as our chair, Sir George? And Mr King, we would also benefit greatly from your experience."

How could they refuse?

Pam said, "Miss Cairns you already know. She will be our new managing director. There is a lot to do, vacancies to fill. Unless there are any questions, I propose to get started."

There were no questions, and, after confirming a date for an update meeting, a week hence, she closed.

Some minor small talk could not be avoided, but Sir George and Leo King were more interested in talking to Pam and Ali than either Jack or Amanda. He caught Amanda's eye and feigned a scream.

She laughed and squeezed his arm. "Had enough?"

"No, of course not, but they don't need us. They're busy now. They don't need us here."

Amanda said. "Ok, I don't want you exhausted on your first day. Come on."

They skipped out of the boardroom and handed back their badges. Jack breathed in the foul London air. He was free.

Chapter 54

"They sure grow up fast," Jack said.

"Yes." Amanda agreed.

He said hopefully, "Tell me we're finished now?"

She linked her arm in his. "Nearly. Come on." She led him along the pavement for about half a mile. It was only a quarter past nine in the morning, but the bars of Smithfield meat market had been open for hours. There were a couple of modern bars, but Amanda went for authenticity and, in a bar that had last been redecorated when Queen Victoria was in her pomp, secured pints of Guinness and the house speciality of salt beef sandwiches.

This was much more agreeable than a working day and they both said nothing, focusing instead on the food and drink. When Jack returned with another round of Guinness, he risked a few questions.

"Is Selena Thornton talking yet?"

"A little. Not everything I want, but she will," Amanda said confidently.

"Hmm."

"What does that mean?"

"It means that I was wondering what you were offering her to spill the beans on the bank accounts."

Amanda took a sip of Guinness. "It's top-quality intelligence if we can get it. I have to try and save lives."

"And put one over on the Americans?"

"If you mean helping our allies, yes."

Jack said, "Oh, I can see that, but she killed Paul. I can just about see why you might have to overlook that, but Pam. I'm not so sure. She might not see it as justice."

"There's that word again," Amanda said. "I try never to think about it. I'm never sure what it means."

"Me neither," Jack admitted, "but it's the sort of thing that you know when you see it. So, what happens now?"

"I'm in the reality business, so all I can do is start from here and do whatever is best."

"And what is best?"

"I'm still thinking about that."

"At least you've got the whole story now. Quite good work."

"Not really. I've got the whole of the state behind me. It would have been tougher to fail."

"So did you ever believe Selena Thornton?" he asked.

"At first, but that changed when I discovered her connection with Sebastian Mann. You see, I had the photographs of her with Sebastian Mann when I met you at the airport. That didn't prove anything really, but obviously it was strange that Selena didn't mention it."

"But she might have been killed. I was there, remember."

"Yes, but what did you really see?"

"I saw Ferguson blow her off and then try to kill her."

"That's your assessment, but what did you really see?"

"I saw Selena fiddling with the airplane, then Ferguson and Mann arrived. Mann went into the plane and Ferguson and Thornton spoke. And then Ferguson produced a gun." He shrugged, "I just don't get it."

"No, but to be fair, I've got an advantage. I can find out things that you can't."

"Like what?"

"Like finding out that that Thornton was sleeping with Sebastian Mann. Like Mann had the technology to remotely drive a car. Like Selena knew how to drive Paul Riordan's car."

Business as Usual

"Is that driver identification science accurate?"

"Apparently it is. Anyway, you told me about track days. I sent people to the track. You'd be surprised how good their records are at these sorts of places. Also, these supercars are not easy to drive, and I know that the car was remotely driven at high speed for several minutes. That needs skill."

Jack said, "But you still haven't explained the airport incident."

"I forgot about that. I believe it's true that Ferguson was going to kill Selena, but in reality, Selena was way ahead of him. She, or probably Mann, was going to kill Ferguson."

Jack shook his head. "Did she admit that?"

"More or less, but remember the gun."

"What about it?"

"Jeez, weren't you listening? It was loaded with blanks. He couldn't have killed anyone."

"So, I shot him unnecessarily?"

"Theoretically yes, but actually you saved him."

"And you killed Mann."

"I'm a better shot than you, and, after all, he was going to kill you. And he didn't have blanks in his gun." She looked at him affectionately, "I wasn't going to allow that."

Jack screwed up his eyes. "I've just realised about that keypad code. That's why you knew the code when we arrived?"

"Yes. Max had gotten in there earlier, but I wanted to test it. As you saw, we walked straight in."

"Are you sure that Ferguson didn't know anything about Selena and Mann?"

"Why would he? He didn't know that Riordan was investigating. Riordan asked Selena for help, not Ferguson. He must have thought that he could trust her. Men are such fools. Riordan trusted her and Ferguson trusted her. To be honest, I wouldn't have been surprised if she planned to kill Mann as well. She could fly the plane, remember."

Jack shivered, and Amanda went on. "If I had to guess, I reckon the plan to double-cross Ferguson was Selena's idea more than

Mann's, he's not that smart. What could be easier? Let Ferguson proceed, kill a dead man and then clear off into the sunset. Katherine Carver was a complication. Better that she had lived. She would have blamed Ferguson for, as far as she knew, only he was moving the money."

Jack said, "Yes that all sounds reasonable, but what about all that stuff about environmental causes?"

Amanda shrugged. "Maybe she believed it once, although I doubt it. Let's say she became an agnostic."

"Sad," Jack said.

Amanda stared at him. "Wasn't it you that complained about corporate hypocrisy?"

"Yes, but I'm not sure I wanted it to be quite so true."

"It is. Selena's focused on restoring the family fortunes, lost some time ago, apparently."

This was all a lot to process so Jack had quite a few mouthfuls of the Guinness. "You know, I'm almost feeling sorry for Ferguson now. Double-crossed by a lover and a best friend."

"Don't get too emotional. Ferguson was happy to have Common killed and to set these gunmen on you. Besides, he's going to be responsible for a lot of damage in the future. It's a good thing I've got Selena. She doesn't believe in anything other than herself, so she'll do plenty to save her skin. I'll get a pile of information on these transactions."

"And after she gives you information?"

"Maybe I'll let her call one of her hot-shot lawyers."

Jack laughed. "I trust your judgement. I understand that personal feelings have to be put aside."

"I don't always put personal feelings aside. I'm not arrogant enough to claim that."

Jack touched her hand. "That's an oddly reassuring statement. You'll do the right thing."

"Quite a responsibility."

Jack squeezed her arm and complacently sipped at his beer. "And what about Ferguson?"

"Have you a suggestion?"

"In the old days, you could have shot him as a traitor."

"It still happens."

"I'm sure it does. But what are you going to do? Send him off to some unknown location and work on him?"

"Maybe."

"I don't approve of torture."

"Neither do I, but people are strange. Some take longer than others, but most feel compelled to talk eventually. If we can get just one of these terrorist contacts it will be worth it."

Jack said, "He won't talk."

"Maybe, maybe not, "Amanda conceded. "He might change his mind." She added chillingly, "He'll have a long time to think about it, and of course he has yet to learn about Selena and Mann."

"I've got one more question. What about Paul's so-called drug use?"

"I think Thornton spiked his drink at the leaving party."

"Did she say that?"

"Let's say it's our working theory at the moment."

"And that's it. Case closed?"

"As far as you are concerned, yes, except for your new responsibilities on the Canisp board."

"I'm not looking forward to that."

"Even you can manage six meetings a year. Besides, you said you wanted to help your god-daughter."

"I doubt she needs my help."

"Maybe not, but maybe I want to see you when you're in London. Maybe even a bit more than six times a year."

Jack put his hand on her arm. "We were going to talk about that once the case was over. I remember you kissing me at the airfield. I enjoyed that."

She leant into him with her head under his chin. She turned her face to him. Her eyes were big and round. "So did I."

Jack wasn't much of an expert on women, far from it, but the way she was looking at him was unambiguous. He moved his lips forward until they settled on hers and then lingered. It was a long time since he had felt that way.

He thought about another kiss, but a group of teenagers sitting opposite were nudging each other and looking across. Amanda followed Jack's gaze and laughed. "They're right. We're too old to behave like this in public. Another drink?"

Jack laughed as well. "Yes, I'll get them."

He went back to the bar and came back with more Guinness. Alcohol wasn't much of a way to cope with the horrors of life and death, but sitting close to Amanda in a warm bar with a cold beer was going to have to do for the next few hours.

ENJOY BUSINESS AS USUAL?

YOU CAN HELP ME WITH JUST A LITTLE MINUTE OF YOUR TIME

If you enjoyed *Business as Usual,* it would be a great help to me if you could leave a rating with a brief review on Amazon.

Most of the major publishers spend a lot of money on marketing. With just a minute of your time, you can give me something special:

your support.

Many thanks

Adam

Adam Parish

Business as Usual
by
Adam Parish

*Book 4 of the
Jack Edwards and Amanda Barratt
Mystery Series*

Also by Adam Parish
*The Quartermaster (1)
Parthian Shot (2)
Loose Ends (3)*

To sign up for offers, updates
and find out more about Adam Parish
visit our website www.adam-parish.com

Printed in Great Britain
by Amazon